T0000475

AUBREY MCFADDEN
IS NEVER
GETTING MARRIED

Praise for Georgia Beers

Playing with Matches

"*Playing with Matches* is a delightful exploration of small town life, family drama, and true love...Liz and Cori are charming characters with undeniable chemistry, and their sweet and tender small town, 'fake-dating' love story is sure to capture the attention of readers. Their journey reminds readers of the importance of love, forgiveness, family, and community, making this feel-good romance a true triumph."—*Women Using Words*

Peaches and Cream

"*Peaches and Cream* is a fresh, new spin on the classic rom-com *You've Got Mail*—except it's even better because it's all about ice cream!...[A] delicious, melt-in-your-mouth scoop of goodness. Bursting with tasty characters in a scrumptious story world, *Peaches and Cream* is simply irresistible."—*Women Using Words*

Dance with Me

"I admit I inherited my two left feet from my father's side of the family. Dancing is not something I enjoy, so why choose a book with dancing as the central focus and romance as the payoff? Easy. Because it's Georgia Beers, and she will let me enjoy being awkward alongside her main character. I think this is what makes her special to me as an author. While her characters might be beautiful in their own ways, I can relate to their challenges, fears and dreams. Comfort reads every time."—*Late Night Lesbian Reads*

Camp Lost and Found

"I really like when Beers writes about winter and snow and hot chocolate. She makes heartache feel cosy and surmountable. *Camp Lost and Found* made me smile a lot, laugh at times, tear up more often than I care to share. If you're looking for a heartwarming story to keep the cold weather at bay, I'd recommend you give it a chance."—*Jude in the Stars*

Cherry on Top

"*Cherry on Top* is another wonderful story from one of the greatest writers in sapphic fiction...This is more than a romance with two incredibly charming and wonderful characters. It is a reminder that

you shouldn't have to compromise who you are to fit into a box that society wants to put you into. Georgia Beers once again creates a couple with wonderful chemistry who will warm your heart."
—*Sapphic Book Review*

On the Rocks

"This book made me so happy! And kept me awake way too late."
—*Jude in the Stars*

The Secret Poet

"[O]ne of the author's best works and one of the best romances I've read recently...I was so invested in [Morgan and Zoe] I read the book in one sitting."—*Melina Bickard, Librarian, Waterloo Library (UK)*

Hopeless Romantic

"Thank you, Georgia Beers, for this unabashed paean to the pleasure of escaping into romantic comedies...If you want to have a big smile plastered on your face as you read a romance novel, do not hesitate to pick up this one!"—*The Rainbow Bookworm*

Flavor of the Month

"Beers whips up a sweet lesbian romance...brimming with mouth-watering descriptions of foodie indulgences...Both women are well-intentioned and endearing, and it's easy to root for their inevitable reconciliation. But once the couple rediscover their natural ease with one another, Beers throws a challenging emotional hurdle in their path, forcing them to fight through tragedy to earn their happy ending."
—*Publishers Weekly*

Fear of Falling

"Enough tension and drama for us to wonder if this can work out—and enough heat to keep the pages turning. I will definitely recommend this to others—Georgia Beers continues to go from strength to strength."—*Evan Blood, Bookseller (Angus & Robertson, Australia)*

One Walk in Winter

"A sweet story to pair with the holidays. There are plenty of 'moment's in this book that make the heart soar. Just what I like in a romance. Situations where sparks fly, hearts fill, and tears fall. This book shined with cute fairy trails and swoon-worthy Christmas gifts...REALLY nice and cozy if read in between Thanksgiving and Christmas. Covered in blankets. By a fire."—*Bookvark*

The Do-Over

"You can count on Beers to give you a quality well-paced book each and every time."—*The Romantic Reader Blog*

"*The Do-Over* is a shining example of the brilliance of Georgia Beers as a contemporary romance author."—*Rainbow Reflections*

The Shape of You

The Shape of You "catches you right in the feels and does not let go. It is a must for every person out there who has struggled with self-esteem, questioned their judgment, and settled for a less than perfect but safe lover. If you've ever been convinced you have to trade passion for emotional safety, this book is for you."—*Writing While Distracted*

"I know I always say this about Georgia Beers's books, but there is no one that writes first kisses like her. They are hot, steamy and all too much!"—*Les Rêveur*

Calendar Girl

"A sweet, sweet romcom of a story...*Calendar Girl* is a nice read, which you may find yourself returning to when you want a hot-chocolate-and-warm-comfort-hug in your life."—*Best Lesbian Erotica*

Blend

"You know a book is good, first, when you don't want to put it down. Second, you know it's damn good when you're reading it and thinking, I'm totally going to read this one again. Great read and absolutely a 5-star romance."—*The Romantic Reader Blog*

"This is a lovely romantic story with relatable characters that have depth and chemistry. A charming easy story that kept me reading until the end. Very enjoyable."—*Kat Adams, Bookseller, QBD (Australia)*

Right Here, Right Now

"[A] successful and entertaining queer romance novel. The main characters are appealing, and the situations they deal with are realistic and well-managed. I would recommend this book to anyone who enjoys a good queer romance novel, and particularly one grounded in real world situations."—*Books at the End of the Alphabet*

"[A]n engaging odd-couple romance. Beers creates a romance of gentle humor that allows no-nonsense Lacey to relax and easygoing Alicia to find a trusting heart."—*RT Book Reviews*

Lambda Literary Award Winner *Fresh Tracks*

"[T]he focus switches each chapter to a different character, allowing for a measured pace and deep, sincere exploration of each protagonist's thoughts. Beers gives a welcome expansion to the romance genre with her clear, sympathetic writing."—*Curve magazine*

Lambda Literary Award Finalist *Finding Home*

"Georgia Beers has proven in her popular novels such as *Too Close to Touch* and *Fresh Tracks* that she has a special way of building romance with suspense that puts the reader on the edge of their seat. *Finding Home*, though more character driven than suspense, will equally keep the reader engaged at each page turn with its sweet romance."—*Lambda Literary Review*

Mine

"Beers does a fine job of capturing the essence of grief in an authentic way. *Mine* is touching, life-affirming, and sweet."—*Lesbian News Book Review*

Too Close to Touch

"This is such a well-written book. The pacing is perfect, the romance is great, the character work strong, and damn, but is the sex writing ever fantastic."—*The Lesbian Review*

"In her third novel, Georgia Beers delivers an immensely satisfying story. Beers knows how to generate sexual tension so taut it could be cut with a knife…Beers weaves a tale of yearning, love, lust, and conflict resolution. She has constructed a believable plot, with strong characters in a charming setting."—*Just About Write*

By the Author

Romances

Turning the Page

Thy Neighbor's Wife

Too Close to Touch

Fresh Tracks

Mine

Finding Home

Starting from Scratch

96 Hours

Slices of Life

Snow Globe

Olive Oil & White Bread

Zero Visibility

A Little Bit of Spice

What Matters Most

Right Here, Right Now

Blend

The Shape of You

Calendar Girl

The Do-Over

Fear of Falling

One Walk in Winter

Flavor of the Month

Hopeless Romantic

16 Steps to Forever

The Secret Poet

Cherry on Top

Camp Lost and Found

Dance with Me

Peaches and Cream

Playing with Matches

Aubrey McFadden
Is Never Getting Married

The Puppy Love Romances

Rescued Heart

Run to You

Dare to Stay

The Swizzle Stick Romances

Shaken or Stirred

On the Rocks

With a Twist

Visit us at www.boldstrokesbooks.com

AUBREY McFADDEN IS NEVER GETTING MARRIED

by

Georgia Beers

2024

AUBREY McFADDEN IS NEVER GETTING MARRIED
© 2024 By Georgia Beers. All Rights Reserved.

ISBN 13: 978-1-63679-613-0

This Trade Paperback Original Is Published By
Bold Strokes Books, Inc.
P.O. Box 249
Valley Falls, NY 12185

First Edition: April 2024

THIS IS A WORK OF FICTION. NAMES, CHARACTERS, PLACES, AND INCIDENTS ARE THE PRODUCT OF THE AUTHOR'S IMAGINATION OR ARE USED FICTITIOUSLY. ANY RESEMBLANCE TO ACTUAL PERSONS, LIVING OR DEAD, BUSINESS ESTABLISHMENTS, EVENTS, OR LOCALES IS ENTIRELY COINCIDENTAL.

THIS BOOK, OR PARTS THEREOF, MAY NOT BE REPRODUCED IN ANY FORM WITHOUT PERMISSION.

Credits
Editor: Ruth Sternglantz
Production Design: Stacia Seaman
Cover Design by Inkspiral Design

Acknowledgments

This book is a little different, I admit. I woke up one day with Aubrey's name in my head, and I knew instantly that she was a woman I wanted to protect, but also one that I'd want in my corner. Writing her—and this book—was so much fun. Every wedding, every incident, every moment she tries to keep herself and her life from skidding off the very safe path she's been following made me excited to be a writer. Books that do that are so special, and this is definitely one of them. I hope you fall in love with Aubrey the way I did.

A big thank you to Sandy Lowe for the spark of inspiration. I hope I did it justice. Everybody else at Bold Strokes—Radclyffe, Ruth, Cindy, Stacia, thank you for making this career such a joy. And special thanks to Matt for creating such a kickass cover!

Writing is a solitary craft. I say this all the time. And while I live on my own, I now have a crazy unconventional family just two doors down that has made me feel whole again. They can't read my books for another eighteen years (or longer, if I can manage it), but a big thank you to Gemma, Asher, Bennett, and Cyrus for making me a Gigi. It's my most precious title so far, and I love you four with all my heart.

And finally, to you, my readers. I wouldn't be where I am today without you. You've stuck by me through crises and sickness and an absolute disaster of a year that was 2023. I hope to make your devotion pay off in so many ways. Thank you from the very bottom of my heart. I'm still here because you are.

Prologue

AUBREY AND CODY
JUNE 28, 2014
TRADITIONAL CHURCH WEDDING

AUBREY MCFADDEN IS NEVER GETTING MARRIED.

REASON #1
LOVE CAN BLINDSIDE YOU.
AND GETTING BLINDSIDED SUCKS.

A ubrey had never been so happy.

Never in her life. As if to stress that fact, "Happy" by Pharrell Williams began playing, and she did a little shimmy in her wedding dress.

"Oh my God, this song is so overplayed," Trina said with her signature eye roll. Aubrey's best friend had totally perfected the look to be the perfect blend of annoyed and bored.

"On its way to being the number one song of 2014," Aubrey said, studying her reflection in the full-length mirror.

"But it was released last year." The depth of tone would have had strangers thinking Trina's life depended on Mr. Williams not reaching song of the year status.

"I don't care," Aubrey said. "It's perfect. It's the perfect song for the day, don't you think?" She held out her arm. "Come here. Look at us." She put her arm around Trina in her dusty-rose maid of honor dress, and they stood there in front of the mirror. "I don't mind this stupid, overplayed song because this is the happiest day of my life. And I'm so glad you're here with me."

Trina's eyes welled up, and Aubrey felt her arm tighten at her waist. "Me, too," Trina whispered.

They stood like that for a moment, in the bridal room in the church, just the two of them, and gazed at their reflection. Finally, Aubrey gave Trina a gentle little push. "Okay. Go. Tell the others I just need a moment alone, okay? I'll let you know when I'm ready."

"Self-pep talk?" Trina asked with a grin.

"You know me well."

Trina put a hand on Aubrey's shoulder and gave her a tender kiss on her cheek. "I'm so happy for you, Aubs." Then she scooted out, and the door clicked closed behind her, and it was just Aubrey and the mirror.

"It's almost time," she said on a whisper as she pressed a hand against her stomach and studied her reflection. "I've been waiting for this day since I was a little girl. I can't believe it's here. I'm so nervous and so happy and..." She let her eyes mist up but didn't let herself go any farther than that. Her makeup had taken too long and was too perfect. "You got this. It's gonna fly by, but take it all in. Remember it forever." She inhaled a big, slow breath and was pulling herself together when there was a gentle knock on the door. "I'm coming," she called out, giving herself a full-body shake.

The door opened, and it was Cody, and Aubrey gasped.

"What are you doing? Get out! You can't see me before the wedding. It's bad luck!"

Cody's smile was sad. "I'm so sorry," he said so quietly as he approached her that she almost didn't hear him. And Aubrey knew. Right then, she knew. She knew his face, his eyes, his voice, and she knew those three short words were about to destroy her, and what had started out as the happiest day of her life was about to become the worst. Her heart began to pound in her chest and she stared at Cody. At his dark hair, the hair she loved all tousled, but was now tamed neatly. At his clean-shaven face that she knew would be sporting a five o'clock shadow by two in the afternoon. At the devastatingly handsome tux that he looked like James Bond in. His dark eyes were sad and wet, and she could smell that he'd already had a drink, or maybe more. Probably more. But there was something else in his eyes as he spoke. After his apology, he began with, "I can't do this," and those were the only words Aubrey had been able to hear before the rushing of her own blood in her ears drowned out the rest. But his eyes...

His eyes.

She could see it. She could see it beyond any shadow of any doubts. And she knew what she saw.

Relief.

He kept talking, but all she could register were his moving lips and the tears on his face. He was crying, but now she wondered if they were happy tears, because his relief was so plain, so clearly obvious, he might as well be wearing a sandwich board with the words I AM SO RELIEVED painted on it in red block letters. He was cutting himself loose of her. After four years. They'd been dating since their freshman year of college. They'd graduated only a few weeks ago. And yes, they'd stepped up their plans to wed, but getting married, having a family, that had always been the plan. Their plan. Hadn't it? She tried to zero back in on what he was saying because yes, he was still talking. It was like he'd broken a seal, opened the floodgates, and the words wouldn't stop now. He just kept talking, no matter how hard she wished he would stop because his words were killing her.

"I don't want to work in my dad's law firm. I never did. I want to travel. I want to go see other countries. And I want to help those without a voice, you know? I'm twenty-two. I don't want to be locked into a nine-to-five already. Already! You know?" He grabbed her hands, and she didn't stop him, but he kept asking her if she knew. He kept saying, "You know?" And she wanted to scream at him, *No. No.* She did *not* know. But her voice was hiding, and she couldn't find it, and he kept talking, and all she could do was stand there and listen to his horrible words as they sliced her skin like a thousand tiny paper cuts. "I love you, Aubrey. I do. But we want different things. I've known that for a while, but I've never had the balls to talk to you about it, and then with stepping everything up...it just started to move so fast." He glanced down at his feet, then back up. "I was trapped. And I couldn't tell you because..." He shook his head. "I just couldn't, you know?" There it was again, that question.

Did she know?

"No, I...I..." Where were her words? Why couldn't she form any? Did her mouth not work anymore? Had she lost the ability to speak?

"Look, I know, *I know* I screwed up. I should've told you,

should've talked to you so much sooner. But going through with this wedding would be worse. There would be resentment and frustration. When I was talking to Monica about it, I realized. It was suddenly so clear. I just…" And here, he looked her right in the face, his dark eyes locked on hers. "I just don't want the same life you want, Aubrey. I'm so sorry."

Another light rap sounded on the door. It opened just a crack, and Monica Wallace peeked in, her blond hair in some kind of beautiful updo, her makeup on point, looking stunning and gorgeous.

Aubrey hated her.

All Monica did was raise her light brows expectantly, and Cody nodded at her. Turning back to Aubrey, he apologized once more, kissed her on the cheek—something she would be laser-focused on for weeks, she knew—then hurried out the door, leaving Aubrey staring at the back of Monica's head.

That was it? Just like that?

She glanced out the window of the bridal room, which was on the side of the church nearest the parking lot, and she saw Cody hop into the passenger side of a car she didn't recognize and speed off.

Okay, clearly that really was it. Just like that.

She followed the taillights until she could no longer see them, and then she stood there after, unable to come up with a single thing to do next.

"You okay?"

She'd forgotten Monica was still there. Why? Why was she still there? She replayed some of Cody's words, and something inside her understood that she'd be doing exactly that for the rest of her life, but she recalled him saying that after he'd talked to Monica—who had been his best friend from the time they were in elementary school—that was when he'd realized he couldn't marry her.

She whipped around and glared. "You."

Monica was fully in the room now, leaving the door open behind her. She held up her hands in a placating gesture that only served to piss Aubrey off more. "Listen, I know this is hard…"

"Do you? How? How do you know this is hard? Have you

ever been dumped by your fiancé on the *actual day of your fucking wedding*? No? Then you *don't* know."

Monica had the good sense to look at least a little bit chastened, but she continued with the hand gestures and the attempted explanation. "He wasn't happy. Doesn't that matter to you?"

"Of course it does. But he should've talked to me about it. Not you."

"Maybe if you'd given him a second to breathe instead of fast-forwarding the entire wedding, so much so that it made his head spin." Monica had always been protective of Cody. Aubrey knew that. But this was beyond.

"His head wasn't spinning. And we sped things up together. He was fine. He helped pick stuff out. He was in on the planning. He was totally fine."

"He's been drunk for the past month." Monica didn't shout it, but the words were loud and steely. There were people outside the room, in the hall, and Aubrey knew they'd heard. They couldn't not. "How have you not noticed that?"

Okay, those words hit hard. Because she *had* noticed. Cody had always been a drinker. From the beginning, she knew he liked his beer. Occasionally, something harder. But recently, it had gotten more frequent. Monica wasn't wrong, despite the hyperbole. But coming from her made it so much worse, and Aubrey felt her blood start to boil. "He was stressed. We all were. Planning a wedding is a lot." And as soon as she'd said those words, she thought about all the people sitting in the church right now. Waiting. Expecting. There to see her walk down the aisle within the hour. A hundred of them in the church. Two hundred and fifty at the reception later that day. Oh God. It was as if the sheer scope of it all waltzed into the room and sat down in front of her. Waved at her. Smiled. *Hi, I'm your worst nightmare come to life.*

She shook her head, the humiliation she felt bubbling in her stomach like a sour stew. "How…" She had to clear her throat of the bile that was threatening to make an appearance. "How could you do this?" Her voice came out strained. Choked. But goddamn it, she would not cry in front of this woman. "Because I know it was you. I *know* he talked to you and you pushed him to do this."

Monica's expression was a combination of sympathy and irritation, and for a moment, she looked as though she was going to deny talking to Cody. She began with, "I didn't—" but then cut herself off. She seemed to rethink, and when she finally said something, her voice was quiet, even if her words weren't. "I'd think you'd be relieved to not end up married to a man who clearly doesn't want to be married to you."

And Aubrey thought, *Ladies and gentlemen, Monica Wallace, the very worst version of every ice queen you've ever seen in a movie or read about in a book: tall, blond, stunningly beautiful... and fucking brutal in her delivery.*

"Now you can move on, find somebody who wants what you want, and not be tied forever to somebody who wants different things out of life."

Everything within Aubrey was on fire. Her blood. Her heart. Her brain. Her thoughts and emotions and future. All of it. Up in flames. When she focused on Monica's blue eyes, she hoped she felt it, the heat. The searing pain. The anguish. She only had four more words for this woman, and she spat them in disgust.

"I'm pregnant, you bitch."

The widening of Monica's eyes and the clear shock on her face told Aubrey everything she needed to know.

Cody had left that part out.

Part One

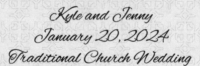

Kyle and Jenny
January 20, 2024
Traditional Church Wedding

Aubrey McFadden is never getting married.

Reason #2
People are selfish.

W hy can't I go and be your date?" Emma wanted to know. "You shouldn't go to a wedding without a date. It's just sad."

Aubrey looked at her nine-year-old daughter in surprise. "Why? Why is it sad?"

"Because you won't have anybody to dance with." There was an unspoken *duh* at the end of her statement, and with that, she twirled herself in a perfect circle. That was her new thing. Twirling. She twirled constantly, like it was part of walking. Aubrey got dizzy just watching.

"I'm sure I'll find somebody to dance with. Don't you worry about me." She checked herself in the mirror. Maybe she actually *would* find somebody to dance with. She looked pretty good, if she said so herself. Her dress was black and white in a geometrical design, and she hoped she wouldn't be cold later at the reception. But the look was worth the discomfort, as were the heels. Her dark hair was freshly styled, looking both slightly disheveled and very carefully done at the same time. Her makeup was perfect. So, yeah. Maybe she *would* find somebody to dance with tonight.

"You look really nice, Mom." Emma had stopped twirling and was looking at her with that look she got sometimes, the one that said she thought Aubrey hung the moon. That look was showing up less and less the older Emma got, so Aubrey knew she needed to grab it and cling to it when she could. She was going to blink, and Emma would be a teenager, and she was so not ready for that. She bent down and wrapped her daughter in a hug.

"Thank you, little bean. You be good for Nana and Papa, okay?"

"Please. She's an angel." Aubrey's father was suddenly there, smiling down at them. "And she's not wrong. You look gorgeous, honey."

Aubrey stood and gave her father a kiss on the cheek. "Thanks, Dad." Then she tousled Emma's light brown hair, grabbed her clutch, and headed out to her car.

This was going to be a hell of a year.

The thought ran through her head as she drove to the church for the wedding of her college friend Kyle. Kyle's was the first of five weddings she'd participate in this year. Five. In one year. For two of them, she was merely a guest. But the other three? She was a bridesmaid. Seemed all her college friends had chosen this year to tie the knot.

Fools.

Okay, that wasn't fair. Not really. Yes, Aubrey had a bias against weddings in general, given her own history, but did that mean marriage was an overall stupid thing?

"I mean, maybe?" she said out loud as she hit her turn signal and waited for somebody backing out of a spot in the church parking lot. The person waved to her as they drove past, but before she could turn into the spot, somebody driving a white Prius zipped into it. "Are you kidding me? Do you not see me sitting here with my turn signal on?"

But the driver of the Prius and his passenger didn't even glance her way as they got out of the car and headed toward the church doors.

For a short moment, she thought about leaning on her horn and holding it until Mr. Prius came back out, realized his mistake, and moved his car so she could have the spot that was clearly hers to begin with. Then reality set in, and she sighed, shook her head, knowing her Towanda moment had passed, and moved on to another spot that was much farther away. People were selfish, that was for damn sure. It was a lesson she'd learned the hard way. Making her way through the wet slush of the freshly plowed lot wasn't easy in the heels, but she managed and reached for the church's door handle in relief.

It was cold out, but the sun was bright, so Aubrey needed to stand inside the church for a moment and let her eyes adjust, as did the people in front of her, clearly. The church was stunning. Even in all her anti-everything-that-had-to-do-with-church glory, she could admit that. The high ceilings, the gorgeous art of the stained glass windows lining each side, the solid oak of the pews, it was all absolutely beautiful. She and the people in front of her all moved at once down the center aisle, ushers asking if they were friends of the bride or the groom, and seating them on the corresponding side.

"Hey," Trina said as Aubrey slid into the pew next to her, and they hugged. "You made it."

"I had to drop Emma off at my parents'. What did I miss?" She shrugged out of her coat and scanned the attendees, finding a few familiar faces from school and gatherings over the years.

"Not much, though Kyle looks like he's gonna hurl all over his wingtips."

Aubrey looked toward the front of the church where Kyle stood, looking very handsome in his tux, and—Trina wasn't wrong—a little ill. "He's so nervous."

"He hates being in front of people," Trina agreed. "Poor guy."

"Will that be Jeff?" Aubrey asked with a teasing bump of her shoulder. Trina and her longtime boyfriend were getting married later in the year.

Trina laughed. "Doubtful. He loves a good audience."

Aubrey continued to scan the crowd, waved at a few familiar faces. She'd catch up with them at the reception. Just as her eyes snagged on a familiar blond head, the wedding march began and everybody stood.

It was always a little bittersweet to Aubrey when she saw a groom see his bride walking toward him—something she didn't get to witness at her own non-wedding—and the familiar poke of envy stabbed at her, because that's how weddings were for her now. She watched as everything in Kyle's face relaxed. The green-around-the-gills look vanished. His face lit up and beamed—literally beamed with love for Jenny. Who, to be fair, looked drop dead gorgeous in her mermaid wedding gown.

"God, she looks amazing," Trina whispered as Jenny's father walked her past them. He handed her off to Kyle, and the crowd sat, and the wedding continued.

It had been nearly ten years since her own bridal disaster, and Aubrey liked to think she'd gotten past it. Aside from the fact that she was never going to put herself through anything even close to that again, she had pretty much moved on. Come on. Almost ten years had passed. Cody had gotten what he wanted—to take a gap year, go off to Europe with a backpack, and explore the world. And she'd gotten Emma. Definitely the better end of the deal. But none of this meant that she didn't wonder. That she didn't wake up in the night occasionally after having dreamed of a life where she and Cody had gotten married, had raised Emma together, had had more kids and a sweet little life. Those dreams didn't happen nearly as often anymore, but they still happened.

As the ceremony progressed, Aubrey let her gaze wander. She recognized many people in the crowd, all on her side—which was Kyle's side—of the church, as many of them had gone to college together and were from the same general vicinity in upstate New York. She saw Kyle's parents in the front row. Both his brothers and his roommate from college were standing up with him as groomsmen. A handful of his frat brothers sat in the pew in front of Aubrey, dressed smartly and with dates she didn't know. And in that same pew, just down a ways, was Monica Wallace.

"Fix your face," Trina whispered to her. "You're glaring. If you could kill her with your eyes, she'd have been dead a hundred times by now."

Aubrey smiled at that. She couldn't help it. Because Trina was absolutely right. If wishes came true, Monica Wallace would have ceased to exist long ago. Her wavy golden highlighted hair, her knockout figure, dressed today in a sexy royal-blue number that easily brought out the color of her eyes, her gravelly voice Aubrey could still hear in her sleep sometimes…yeah, all that would be gone.

She cleared her throat and gave herself a shake. Enough. Enough about Monica Wallace.

She returned her focus to the ceremony.

❖

Kyle and his new bride had seated all his college friends together at the same table, which made perfect sense. Their table of eight consisted of Aubrey, Trina and Jeff, her fiancé, Harlan and Eddie—two of Kyle's frat brothers—and their dates, and Monica.

"Aubrey McFadden," Monica said, and something about the way she said her name wiggled into Aubrey and tickled her. "Been a long time."

"Monica," she said with a nod, adding *not long enough*, but only in her head.

"I guess they figured they'd put the two attending solo next to each other," Monica said softly as she pulled out her chair and sat.

Aubrey nodded. "I guess so." God, she smelled good. Why? Why did she have to smell like warmth and sunshine? It was so annoying. She felt Trina squeeze her knee under the table.

The music was low and playing what Aubrey thought of as dinner mode. Frank Sinatra. Some Motown. A little classical. Tunes that were unobtrusive so the guests could mingle and sip cocktails and catch up while the bride and groom were having pictures taken.

"So, what have you all been up to?" Harlan asked. Always a nice guy, he hadn't changed much, except that his hairline had receded about an inch since graduation. He gave Eddie a playful punch. "Except for you. I know what a loser you are. How about you, Mon? You still at that payroll company?"

Monica nodded and sipped from her glass of red wine. "I am. Moved up a bit. I'm a VP now." Aubrey wanted to roll her eyes, but Monica had said it modestly, not at all being showy or flaunting.

"And Aubrey? How's your little girl?"

At the mention of Emma, Aubrey felt herself straighten up a bit, her spine strengthening with pride. "Emma's amazing. She's going to be ten this year."

"Ten? Holy shit. No kidding. She with Cody this weekend? Or is he still in Lake Placid?"

"She's with my parents tonight," Aubrey said.

And Monica added, "He's in Lake Placid until Tuesday. That's why he couldn't make it tonight." Of course *she* would know where Cody was. She was his best friend, after all. Still. But then Monica surprised her by turning to her. "Emma *is* amazing." She addressed Harlan as she continued. "She's just the coolest kid. Smart and hilarious. She's always making me laugh."

While she didn't enjoy her daughter being described in great, very accurate detail by Monica, she couldn't deny her words. "She's super funny. She'll say something to me that cracks me up, and I always think, But you're nine. How do you know this stuff?"

"I've seen pics," Eddie added. "Last time I saw Codes—God, like, six months ago?—he showed me a few pics of her. She's a gorgeous little girl."

"Thank you," Aubrey said. More with the pride. She couldn't help it. She loved hearing good stuff about her daughter, and she glanced down at her lap to hide the slight blush she felt coloring her face.

"She looks just like you." That was Monica, and it was said very quietly. Aubrey looked up, but the others had broken off into their own small conversations. She met ice blue eyes with her own. Monica was smiling a soft smile, and then she looked away and sipped her wine and, suddenly they were interrupted by a loud voice over the speakers, and the moment was broken.

"Ladies and gentlemen, it's time to introduce the bridal party!"

❖

"It was obviously an olive branch," Trina said later as she fixed her makeup in the mirror of the ladies' room.

A little snort escaped Aubrey's nose. "She's gonna need to hand over the whole tree."

Trina laughed at that, then met Aubrey's eyes in the mirror. A woman who'd been in a stall when they'd arrived had left, so it was just the two of them now. "You know, sometimes I worry that you're not completely past the whole Monica-slash-Cody-slash-ruined-wedding thing. But then I take time to think about what went down and how, and I completely get you holding on to that grudge."

Aubrey squinted at her. "I mean, is it a grudge?"

Trina stopped, mascara brush halfway to her lashes, and met her eyes in the reflection. "Oh, it's *so* a grudge."

A sigh. "I guess it is."

"Hey, no judgment over here." Trina went back to her lashes.

"I mean, there's a little judgment."

"No."

"A smidge." Aubrey held her finger and thumb scant millimeters apart. "Like, this much."

Trina grabbed her hand and kissed her fingers. "I just want you to be happy is all. You're my bestie, and I like it when you smile. And grudges are smile stealers." She snapped her makeup bag closed, swiped at the corner of her mouth with a red-nailed finger, and ordered, "Now, let's go dance the night away."

❖

Aubrey loved to dance.

Like, *loved* to dance. The dance floor was a place you could lose yourself, a place where you didn't have to think about your job or your bills or the chores you hadn't done yet. The dance floor was for setting all that aside, at least for a little while, and just losing yourself.

The reception was in full swing. Dinner had been eaten, the first dance was done, the cake had been cut. The bar was still open, and Aubrey had had just enough alcohol to take away her dancing inhibitions. Trina, on the other hand, was *lit*. She draped herself against Aubrey as they both stood at the bar to get new drinks and pointed toward Kyle and Jenny, who were making the rounds, going from table to table and greeting their guests. "See that? That's gonna be me in a few months."

"It is."

"She looks happy, right?" And for some reason, Aubrey knew the answer to Trina's question was hella important to her.

"She looks blissful," she said and felt Trina give her a squeeze. "You okay?"

"Me? I'm good." Trina drew out the *good* for a couple extra seconds, then stood up a little straighter and ordered two shots of tequila. Aubrey studied her friend. They'd been roommates in college, one of the few pairings that had been perfect and lasted through all four years, and they'd had a blast together. Trina was shorter than Aubrey, curvier, with blond hair cut just above her shoulders, wide hips, and a gorgeous chest that was the envy of almost anybody who met her, Aubrey included. She was hilariously funny and could also be super insecure when it came to her relationships—and she'd had several. But Jeff was a keeper. He was The One. Aubrey had known it the first time she'd met him. He loved Trina inside and out and made it clear often.

"You sure? You seem a little…concerned."

Trina reached for the glass of water Aubrey held and drained it dry. "It's not the getting married part, it's that this is it." Her gaze was slightly unfocused. She was like a balloon slowly rising, about to float away, and Aubrey grabbed the string to tether her back down.

"This is what?"

"*It*." Trina gave the word four syllables. She turned her gaze from the newlyweds to Aubrey and stage-whispered, "That's it for them. They'll never have sex with somebody new again. Ever."

Aubrey stifled the laugh she wanted to bark out at the overly wide-eyed look of horror Trina was giving her and, instead, forced herself to be serious. "You're right. That's true." She glanced back in the direction of the couple. "But just look at them." As if they'd been cued, Jenny looked up at her groom with such love in her eyes, and Kyle returned it a hundredfold. "Look how much they adore each other. And you *know* Jeff is crazy about you."

Trina scanned the room until her eyes landed on her fiancé on the other side. He grinned at her and blew a kiss. She turned back to Aubrey, waved a dismissive hand, said, "Eh. You're right. Fuck it," then held up her shot glass and waited until Aubrey touched the other to it. They downed the shots—no salt or lemon and against Aubrey's better judgment—and it burned all the way down her throat. "I gotta pee."

And then Trina was gone, leaving her standing there at the bar alone, watching after her and wondering if she'd just completely fried her entire esophagus.

"Who decided shots of tequila were a good thing?" Aubrey didn't hear the voice often, but she'd recognize it anywhere. Wasn't that weird? Low and a little husky. She turned and met cool blue eyes. "Like, if you need salt at the beginning and to suck on a lemon wedge after, that's a pretty clear sign that the middle part is awful, right?" Monica smiled tentatively at her.

"Seems obvious."

"So, I wonder who decided that was going to be the delivery method. Salt, shot, lemon. Who came up with that?"

"Mr. Tequila? I don't know." Aubrey shook her head, beginning to feel the effects of the shot on top of the wine with dinner, the champagne toast, and the Baileys in her coffee with the cake. The world had softened a bit, all the edges blurring just a little, and she felt warm inside.

"Is there a Mr. Tequila?" Monica laughed, and the sound was musical, higher than expected given the low register of her voice. A beat went by, and it wasn't until Monica asked, "What?" that Aubrey realized she'd been staring.

"Nothing." She shook her head, both in response and to hopefully shake her own brain back to normal.

Monica held her gaze for a moment, then ordered herself a glass of merlot. She pointed at Aubrey. "Do you want something?"

"Water. Please."

A few seconds later, she had a glass of ice water in her hand,

and while part of her wanted to flee, to get as far away from Monica as possible, some other part wouldn't allow her feet to move. What the hell?

Monica took a sip of her wine. "It was a nice ceremony, wasn't it?"

"It was. Way nicer than mine." Her intention had been to say the second line silently, but when Monica flinched ever so slightly and glanced down into her wine, she knew she'd said it out loud.

"And that's my cue," Monica said quietly. "Take care of yourself, Aubrey." And with that, she pushed away from the bar and headed…away. Probably anywhere that was far away from Aubrey.

She watched her go, watched her hips sway gently from side to side in the dress that clung to her body like a lover. Aubrey hated that her nemesis was gorgeous. It was so unfair. And then her brain flashed her the image of Monica's face after Aubrey's snarky comment. The way her eyes had shadowed and the corners of her lovely lips had turned down and the way her throat had moved when she'd swallowed, and Aubrey felt like a complete asshole. She sipped her water and wondered where the hell Trina was, annoyed all of a sudden that she'd made her do a shot in the first place. Her eyes found Monica again, near the stage, talking to somebody she didn't recognize and clearly *not* looking back at Aubrey. Because why would she?

"Stupid tequila," she muttered.

As if she materialized out of thin air, Trina was suddenly back, grabbing her hand and shouting at her to get her ass on the dance floor now. Aubrey's brain shot back into the present moment, and that's when she realized the DJ was playing Snoop Dogg and just about everybody left in the reception hall was dancing.

She let go. She let go of all the stress right then and simply let herself feel the music, pretend she felt as young, wild, and free as the song implied. No worries. No responsibilities. And none of the envy, sadness, or pain she normally felt at weddings, even this many years later. She raised her arms over her head and swayed, let everything go, and just danced.

There was a whole group of them, dancing as one living form

of limbs and heads, rolling and waving and rocking to the beat. The whole gang of them had gone to school together. Kyle and Jenny—well, not Jenny, but now that she was married to Kyle, she'd be absorbed into the group by osmosis. It would be the same with Harlan's and Eddie's girlfriends if they hung around. Trina and Jeff. Monica, yes, because she was part of the gang as well, whether Aubrey liked it or not, and she found herself watching Monica dance. She was a self-conscious dancer—Aubrey could tell right away. Monica definitely had rhythm, but her moves were subtle, like she was afraid to just cut loose. She moved her hips a little. Her shoulders...kind of. Her feet stayed planted, as if they'd rooted to the dance floor. She held her hands in loose fists.

"Just a little news update to tell you you're staring, and everybody knows it." Trina's singsong voice was right in her ear, and it yanked her roughly out of her dance analysis of Monica Wallace.

Shit.

She closed her eyes for a second, gave herself a mental shake, and then forced her gaze to look at anything but at Monica. Literally anywhere else. She shot Trina a look of gratitude.

Trina smiled and got close to her ear again. "I mean, I get it. She's fucking hot." She seemed to watch Aubrey's face. Then she looked at Monica and back to Aubrey and seemed to be debating something. Then she leaned in close again and said, "You know, we all wondered if she had a thing for you. Back then."

Aubrey was astonished. "What?" This was news to her.

Trina shrugged and wobbled a bit but rebalanced herself. Definitely drunk. "I mean, we know she had her reasons for doing what she did with Cody, but there were always whispers of an... unspoken thing for you."

This was *so* news to Aubrey. Like, it wasn't something that had ever even crossed her mind. Monica having a thing for her, not Aubrey thinking Monica was hot. Because she did. She always had. You could intensely dislike somebody and still think they were hot, couldn't you? That was allowed. She must've gotten lost in thought as she danced because when she glanced back at Trina, she looked stricken.

"Should I not have said anything? I'm sorry. I was overserved, and you know how I like to run my mouth when I've had too much."

Aubrey smiled and reached to give Trina's hand a squeeze. "No worries at all, Tree." She honestly wasn't sure if she was better off with this new information or if she would rather not know. But Trina only ever looked out for her. Always. So there was no way she could be mad at her. "It's a weird night."

Trina's grimace and nod said *I get it*, and they kept dancing, and Aubrey kept her eyes on her own paper, so to speak. Guests had been filtering out little by little until there were only about twenty left. A glance at her phone told Aubrey it was after midnight, and eventually, she made a slashing move across her throat as she said to Trina, "I'm out."

The place cleared out fast after that. She left her car at the reception hall, taking Trina and Jeff up on their offer to drive her home. She wasn't drunk, but she'd had a few, and it would be better to Uber to pick up her car tomorrow than get pulled over tonight. Trina hugged her tightly when they dropped her off, and Jeff stayed in the driveway until Aubrey was inside her house and waved out the window.

The house always felt so quiet without Emma. It was a weird dichotomy, though, because on the one hand, having the place to herself—something that happened rarely—was a joy. She'd always been a person who was perfectly comfortable with her own company. On the other hand, the mother in her missed her child. Would always miss her child, whether she was on the other side of the world or at the next-door neighbor's. It had been ingrained the second she'd pushed Emma out of her body. She would miss her and worry about her every single day for the rest of her life. Forever.

Sleep should've come easily given the combination of the alcohol in her system and all the dancing she'd done. Her body was bone-tired. Her mind had other ideas, though, and she lay in her bed until nearly two thirty, watching her brain play movies on the ceiling. Weddings and dancing and a very attractive blonde dressed in royal blue.

❖

"Morning, Mom." Emma's smiling face graced Aubrey's phone, filling up the screen.

"Hi, baby. How was your night?" Aubrey was still in bed, and it was after eight. Just as she was hoping she didn't look like she felt—run over by a truck—her father's face appeared behind Emma's.

"Looks like the wedding was a blast," he said with a knowing wink.

"Quiet, you," Aubrey said with a hoarse chuckle.

"Scrambled eggs and bacon will fix you right up," her father said. "Grease is a great hangover cure. Meanwhile, your daughter and your parents are going to get crepes for breakfast."

"That's why we're calling," Emma chimed in. "To see if I can stay later."

"Not to say good morning to your poor lonely mother?"

Emma snorted. "Please, Mom. I'm almost *ten*." She stressed the number as if that was all Aubrey needed to know to understand her. "I don't need to say good morning to you *every* day."

"You do if you don't want me to cry."

Emma had perfected the sarcastic eye roll by the time she was seven, and she used it now, while adding, "You're so weird."

"I know. Go. Have breakfast with your grandparents. I'll pick you up later. Love you."

Her father waved from the background and shouted, "Toast, too!" just before the call abruptly ended.

"And now I know I rate well behind crepes," she said to her empty bedroom. Not that she could blame Emma because crepes were food of the gods. She tried to go back to sleep for a bit. It was so rare that she had the opportunity to sleep in, but visions of scrambled eggs and bacon were too vivid to let her drift off, and soon she was up and shivering in the January cold. She pushed her legs into joggers and then pulled her favorite red hoodie over her head. The mirror told her she looked about as good as she felt, so she brushed her teeth with her back to it, then gathered her dark hair into a messy bun and went down to the kitchen to whip up some eggs.

Aubrey was proud of her little house. She'd had to work her ass off to afford it, and she'd had to take some call center jobs she could do from home, since childcare had been way out of her budget. But she'd worked, and she'd learned, and she became excellent at customer service. She could de-escalate an escalated call in a matter of minutes, and she made herself invaluable. When she'd been promoted to customer service manager, she'd vowed to save as much as she could so she could buy a little house for herself and Emma, get them out of the teeny tiny apartment they'd lived in for five years. And she'd done it.

It was small, a little Cape Cod on a tree-lined street in a decent neighborhood. Barely twelve hundred square feet. Her furniture was inexpensive, but she had a good eye for decorating, and now, as she sipped her coffee and leaned back against the counter in her kitchen, she felt a surge of pride at how far she'd come on so little. She watched the birds in and around Emma's feeder as they scrabbled in the snow to get every last bit of seed that had fallen to the ground. Her kitchen was a sunny pale yellow with white cabinets and a marbled gray countertop that wasn't marble or granite or anything expensive, but a terrific laminate she'd found that looked shockingly like granite and had cost about a quarter the price. The knobs and handles on the cabinets were a brushed nickel, as was the faucet curved above the stainless steel sink. She hadn't been able to afford stainless steel appliances, but the white ones she'd chosen looked great and gave the whole room a clean, fresh feel. Plus, despite all the white, it was a warm and inviting kitchen, which went a long way in the cold, dreary months of January and February in the Northeast.

She took her time scrambling eggs and frying bacon, and about an hour and a half later, after eating breakfast and downing a handful of Motrin, she called herself an Uber and headed out into the cold, snowy morning to pick up her car, then go get her kid.

While Aubrey didn't love winter, she did love when it snowed big, fat flakes, when they seemed to float slowly to the ground like they had all the time in the world to get there, covering it like a fluffy white blanket. She wasn't a fan of the cold, but she loved the beauty of winter. There was something about a fresh snowfall that made the world feel clean again. Like you could start fresh. A clean slate and all those clichés. She gazed out the window of the sedan, thankful that she'd ended up with an Uber driver who didn't do small talk. He said hello and said good-bye and that was it.

Her leased Toyota and one other car—a silver SUV—were the only ones in the lot. Hers should have been covered with snow, and half of it was. As her Uber drove away, Aubrey was shocked to see Monica brushing off the other half.

"No way," she whispered into the cold air when she saw her. *What in the unfair-surprise-visit-when-you're-hungover is this?*

"Well, hi there," Monica called as she stepped around to the front of Aubrey's car and brushed off the headlights. "Looks like we think alike."

Aubrey nodded, brushing the snow absently. "I guess so."

"You want to get it started to warm it up?"

That's when Aubrey realized the SUV was running, the snow beginning to slowly melt, clearing two twin spots on the windshield. She got into her own car and started the engine.

"How do you feel this morning?" Monica asked, then telescoped her snow brush so she could reach across Aubrey's roof. "I don't know about you, but my head and my stomach were not happy with me when I woke up. Felt like I'd been hit by a train."

On what planet was it fair that Aubrey woke up looking like somebody who'd been sleeping in a dumpster and Monica looked like, well, *that*? Completely put together. Her hair styled, her face smooth, her blue eyes bright. Aubrey became painfully aware of her decade-old sweats and her rat's nest hair and her pale, un-made-up face the more she looked at casual, fashionable, Sunday morning Monica. God, she hated her and her very sexy ass, which she got a terrific look at as Monica bent to pick up the snow brush she'd dropped.

"Yeah," Aubrey said. "Bacon and eggs helped."

"I was thinking of grabbing an Egg McMuffin on my way home."

"Universal hangover cure."

Monica barked a laugh. "So true."

It was only fair that Aubrey help brush off Monica's SUV—despite Monica telling her she didn't have to—so in the next moment, they were working together. It was weird. And also not weird at all, like it was something they did every day. Aubrey found herself taking her time. Probably because she was very safety conscious and didn't want to leave a lone woman on her own in an empty parking lot, so she was helping Monica avoid that.

Yeah. That was surely it.

"Kyle and Jenny seemed really happy," Monica said, not looking at Aubrey as she brushed off the back window. "I liked seeing that. It was nice."

Aubrey nodded her agreement. "It was." Did Monica's voice have an element of…wistfulness to it? She wasn't sure. She didn't know her well enough. But it seemed like it.

"And we get to do it all again in March, but at least it won't be in the snow." And then she laughed what Aubrey was starting to think of as the Monica laugh: a quick bark at the beginning, then a little bit of a musical tinkle to it. Like it started out harsh and ended kind of girly. It was cute, if Aubrey was honest. And then Monica's words registered.

"In March?"

Monica kept brushing snow as she said, "Sarah and Bailey? On the Outer Banks?" Then she stopped brushing and looked at Aubrey, stricken. "You are going, aren't you?"

Aubrey decided the panic was because if she hadn't been invited, Monica just made a big faux pas. She didn't have to worry. "I'm actually in that one," she said.

"You're a bridesmaid? That's great." And Monica seemed to really think so if her smile was any indication, and what was that about? "You and Sarah always did seem pretty close in college."

"She was probably my closest friend there after Trina."

"Makes sense," Monica said with a nod. "She and I have become pretty good friends. I go to her for my massages. She does wonders on my shoulders, which is where I hold all my stress, I'm told." She laughed softly and continued to brush the snow as she said, "I've never been to a destination wedding. Have you?"

The small talk was surprising Aubrey, but she went with it and shook her head. "I never have, no. I both love and hate the idea. I mean, it'll be fun to get out of the cold in March, but it's also expensive. I'll have to miss work, and I can't afford to bring Emma, so it'll just be me." Why? Why was she telling all this to Monica. It was none of her business. "Not that you asked for all that info. Sorry."

"No need to apologize. I get it." Monica finished her side of the car and asked, "All set? I don't think either of us should stay here alone."

"Yeah. I'm good."

"Okay." Monica opened the door to her SUV and tossed her snow brush in, then turned to Aubrey and smiled at her like they were old friends. "I guess I'll see you in North Carolina, then." She gave a little wave and got into her car before Aubrey could say anything more, like thank you—God, she was such an asshole—and she gave a little wave back, watching as Monica drove away.

She got into her own car, which was toasty warm now, and thanked the stars above once again for her seat warmers. "What the hell just happened?" she muttered to the empty interior of her car. Then she glanced into the rearview mirror, which was a mistake because she was reminded again that she looked like she'd slept in her clothes and had no idea how to brush her own hair. With a loud groan, she shifted the car and headed toward her parents' house.

She put away the knowledge that she'd see Monica again in less than two months, because she wasn't sure what to do with that, and focused on her drive. It was time to pick up Emma.

❖

Aubrey wasn't a huge fan of football, but her father was, and he was doing his best to teach the rules of the game to his granddaughter.

That was how Aubrey ended up talked into spending the afternoon at her parents' house. Emma *really sooo bad* wanted to watch the game with her papa, and Aubrey's mom was making chili and said she could use the company. Then she mentioned that she was also going to make cornbread, and that was all Aubrey needed. Sold.

"How was the wedding?" her mother asked as she sautéed onions and peppers for the chili. "Did you get to see all your college friends?"

Aubrey nodded as she made herself a cup of coffee, extra strong, and stirred in some cream. "Yeah, it was a lot of fun. A really beautiful ceremony, good food, good music." She pulled out a stool nestled under the peninsula, sat, and blew out a long breath. "Do you know I have five weddings to go to this year? Five! All friends from college. And Cody."

"Oh my God, that is a whole lot of marriage. Wow."

"It's a whole lotta marriage, Mom." And then they both laughed.

"Your friends all seem to be on the same page this year. Have they all been together around the same amount of time?"

"I mean, the next one in March is Sarah and Bailey, and they're the only ones who've been together since actual college."

"And you're all set with your dress for that one? You're in it, right?"

"I am, and you might need to take Emma for the weekend because"—she lowered her voice to just above a whisper—"who knows if Cody will be at the wedding or here or gallivanting or what?" Her mother shot her a look and she amended her words. "Fine. Working, not gallivanting."

"He does a good thing, honey."

Aubrey sighed loudly. "Yeah, yeah. I know. He's Mr. Legal Aid. He helps the downtrodden. He's admirable. I get it. Too bad he wasn't more helpful when his kid was born." At her mother's expression of pity, she waved her hand in a dismissive gesture. "Forget it. Never mind. It's old news. I know." And as if sent to alleviate any tension, Emma came bounding into the kitchen.

"Papa wants me to get the salt and vinegar chips," she said, her eyes and tone all perfectly innocent.

"Oh, *Papa* wants them?" Aubrey asked, grabbing her daughter by the waist and hauling her into a hug.

"He does!" Emma squealed.

"And do you get to eat some if you get them for *Papa*?" Aubrey asked, digging her fingers into Emma's side where she knew her daughter was particularly ticklish.

"I mean, duh." Then she broke into a fit of giggles, and it was Aubrey's favorite sound in the whole wide world.

"What do you think, Mom?" Aubrey asked. "Do you believe this garbage story about the chips being for Dad?"

Her mother was laughing at the two of them. "Your father used to send you in to get ice cream, and you always ended up with a bowl, too, so yeah, I believe it." She went to the pantry, grabbed the bag of potato chips, and dumped them into a bowl. To Emma, she said, "Do you want your own bowl, or can you get him to share?"

"He'll share," Emma said with supreme confidence. "He says I'm his favorite person." At Aubrey's gasp of mock horror, she turned and ran out of the kitchen, her giggles still hanging in the air.

"You know," her mother said as they stood in the wake of Hurricane Emma, "it was a terrible time for you, and it would've been nice if things had worked out a little differently, but I wouldn't change a thing because look who we ended up with." She waved a hand in the general direction Emma had gone, and her eyes were wet.

"Oh, Mom, you're such a sap," she teased. "But I get it. She's my heart, too." They chatted for a bit, mixed up the cornbread batter, and slid the pan into the oven. Aubrey's phone rang the second the oven door closed, and she glanced at the screen. Cody.

"Hey there," she said.

"Hi, A, how's things? How was the wedding?"

She filled him in on the ceremony, who was in attendance, and what kind of music they played. It was funny—sometimes, if she closed out any details about their past, she could almost fall right back into conversations with him like they had when they were together. It had been ten years, but the memories were often still so vivid, they could make her heart ache just a little. Not because she missed Cody himself. She didn't anymore. But she did sometimes miss what might have been.

"You're in Sarah and Bailey's in March, right?" he asked.

"Yep."

"The Outer Banks should be nice that time of year. Not super hot, but much better than upstate New York."

"True. You going?"

"I think so. Depends on Kimmy's work schedule." When she didn't respond right away, he went on, asking, "Is my little nugget there?"

"Yup. She's watching football with Papa. Hang on." She called to Emma that her dad was on the phone. As Emma ran into the kitchen, took the phone, and said hi to her daddy, Aubrey watched as her face lit up and her whole body became animated, and her voice got a little softer, a little more little girlish. It was always like that, and it had always been like that. Cody was a treat, a special appearance, while Aubrey was the same old, boring usual. Steady and reliable, yes. Also boring.

"Will he be at the next wedding?" her mother asked as Emma took the phone and her conversation to another room.

"Depends on Kimmy. Seriously, what kind of name is that for a grown woman?" She caught the look from her mother and said, "I'm not bitter. I'm not. But the woman is thirty-five years old and a lawyer. Why isn't she Kim? Or Kimberly?"

Her mother's chuckle could be heard from behind the refrigerator door as she took a bottle of beer out of the fridge and popped the cap. "Well, she's gonna be Emma's stepmother, so you'd better get used to saying her name." As she walked past her to deliver it to Aubrey's father, she ran her hand across Aubrey's shoulders in a subtle show of support. She knew Aubrey well.

"Yeah, I know," Aubrey said. "I know."

Later that night, she was helping Emma get ready for bed. She'd taken a bath—because she hadn't showered at her grandparents' that morning—and was in her pj's in the living room, curled up on the couch under a blanket watching television.

Aubrey gave her foot a pat. "Just about time for bed, kiddo."

"Mom? Will you read to me?"

Aubrey couldn't hide her surprise. "Of course I will. How come?"

"I just like your voice when you read to me. Makes me feel safe."

Aubrey felt her heart squeeze in her chest a little, and they headed upstairs to Emma's bedroom.

A few minutes later, they were curled up on Emma's bed, Aubrey with her legs stretched out and Emma all snuggled into her side. They were reading *Because of Winn-Dixie* for what had to be the tenth time. They both knew the book by heart, but for Aubrey, this moment wasn't about the story. It was about the moment. Emma was almost ten. She was in fourth grade. These nights of snuggling were becoming fewer and farther between, and she wanted to capture each one, wished she had a movie reel of all of them so she could go back and visit these moments.

She read until she felt slightly hoarse, and Emma was snoring softly next to her. And after she closed the book, she stayed for a while, just watching her child sleep, listening to her breathe. Life hadn't been easy. Getting to this point, where she had a house and a job and an actual savings account—with money in it!—had been a struggle. But these moments? These were the times that made that struggle worthwhile. Her daughter. Her child. The most important person in the world and the one who gave meaning to her life.

People thought Emma looked like her, and Aubrey could admit to taking some pride in that, though she did see a lot of Cody. Aubrey's hair had been lighter as a child, so that's where Emma's hair came from. But she had Cody's dark eyes and his dark lashes and brows. Her brows were thick, straight lines, not arched. She hated them now, but Aubrey knew when she was a woman, those straight, dark brows were going to be a main feature. They already gave her a look of intensity, of mystery. Those would only be accentuated, she knew. Emma also had Cody's strong jawline and square chin. Watching her grow into her features was one of the things Aubrey most looked forward to, because while she might have her issues with her ex, she'd never deny his good looks. They'd made a beautiful baby. That was a fact that could never be changed.

She gave herself a few more minutes to gawk at her adorable kid before she finally extricated herself from her daughter's grasp. She had no worries at all about waking her up—Emma slept like she'd been drugged. She always had. Thunderstorms, fireworks, the house exploding, none of it would wake her up. She turned off the light on the nightstand and pulled the door shut behind her.

Tomorrow was Monday. Back to school for Emma. Back to work for Aubrey. The wedding had been a nice break from reality, but it was almost time to get back to it.

In the kitchen, she got her coffee ingredients ready for the morning, as well as a spoon and bowl set out for Emma. Whether she ate a bowl of cereal or a granola bar on the run would depend on how quickly she got out of bed in the morning. That was anybody's guess, and Aubrey found herself smiling at the unpredictability of her kid. Not that she'd be smiling tomorrow morning if it took a crane or a crowbar to get Emma out of bed.

She turned off the lights downstairs, poured herself a small glass of cabernet, and took it and her book upstairs to her bedroom. No cute dogs named after grocery stores for her, no sir. Her book was a thriller, and the main character was a tall, beautiful, blond woman who was doing her best to figure out who in her small town was lying to her about her childhood. She'd read a good three chapters before it occurred to her that she'd given the main character a face. Monica's face. She slammed the book shut.

"Yup. Okay. Time for bed."

Lights out, curled into her pillow and under her thick, downy comforter, it didn't take long for her to drift off. It also didn't take her long to start dreaming about Monica.

WEDDINGS DOWN: 1
SUCCESS IN AVOIDING MONICA WALLACE: 0

Part Two

Sarah and Bailey
March 30, 2024
Destination Wedding

Aubrey McFadden is never getting married.

Reason #3
Everybody lies.

The drive from upstate New York to the Outer Banks in North Carolina was about eleven hours and change, and Aubrey had seriously considered driving. But between getting Emma all settled in at her parents', going over homework assignments and her nighttime schedule, and dealing with trying to take time off at her own job, she couldn't spare the extra day she'd have spent in the car. She hadn't really wanted to fork over the money for a plane ticket—she was already several hundred dollars in the hole after buying her bridesmaid's dress, having it altered, and what her hotel room was going to cost—but if she'd driven, she'd have missed some of the stuff that Sarah had set up for her bridesmaids to do. And she knew it would be fun once she got there. It was always the prep that was hard.

Sarah was already in North Carolina, as was her sister, but the other bridesmaids, like Aubrey, were headed there on Wednesday. Aubrey didn't know the other two—friends from the massage place where Sarah worked—and assumed they were flying in from Philadelphia, where Sarah and Bailey lived.

She'd gotten through security with no problem and made it to her gate, and that's when the nerves began to kick in. Because that was the main thing about Aubrey and airplanes—she hated to fly. Hated it. Was terrified. And if she had to, she would do her best to find a direct flight because there was always the possibility that once she deplaned at her connection destination, she wouldn't be able to bring herself to get on the next one.

She didn't fly often, but she wasn't a flight virgin either. She preferred to fly with a buddy, somebody whose forearm she could hold in a viselike grip while they took off, and again during landing. But she was on her own today.

Her phone kept her occupied until her flight was called to board. There was no assigned seating with this airline, but she had grudgingly paid a little extra to ensure she'd be able to board fairly early and get herself a window seat. No, she didn't want to look out—the first thing she'd do was slam that shade down so she didn't have to see how fast they were speeding along the runway or how high they were above the smart people who stayed on the ground—but she needed to lean. Additionally, the idea of being in between two strangers while she was quietly losing her shit did not sound like her idea of fun.

Seat A in row seven was hers, and she claimed it quickly, plopping into the seat, buckling her seat belt, and sliding that shade down. The flight attendant announced that they would be a completely full flight and that every seat would be taken. With a glance at the currently empty middle seat next to her, she sent up a prayer that whoever sat there would be forgiving if she had a panic attack. She dug out her AirPods and stuck them in her ears, tuning her phone to Taylor Swift—she didn't listen often enough to be considered a Swiftie, but Emma did, so Aubrey labeled herself a Swiftie-by-Association. Plus, the music would keep her from hearing every knock, bump, and ding the plane made, sounds that apparently did *not* mean the plane was about to crash, or so she'd been told more than once. Then she tightened the seat belt until it was just this side of too tight, leaned her head back, closed her eyes while the rest of the passengers boarded, and let herself get lost in the music.

When she sensed that people had stopped boarding, she ventured to open her eyes. Everyone was seated, and the middle seat next to her remained empty. So, not *completely* full, she thought, pausing her music to listen to the announcements. She was contemplating whether she'd rather have it empty or occupied by a stranger when the flight attendant added that they were waiting on one more passenger and then they'd be ready to pull back. There was the typical grumble from people who were impatient or unsympathetic or who had never run late ever in their lives, but Aubrey just shrugged. Whoever it was would clearly be sitting next to her, and she decided right then that another person would be better than the empty space, that she'd feel safer.

Closing her eyes again, she let Taylor serenade her some more until she felt the air shift next to her, and she opened her eyes to see her seatmate.

No. Fucking. Way.

"What...? How...?" Apparently, all the other words in the English language had fallen out of her brain, because she just sat there, gawking, while Monica Wallace shoved a bag under the seat in front of her, buckled her seat belt, and blew out a huge breath.

"I know." Monica kept her voice just above a whisper, but she was clearly stressed. "Trust me, I'm very aware that you'd rather not sit by me. And if my alarm had gone off when it was supposed to, and if I hadn't had trouble finding a parking spot, and if they hadn't decided to pull me out of the security line for a *more thorough* search"—she made air quotes—"I'd have picked another seat. Unfortunately, this is the only one left. I'm sorry."

Aubrey glanced down at her hands and felt like a jerk. "No, I'm the one who's sorry. Sounds like you had a rough morning."

"Yeah." Monica pulled out her own AirPods and stuck them in her ears, not looking at Aubrey again.

The Powers that Be were definitely messing with her, she decided. She was mulling that over when the airplane jerked and started to move, and then they were headed for the runway.

This was when the panic started to bloom. It started right in the center of her chest, like somebody flicked a switch and flooded her with heat. A lump formed in her throat, and things started to tense up without her permission. Her jaw clenched, her fingers balled into fists, her shoulders rose up a bit, and one leg started to bounce uncontrollably. She closed her eyes and tried to focus on her breathing like Trina had taught her, but when she felt the plane lurch forward and pick up speed, she squeezed her eyes shut harder and grabbed for the armrest on her right.

Monica's arm was there.

Before Aubrey could jerk her hand back, Monica put her other hand on top of it and held her tight, Aubrey's hand sandwiched between Monica's forearm and her hand. And God help her, it was exactly what she needed. She hazarded a glance at Monica, but she was facing forward, eyes closed, head back on the headrest. What must it be like to be that relaxed during takeoff?

And then the plane was lifting off the ground. Aubrey squeezed her eyes shut again and tightened her grip on Monica's arm, didn't let up until the plane leveled off and the flight attendant announced they could get their larger electronic devices out for use.

Forcing her brain to tell her fingers to ease up, she gave Monica what she hoped was a sheepish grin. "Sorry about that," she said quietly.

Monica took out one AirPod. "Not big on flying, huh?"

"Hate it."

"Sorry. That's rough." Back in went the AirPod, and Monica's eyes closed again.

For the next hour, Aubrey couldn't decide which would have been worse, having Monica ignore her completely or being forced to carry on a conversation with her for the whole time. It didn't matter, though, because Monica made the decision for her by keeping her AirPods in and her eyes closed for the entire flight. She might have been sleeping, Aubrey wasn't sure. But she felt a little silly sitting next to somebody she knew and not talking at all.

Oh, well. She wasn't about to *make* her chat.

The flight was short—less than ninety minutes—and when the flight attendant announced they were making their descent into Norfolk, Aubrey's nerves took that as a sign to wake up and begin the whole tension thing all over again. Landing was always a little bit worse for her because of touchdown. That jolt when the wheels touched the ground always sent her fear through the roof as her brain sent her images of landing gear snapping off and planes sliding on their bellies at a bajillion miles per hour along the asphalt until they exploded into balls of flame and—

She glanced down at the armrest, and Monica's hand was there and open, as if she was waiting for Aubrey to grab on. Her eyes were still closed, her AirPods still in, but there was her hand, like a lifeline. Aubrey blinked at it. Once. Twice. Three times. And then the plane hit a little turbulence that seemed to toss her stomach around inside her body and she didn't even have a chance to think *fuck it* before her hand was on Monica's, *in* Monica's, their fingers interlacing like they were lovers that held hands all the time. Monica never looked at her. She just closed her fingers around Aubrey's hand, pulled it into her body, and closed her other hand over it.

Aubrey had never felt so safe on a flight before.

It didn't keep her from squeezing her eyes shut again or clenching every muscle she could, but it did keep the deadly visions away. It kept her knee from bouncing. It kept her breathing steady.

And then the wheels touched and the brakes went on and they were safe on the ground, dear sweet Jesus, they were safe.

It was another moment or two before she relaxed her grip on Monica's hand and Monica let her go as she finally opened her eyes.

They taxied for several minutes until finally making it to their gate, and the sound of everybody's seat belt being unfastened at once was music to Aubrey's ears. People were on their feet and pulling bags out of overhead compartments and chatting and moving, and all Aubrey felt was relief. She was awash in it. Her muscles all relaxed, and she felt like she could breathe normally again.

"You got a bag up here?" Monica asked her, just as a man from several compartments back handed one up the aisle until Monica had it in her hands. She smiled a thank you to the man, and it changed her face completely. Monica was gorgeous, there was no way around that fact. As if to punctuate Aubrey's thought on the matter, the man's cheeks bloomed red, and he told Monica she was very welcome and then glanced down at his feet like a schoolgirl with a crush, and it was all very interesting to watch. The smile was not meant for Aubrey, though, as it disappeared completely when Monica turned back to her, eyebrows raised expectantly.

"Oh. No, I checked a bag."

Monica nodded once, hauled her backpack over a shoulder, and stood with her carry-on in the aisle as passengers began to file off the plane.

"Hey," she said, just as Monica was about to move. When she turned and those blue eyes locked on her, Aubrey felt something in her body shift. "Thank you," she said, then held up her hand and wiggled her fingers to specify exactly what she was talking about.

Monica nodded, gave her a half smile, and followed the guy in front of her up the aisle.

A gentleman across the aisle waited for Aubrey to scootch out and deplane before him, so she did but took her time once she was in the tunnel that would lead her into the airport. It always went like that. She needed time to reacquaint her feet with solid ground, time to let her lungs take in full breaths instead of panicked short ones. People always hurried past her, and sometimes they were annoyed with her lack of speed, but she didn't mind. She went at her own pace until the tunnel spilled her into the bright and open air of the airport and she felt human again.

As she followed the signs to baggage claim, it occurred to her that she hadn't asked Monica why she was headed to the wedding location so early. As far as she knew, it was only the bridal party who needed to be present for the two days before the wedding. But Monica was clearly one of the passengers who walked at a hundred miles an hour because she was nowhere to be found. She'd disappeared into the sea of people, and Aubrey couldn't find her at all.

With a mental shrug, she made her way to the correct baggage carousel and waited for her bag. It was a good twenty minutes before that happened, but it was okay, because she was going to rent a car and make the drive to the Outer Banks. What would've been super convenient would have been if Sarah and Bailey had chosen to get married in Virginia Beach instead. Then she wouldn't be spending yet more money on renting a car and driving for two hours and change, but if Aubrey was being honest, she was kind of looking forward to such a long drive. It would give her time to decompress.

What was not going to help her decompress was the line to the rental car counter. "What in the I'm-going-to-be-in-this-line-forever is this?" she muttered to herself as she stood there. Doing a very good impression of a very long snake, the line turned back on itself several times as people wove around the ribbon thingies that made them look and feel like cattle. There had to be close to fifty people in line ahead of her. *I'm going to be here until the end of time.*

It wasn't like she had a choice. She pulled out her phone to see what time it was and to see what options she might have. There were a couple other rental car places, but apparently, everybody in the airport needed to rent a car right then because each counter had a significant line of people.

Just when Aubrey was about to accept her fate—that Sarah and Bailey would not only be married, but would probably have a couple of kids by the time she actually got to the front of the line and rented a car—there was a tap on her shoulder. She turned and locked eyes with a familiar figure.

"Come with me," was all Monica said, and then she turned and walked away. Aubrey blinked at her in confusion, and when Monica noticed she wasn't coming, she said simply, "You can stand in that line until midnight, or you can ride with me. My car is ready."

Okay, yeah, that was some pretty easy math.

Aubrey jumped out of the line, hauling her suitcase and mentally congratulating the person in line behind her for getting one spot closer, and she followed Monica as she walked between two rental car counters and under a sign that read *Hertz Gold Plus.*

"No lines for you, huh?" she asked as she hurried to catch up, realizing they were headed for the parking garage.

"I travel a lot for work. This is the only way to go. The lines never used to be that bad, but after the pandemic—between staffing shortages and car shortages—it just became unbearable. There was one time I stood in line for almost three hours to rent a car. That was enough for me. This is so much less stressful."

They passed a large sign with a list of people's names and then a number which she figured out were parking sections. *Monica Wallace D27* was the fourth name down. They kept walking until the reached the well-labeled D27.

"What do you think?" Monica asked as she stopped and seemed to survey the cars.

"About?"

Monica looked at her for the first time since Aubrey had started following her. "Which car should we take? We can choose."

"Seriously?" Aubrey didn't know such a thing existed, and she scanned the Rogues and RAV4s and Altimas and even a Corvette convertible off to the left.

"Yeah, not the Corvette. I'm two levels down from that. *For now.*" She emphasized the last two words with a grin.

Together, they chose a candy-apple-red Nissan Rogue, a nice middle-of-the-road SUV that easily carried both of them and all their bags. The keys were inside, and Monica started it up, then hooked her iPhone up to the dash and called up directions to the hotel. Then they drove to the exit booth, checked in with the employee there, and were on their way.

As they pulled out into the lovely spring sunshine, Aubrey thought back to the line-that-never-ends back at the rental counter and gave a mental shudder. "Thank you so much for this. Who knows how long I might've been in that line."

"My prediction? Six months to a year."

Aubrey grinned as she dug her sunglasses out of her purse and slipped them on. "How come you're coming so early?" She asked the question that had been hanging out in her brain since the moment she first saw Monica on the plane. "I didn't think guests had to be there until Saturday morning."

"I've been promoted to bridal party. One of Bailey's friends had to cancel at the last minute because of a family thing, so Bailey asked me if I'd step in."

"*Oh*," Aubrey said, giving the tiny word three syllables.

"She and I spent some time together during school, and we've kept in touch over the years."

Aubrey squinted at her, something about her tone making her

think. "I see. And does *spent some time together* equal *dated a little bit*?"

Monica threw her head back and laughed, a big, hearty laugh that Aubrey couldn't help but smile at. "Oh, you're good. Yes, we dated for about four and a half minutes back in sophomore year."

"I can't believe I never knew this."

"I mean, it literally was a super short thing. We realized pretty quickly that we made better friends."

"And then she met Sarah, and the rest is history."

"Right."

Aubrey thought she saw a shadow cross Monica's face, but she said nothing more, and they were quiet for several miles.

Finally, Monica spoke again.

"Hey, I didn't have time for breakfast, and my stomach is eating itself. You mind if we grab something?" Before Aubrey could say a word, her stomach rumbled loudly, and Monica laughed. "I guess that's my answer." They swung through the drive-through of a McDonald's, and then they were back on the road, loaded down with fast food.

Aubrey took it upon herself to get it all organized. She unwrapped Monica's cheeseburger and spread the paper on her lap below the steering wheel like a tablecloth, mentally reminding herself that Monica's designer jeans likely cost more than Aubrey's entire outfit. She set Monica's container of fries up in one of the drink holders for easy access and her soda in the other. Then she got her own food situated, and they ate as Monica drove.

"You're pretty good at this setup thing." Monica offered the compliment after she'd taken a bite of her burger and set it back onto her makeshift tablecloth lap.

"I have a nine-year-old."

"That really is all the explanation you need, isn't it?"

They ate and drove, and it occurred to Aubrey that it almost felt like they did this all the time. Traveled together. Ate together on the road. It was comfortable—at least in that moment—and she wasn't sure how that was possible.

When they'd eaten all but a few of the fries, Aubrey gathered everything up and put it all neatly into the McDonald's bag, leaving just their drinks in the drink holder. She really wanted to hunker down in her seat and put her feet up on the dash, but she wasn't sure how that would go over, so instead, she sat up and watched the road and the shops go by, and every so often, she'd glance over at her driver, using her sunglasses as cover.

Monica was stupidly good-looking. There was no way around it. She had natural beauty, and Aubrey had always hated her for that. Which was silly, she knew. Now, she looked at her with no bias. Factually. Her skin was smooth, and Aubrey had a feeling she would go home with a lovely bronze suntan by the time Sunday rolled around. She'd shucked off her jacket while in the drive-through and now wore a simple long-sleeve white T-shirt and jeans, and how was it that she made such basic, everyday clothes look like they were made for her. She had an elbow up on her driver's side door, her hand supporting her head. Her blond hair was down and wavy, and Aubrey could smell her shampoo—coconut and something else tropical…maybe mango? She'd gotten a manicure, her nails neatly filed, not long but not short, and polished a deep plum.

"So, what's the schedule for the next couple of days?" Monica's voice startled her, and she felt her body flinch. She'd been staring, but she didn't think she'd been caught. She sent up a silent thank you to the stars above.

"Let's see…tomorrow is the bachelorette party. It's at a bar and restaurant that's right on the beach. I looked at the weather last week but haven't had a chance to check it more recently. Hopefully, it won't be freezing."

"Listen, there's no snow and it's above fifty degrees. I'm good."

"Same," Aubrey said. "Then Friday is a spa day for the bridal party and then rehearsal and dinner. Saturday is the ceremony, obviously. On the beach. I hope we don't freeze to death. Yes, it's warmer than home, but it's March. It's not *warm*-warm."

Monica nodded at the words, then turned to her and lifted one shoulder in a half-shrug. "Maybe we'll get lucky."

❖

Sarah and Aubrey had been pretty close in college, despite the fact that Sarah dated women exclusively and Aubrey had been all wrapped up in Cody. They had a few classes together, lived on the same floor in the dorm, and just generally hit it off. Seeing her yesterday after she and Monica arrived at the hotel, it was like no time at all had passed. They hugged, they joked, they laughed, and Aubrey was finally glad she'd come. She was introduced to the other bridesmaids, she lost Monica somewhere in the shuffle, and the celebration began.

The luncheon the next day was at the hotel restaurant, Ricardo's, and when Aubrey had looked it up on Tripadvisor after the schedule was handed out, the reviews had been impressive. So she'd looked forward to it all morning, skipping breakfast in favor of coffee so she'd have more of an appetite at one o'clock.

She and Monica sat on opposite sides of a long table in a room that was closed off from the rest of the customers. There were Sarah's three bridesmaids, plus her sister, Charlene, her matron of honor. There were also Sarah's mom and her grandmother, plus her aunt Marcia. On the other side of the table were all Bailey's people, including Monica, Bailey's mother and grandma, and a great-aunt. Sarah and Bailey were at the end of the table, and when they stood up, champagne flutes in hand, the rest of the room went quiet, and Bailey spoke.

"Sarah and I just want to take a moment to thank you all for making the trek to the beautiful Outer Banks to celebrate our day— well, our _three_ days—with us. It means so much that you're all here, and hopefully, we're going to get a nice day on the beach on Saturday. So far, it's looking good." She put an arm around Sarah and pulled her closer. "And if it takes a turn and the weather tanks, blame my lovely bride-to-be, who always wanted to get married on the beach." A ripple of laughter went around the room.

"Seriously, though," Sarah said, "thank you all so much. Special thanks to Monica, for stepping in at the last minute." Then she lowered her voice to a stage whisper and said, "Please don't talk her out of marrying me."

Ouch.

Another ripple went around the room, though Aubrey noticed that Monica didn't laugh, nor did she look in Aubrey's direction. In fact, she turned slightly pink, and while she did smile, it looked pained, probably a mirror image of Aubrey's face.

"Sorry, Aubrey," Sarah said, holding up her flute. "I couldn't resist. You know I'm just playing."

Aubrey smiled dutifully and nodded, and they toasted and sipped and things moved on. But her appetite had taken a hit, and much as she'd wanted to dig in to the dishes she'd read up on, her stomach had a different idea. She managed some salad and a few bites of a delicious salmon dish, but mostly the food just sat in her belly like rocks.

"So, what do you do, Aubrey?" asked the woman next to her, Jordan, who she knew was one of Sarah's coworkers.

"I'm a customer service manager for the pharmacy end of a drug store."

"Oh, wow, I bet you've got stories," Jordan said, then took a sip from her wineglass. Hers was red while Aubrey had a rosé. "Customers can be horrendous when they feel slighted."

"So many stories," she said with a laugh.

"How long have you been doing that?" Jordan asked. Aubrey decided she liked her. She seemed down to earth and her curiosity, genuine.

"About eight years. I started right out of college taking customer service calls at home when Emma was a baby."

"Right out of school? What was your major?" Jordan scooped a forkful of fruit salad into her mouth, her eyes on Aubrey.

"History," she replied. "I wanted to be a history teacher."

"Oh, wow. Didn't work out, huh?" It seemed she genuinely might not know the story, which seemed unlikely after Sarah's comment to Monica, but Jordan's face was still open and curious.

"No, I had a baby. Not planned, but the best thing that's ever happened to me, so…" She shrugged and knew without looking that Monica's eyes were on her from across the table.

"Oh, wow," Jordan said again. "Go, you. I can't imagine having a baby now, let alone straight out of college."

"It definitely wasn't ideal, but…" She shrugged again.

"Do you have pics?" Jordan asked.

"Of?"

"Of your kid, weirdo." Jordan's laugh was soft and cute, and she bumped Aubrey with a shoulder.

"Oh!" Then she gave a snort. "Do I have pics. Be careful what you wish for, woman." And she pulled out her phone.

Lunch wasn't so bad after that.

❖

"I miss you, sweetie. So much." Aubrey made a kissing face and sound into the screen of her phone as she FaceTimed with her daughter.

"You too," Emma said, but she was clearly distracted as Aubrey's father held the phone in front of her. "We're going to have pizza and we're gonna be *late*."

"Late? For what? Does the pizza have someplace else to be and if you're not there at a certain time, it's leaving?" She forced herself to chuckle so her daughter wouldn't see her hurt feelings.

"*Mom*," Emma said, giving her name three syllables and punctuating it with an eye roll that told her how very uncool she was without actually saying it.

"Hey, your mom said she misses you," Aubrey's mother said off-screen. "Be nice."

"It's okay," Aubrey said, making a shooing motion with her hand. "Go have your pizza. I just wanted to check in while I had a minute."

"Love you, bye," Emma said, and this time, three words came out like one. Suddenly, Aubrey was looking at her father.

"Kid's a whirlwind," he said with his gentle smile and kind, dark eyes.

"Is she being good?" she asked. "Don't let her run you ragged."

"She's keeping us young. Stop worrying. We got this." And then his face disappeared as her mother took the phone from him.

"How's it going down there? You doing okay? I know how much you don't enjoy weddings."

Bless her mother. Just bless her for getting it. Somehow, just her understanding made some of Aubrey's stress dissipate. "It's fine. I'm good. Having a decent time so far."

"How's the weather?"

"Kinda gray and gloomy today. The forecast for Saturday is promising, so keep your fingers crossed for me. I don't want to be standing on the beach in a hurricane."

"Grandma, come *on*," came Emma's voice from somewhere off-screen. Her mother gave her a slight grimace, which made Aubrey laugh.

"Go. Don't keep the pizza waiting. I'll call you tomorrow." Raising her voice a bit, she said louder, "I love you, Emmy!"

And then they were gone and the screen was back to her icons, and she didn't like how alone she felt. With a sigh, she tossed her phone onto the hotel's queen-sized bed and thought *story of my life*, just as there was a knock at her door.

She wasn't due anywhere for another three hours and had hoped to grab a nap, so the knock surprised her. She was even more surprised when she looked through the peephole.

"Sarah, hi," she said when she opened the door. "What are you doing here? Don't you have bride-to-be stuff to do? Shouldn't you be enjoying your last couple of days as an unattached woman?" She stood aside and waved her in.

Sarah gave a small chuckle. "Are you kidding? I've been waiting to get married since the second week I knew Bailey. I will be *thrilled* to be unavailable." Aubrey watched as Sarah's hazel eyes went slightly wide and then slammed shut, and she shook her head slowly from side to side. "God, there I go again."

Aubrey frowned, confused. "What do you mean?"

"I came here to apologize." Sarah was cute, petite and athletic, with chestnut hair that was currently pulled back into a ponytail. She wore simple leggings and a T-shirt with the Nike swoosh across the front. She'd dressed in athleisure before it was hip to do so, and Aubrey had always envied how put together she could look in workout clothes. "And instead, I just hit you with another zing about marriage. I suck. I'm so sorry."

Aubrey made a face. "I don't understand. *Why* are you here to apologize?"

"For my stupid crack at the luncheon about Monica not talking Bailey out of marrying me!"

"Oh my God. Please." Aubrey waved it off but, deep inside, felt more seen than she had since she got here.

"No, seriously. It was cruel and unnecessary, and Bailey almost killed me."

"It was ten years ago."

"I know." Sarah's eyes softened, as did her tone. "But it sucked. And it can't be easy for you to see all of us who were there getting married. I mean, it's the weirdest year, right?"

"So weird. Did you guys have a Zoom meeting and decide you'd all get married this year?"

And then they were laughing, and any tension or discomfort that had been in the room vanished. They were college friends again, standing in a dorm room, talking about what time tonight's soccer game was.

"I heard you and Monica drove together from the airport," Sarah said, changing tack completely.

"She's clearly much smarter about car rentals than I am. I'd probably still be standing in line at Budget if she hadn't saved me."

Sarah's expression was unreadable to Aubrey. "Then I'm hoping you won't mind doing your entrance together at the ceremony Saturday?" She grimaced in obvious anticipation of Aubrey's answer. "She's filling in for Jessie, whose mom fell down some stairs and needs her there to help. Jessie was going to walk the beach with you. So, now it's Monica." She put a hand on Aubrey's shoulder as she hurriedly continued with, "But if you want me to change things up, I can. Just say the word. No big deal."

I am not going to be that person.

That was the first thought that zipped through her head. She was not about to force Sarah to switch up things at her wedding just so Aubrey didn't have to walk down the proverbial aisle with somebody she hated ten years ago. "Absolutely not," she said. "Leave it all as is. I have no issue standing up with Monica. We're all grown-ups, right? And ten years is a long time."

Sarah's relief was evident. "That's what I thought, too, but Bailey wanted me to make sure."

She reassured Sarah some more, wanting to be certain she wasn't worried about Aubrey when she should be focusing on getting married. Then she sent her on her way, telling her she'd see her at the bachelorette party that night. As she closed the door behind her, she couldn't decide if she was touched that her friends were concerned enough about her to make sure she was okay, or embarrassed because her friends were still concerned about how she'd be in any given wedding-like situation, even after ten years.

After *ten years*.

It had literally been ten years.

An entire decade. That was a long time. But if Aubrey closed her eyes, she could still see Cody's face as he broke her heart. She could still see Monica, hear her voice telling her it was better that she knew now.

In her experience, some things didn't fade if you didn't let them, and ten years could vanish just like that.

She flopped back onto her bed and blew out a frustrated breath. A nap now was damn unlikely.

❖

While strippers were not really her thing, Aubrey had to admit she was having a great time. They were at a classy strip club/steakhouse combo called Strip Steak—yes, that was the actual name, and Aubrey still couldn't get past it. The whole bridal party was there, as well as both Sarah's and Bailey's moms, sitting at round tables or just in chairs turned to get a better view of the stage. Her belly was full, the dancers were beautiful, and Aubrey was on her fourth gin and tonic…and wow, look at that woman's breasts!

"Not really a true bachelorette party," came Monica's voice from behind her, very close to her ear, and how weird was it that she'd expected it somehow? She'd been in the general vicinity of Monica Wallace for all of what? Thirty-six hours? And yet there was some part of her body that braced for Monica to be near, that anticipated her presence, that both dreaded and hoped for it. Aubrey had no idea what to do with that, and she didn't care right now, because another drink and a half of these, and she'd be well on her way to being pretty toasted.

"What do you mean?" she asked, and when she turned to look at Monica, her face was startlingly close.

"I mean that bachelor parties and bachelorette parties are supposed to be the last gasps of being single, right? You go out with your closest friends and celebrate your last month or week or night as unattached." Monica pulled up a chair and sat down next to her. Their thighs touched as they faced the stage, the table to Aubrey's left. Monica gestured with her chin across the way at Bailey and Sarah, who were much farther along in their alcohol consumption than Aubrey was, if Sarah's loud hoot as she waved around a couple of ten dollar bills was any indication. "But they're both here. Hard to celebrate your last couple nights of being unattached if the person you're attaching yourself to is right next to you"—Monica tipped her head as she watched the couple—"also sticking money into a stripper's G-string."

"Yeah, but look how much fun they're having," Aubrey said with a laugh.

And they were. It was clear. The two brides-to-be were laughing, falling all over each other, and very clearly having the best time.

"Well, don't you two make a hot couple," said a nearly naked woman who was suddenly in front of them, and before Aubrey could correct her or decline or anything at all, the woman had draped herself across both their laps, and now Aubrey was stuck. She could either stand up, tossing the poor woman off their laps and to the probably sticky and gross floor, or she could let her do her job while she literally felt the heat from Monica's leg pressed up against hers.

And truly, if she hadn't had anything to drink, she'd have definitely gone with option number one. Thank all the stars in the heavens for gin.

The woman had moves. She was a gorgeous blonde with thick, wavy hair and enormous blue eyes. Her bikini was bright yellow and didn't leave much to the imagination *at all*. She didn't so much dance as writhe on their thighs, but she was fun to look at and she smelled like peaches, and when Aubrey glanced at Monica to see what she thought, she found Monica's liquid eyes fixed on hers.

There was an intensity there that Aubrey couldn't describe. Couldn't understand. Couldn't verbalize at all. The sudden lump in her throat took three swallows to go down, and yet she couldn't manage to pull her eyes away. She had to get out of here. But how, when this gaze was quite literally holding her prisoner?

"Listen, I'll let you two off the hook." It was the stripper, who was pushing herself off their laps and to her feet. "Jesus, get a room," she said, not unkindly and with a smile.

Monica pulled her gaze away, and Aubrey felt a need to cry out at the loss, though she managed to keep control of herself. Because yeah, that's all she needed right now. What the hell was wrong with her? Monica was apologizing to the dancer and slid a twenty into her G-string, which put a big smile on the woman's face again.

"I love dancing for sapphic stuff. Y'all are always such great tippers." And then she was off to the next table, climbing up to straddle the lap of an older gentleman who looked like she'd just made his entire year.

Of course, the departure of the dancer now meant that Aubrey was left there sitting next to Monica. Before she could decide what to do about that, Monica stood kind of quickly, and Aubrey had to reach out and steady her chair.

"I need...I'm gonna..." Monica pointed to some undefined spot and headed in that direction, leaving Aubrey sitting there with her almost-empty drink, staring after her, feeling the weirdest mix of disappointment, relief, and confusion. Because what the actual fuck had just happened?

Two hours later, Aubrey was stumbling into her room. Her hair was wet, matted to her neck thanks to the sudden downpour that had caught them as they walked from Strip Steak back to the hotel, drenching the lot of them. She'd had two more drinks before switching to water, but it was too late. She was drunk. Solidly, certainly, good-thing-she's-not-driving drunk. She had leaned on Jordan—wait—had she been the leaner or the leanee? She couldn't remember, but they'd helped each other through the lobby of the hotel, laughing and walking like they were conjoined twins attached at the hip and shoulder, with rubbery legs and a questionable sense of direction. Jordan's room was down the hall, so she'd made it inside first. Now Aubrey closed her own door and was super tempted to simply face-plant onto her bed and go to sleep—and she would have if she hadn't caught a glimpse of herself in the mirror that doubled as a closet door.

Her father would say she looked like a drowned rat, and for some reason, that was hilarious. She laughed the whole time she stepped out of her clothes and into the shower, then continued to chuckle a bit as she stood under water that was as hot as she could stand. Monica had avoided being close to her for the rest of the time at Strip Steak, but Aubrey had caught her eye more than once, held her gaze. Monica had pulled away first every time, and something about that gave Aubrey a little thrill, like she'd won something.

The shower was sobering her up a little, and she closed her eyes and let the water run over her, while her eyelids played her a little movie of Monica…wide-leg beige pants, a blue top with a halter-style neck that showed lots of shoulder and just a peek of midriff, her hair pulled back in some kind of complicated twist, then falling down her back between her shoulder blades, and—

She'd barely registered sliding her fingers between her legs, and she gasped as her orgasm hit her after only a couple minutes. Hit her *hard*. She braced herself against the tile with her other hand and rode it out because she had no choice. What in the inappropriate fantasies was that about? And wow, why was it so good?

"No." She said it aloud as she quickly shut off the water, then grabbed a towel. "No, no, no, no, that is *not* okay." She toweled herself dry. "Oh my God. No. *No.* It was *not* good and it was *so* not okay."

Everything else she did, she did angrily. She brushed her teeth angrily. She shoved her feet into her pajama bottoms angrily. She pulled back the covers angrily. And then she lay there, wide awake, trying hard to ignore the image of Monica Wallace above her. Underneath her. Inside her...

"Goddamn it," she muttered, yanking on the covers as she rolled onto her side. Angrily.

❖

Sleep for Aubrey had been elusive, and when it did come, she had a sex dream about Monica. An honest-to-God sex dream! She didn't have those often, and when she did, they certainly weren't about people she knew. The last sex dream she'd had, she'd been with Dianna Agron, who was her girlfriend in the dream and...well, she couldn't remember any more than that. But seriously, what more did she need to remember besides Dianna Agron was her girlfriend and they had amazing sex? She'd filed that one away for future use when she was taking care of business. And then last night's shower fantasy had happened, and it was clear that Monica had tossed poor Dianna out on her shapely behind and was now taking up all the sex space in her head. Goddamn it.

Friday was a spa day for the brides-to-be and their bridal parties. That's right, a spa day, which Aubrey had been very looking forward to—she couldn't remember the last time she'd been pampered—until the first time they all met in the waiting area in robes. Guess what wasn't at all helpful in getting Aubrey's brain out from between the satin sheets in her mind and into the current present day where she wasn't having sex at all, with anybody? That's right: Monica Wallace in a fluffy, soft, white robe, belted at the waist, hiding the treasures of her nakedness underneath and...

"Oh, for fuck's sake, Aubrey," she muttered under her breath. *Treasures of her nakedness? Who says that?* She stifled a groan, took her glass of cucumber water, and sat in one of the super comfy recliners in the waiting area. They were all there, some looking worse than others. Sarah was low-key, and when she caught Aubrey's eye, and Aubrey smiled at her, she made a face that was probably supposed to be a smile but ended up more like a grimace, which made Aubrey's smile grow bigger. Clearly, she wasn't the only one who'd gone a bit past her limit last night.

"How's everybody feeling this morning?" Monica asked. The responses were a mix of groans, scoffs, and a couple of giggles. "How many never, ever want to see another shot as long as they live?" Of the ten women in the room, eight hands went up. Only Monica's and Aubrey's remained down. Monica said, "Well, I guess we see who the smartest ones in the group are."

"Or just the ones with the longest memories," Sarah pointed out, her eyes on Aubrey. "I seem to remember somebody doing shots of Jäger senior year and nearly missing a final because she was too sick to get out of bed."

As it did every time Aubrey flashed on that day, her stomach gave a little churn, like it was tapping on her shoulder and reminding her how bad it was, and not to do it again. She made her nose wrinkle. "That was a bad night."

"I don't remember that party," Monica said, her brow furrowed, her cleavage trying its best to drag Aubrey's eyes there. Wasn't her robe more open than everybody else's? It must have been...

"You'd already left for your internship, I think," Sarah offered.

Aubrey nodded. That was right. Monica had left for her internship and Aubrey hadn't seen her again until a week or two before the Wedding that Wasn't.

"So, you didn't have any shots last night?" Jordan asked, slumped back in a chair and looking like she was mere moments from hurling.

Aubrey shook her head. "Aside from one shot of tequila Trina and I did at Kyle's wedding in January, I haven't had a shot since that party in college." Gasps of surprise rolled through the room and she laughed. "Please. It's not like I said I haven't had sex since that party."

"Have you?" Monica, snagging her gaze and holding it.

"Of course I have," Aubrey said with a scoff.

Monica looked like she was going to push some more, seeming to know she'd found a hot button, but Aubrey could see the moment she decided against it. She smiled and said, "Good." Whatever the hell that meant.

A door opened and three spa employees came in the room, and thank fucking God, because Aubrey had no idea what she'd have said if that conversation had gone any farther. She was also pretty sure Monica had caught her staring at her chest. And that she smiled about it.

They were split into three groups, one for massages, one for facials, and one for pedicures. Aubrey was in the same group as Monica. Because of course she was. They headed to massages first. Because of course they did.

The spa specialized in bridal parties and group visits, and the room they were led to was a group massage room. Sarah and Bailey had been split up, so this group was Sarah, Jordan, Aubrey, and Monica. The employee waved an arm toward the four massage tables lined up parallel to each other, and Sarah and Jordan got the first two tables from the left, leaving Aubrey and Monica to take the last two. Next to each other.

Thank God for the doughnut was all Aubrey could think because she'd be face down and not have to look at half-naked Monica. That was a relief.

"All right, you can disrobe and get under the sheets on your table, and we'll be right in." With that, the employee left the four of them alone.

Wait. What?

Sarah wasted no time untying the belt around her waist and draping it over a nearby chair. She was athletic in build, solid and muscular, and it was clear why she chose to wear athleisure most of the time. She definitely had the body for it.

"Won't this be weird for you, since you're a massage therapist?" Jordan asked as she dropped her own robe. Aubrey realized she was kind of staring so quickly turned to face the other way.

What in the bronze goddess was she seeing?

Monica had hung her robe on a hook and was pulling back the sheet on her table. She stood on the opposite side of it, facing Aubrey, and if she didn't have the most beautiful breasts Aubrey had ever seen in her life, she'd eat her own robe. Monica wasn't looking at her, but Aubrey was certainly looking at Monica. No, not looking. Not staring. Gaping. Gawking. Ogling.

Get your shit together, McFadden, her brain screamed, and it was enough. She whipped off her own robe and dived under the sheet so fast, her table rocked for a moment. She took a few seconds and did her best to get herself under control, to stop breathing like she'd just run a race, to stop staring at everybody like some weirdo. She was not a person who was ever this discombobulated, but she felt completely out of sorts right now. Her face in the doughnut, she inhaled a long slow breath, held it, then blew it out just as slowly. After three rounds of this, she felt better. The sweating had stopped—thank God, because her poor massage therapist—her heart rate had eased up, and she began to feel human again. She lifted her head once, to push some hair out of her face, and eyes the same blue as a midsummer sky were fixed on her.

Aubrey couldn't look away.

So she didn't.

They stayed like that until there was a knock at the door and Sarah called, "Ready!"

Aubrey put her face back in the doughnut and tried to comprehend what she'd seen on Monica's face.

Her expression had been...knowing.

Aubrey spent the first half of her massage fighting her brain, which wanted to pretend those were Monica's hands on her skin. She finally gave up and let her brain have its way, and the second half of her massage didn't relax her at all. It turned her the hell on.

Clearly, it had been way too long since she'd had somebody's hands on her. That way.

I need to get laid, she thought, thankful her face wasn't visible.

❖

The weather on Saturday, the day of the wedding, turned out to be as gorgeous as it possibly could have been for that time of year at that location on the map. Temps were in the midsixties, which made the normal beach breeze bearable instead of freezing them all into ice sculptures of wedding attendees. The sky was a deep, intense blue, and the sun shone so brightly, like it was specifically there to spotlight the union. There were a few short rows of wooden folding chairs arranged facing an arbor that was entwined with vines, pale green silk, and some sort of white flower Aubrey couldn't identify. She'd seen the officiant wearing a rainbow scarf and mingling among some of the guests as they arrived and were ushered to their seats.

The bridal party had been instructed to wear something beachy and were given acceptable colors by Sarah and Bailey—white, anything pastel, ivory, peach, pink—and they were allowed to choose their own outfits. That was helpful for Aubrey, who didn't want to have to spend hundreds of dollars on a gown she'd wear exactly once. After much online searching, she'd found a soft yellow and ivory sundress with spaghetti straps and a long, flowy skirt that she'd had to get altered, but it was worth it because now it fit like it had been made just for her. It had come with a sheer wrap, in case it turned out to be chilly on the beach, but with the sun high overhead shining down on them with enough warmth, she found she didn't need it. The other request Sarah and Bailey had was that they all be barefoot in the sand, which was why they'd all gotten matching pedicures the day before.

While she'd managed to avoid getting close to or being alone with Monica for the rest of yesterday and all of last night, there was no way to do that today, as they were being paired up. A little pep talk to her reflection that morning helped.

"You're fine," she told the woman in the mirror, who was looking a bit more wide-eyed than usual, as if anticipating a loud noise. "You're totally fine. Listen, it's been a while since you got laid. That's all this is. Okay? You just need some action. If it wasn't her, it would be somebody else. Just chill. You're fine." And it had worked. She'd felt lighter. A bit relieved to have identified the problem. She just had to get through this day, and then tomorrow, she could head home to Emma and her job and everything else that didn't make her feel like she was in some foreign land she couldn't navigate. She was fine. She was good. She had this.

And then she saw Monica.

Wide-leg ivory pants with a yellow halter. She had baby's breath woven into her wavy blond hair. Her feet were bare, her lips were glossy, and just as Aubrey had noticed yesterday, her skin was as bronzed as if she'd just returned from a tropical vacation. If Aubrey had ever seen a sight more beautiful, she couldn't have come up with it, even if you'd offered her a bazillion dollars. Monica was it. She was breathtaking. Stunning. The sun seemed like it was pointing out the golden highlights in her hair. *See this? How about this one here? Isn't this one gorgeous?*

God, shut up, sun!

"Hi," Monica said quietly to her as they lined up in order of how they were to walk through the sand between the chairs to the spot where Sarah and Bailey would be. She lowered her voice more, leaned in close, and said, "You look beautiful."

Compared to her? Pfft. She did *not*. She didn't even come close. How could Monica even say such a ridiculous thing?

Before she could come up with a retort, Sarah was there. "Oh my God, you guys all look so amazing!" And everybody squealed and laughed and bounced a little and Sarah said, "Are we ready? 'Cause it's time. Let's marry me off!"

The rest of the day was a whirlwind, as most weddings were. Getting married on the beach turned out to be the most perfect thing ever for Sarah and Bailey. Guests had begun to arrive the night before, and it was a small gathering, but filled with joy and food and cocktails, and every moment blurred into the next. Except there was Monica, and what the hell was going on with Aubrey that she was so hyperaware of her? Seriously. She knew where Monica was at all times. Not only could she feel Monica's hand in her own from when they marched down to the beach toward the brides-to-be, but she felt every bone, every inch of soft skin, the security of her grip. She could smell her. God, she could smell her, the coconutty, citrusy blend of whatever she was wearing on her skin. Even when she was across the room from her, that scent still lingered in Aubrey's nostrils, teasing her.

This was bad.

This was so, so bad.

Thank God Trina and Jeff had shown up. Aubrey stuck to Trina like she had magnetic pull, but she also had wedding duties. Like being announced. When the DJ shouted, "Aubrey McFadden and Monica Wallace!" it was absolutely surreal to her, especially when Monica caught her eye and met her at the edge of the reception space, hand outstretched.

Then there was the dance.

God. The dance.

It was a sapphic wedding, after all, so girls dancing together was nothing unusual. But when the bridal party was asked to pair up and move to the dance floor while Sarah and Bailey danced to Ed Sheeran's song "Perfect," Aubrey felt every nerve in her body spark to life. And then the bridal party was asked to join in, and she put her hand in Monica's, and Monica's hand slid warmly down her side to rest on the small of her back. Their heads were close. Their lips were scant inches apart. Aubrey felt caught, captured by those clear blue eyes. And they swayed. Slowly, they swayed while the rest of the world seemed to blur and fade until there was only the two of them. Monica never looked away from her, just kept swaying, kept eye contact, and Aubrey couldn't have looked away if she'd wanted to. Which she didn't, she was shocked to admit. Because being held in that gaze, in those arms, did things to her. Sensual things. Confusing things. Things that were wonderful and also so, so bad. What in the world was happening to her?

The applause felt extra loud, and it startled her, made her take a small step back, breaking whatever hold, whatever spell Monica had cast. She turned toward the brides and clapped politely, then hurried off the dance floor back to the table where Trina was seated.

"*Ho-lee* shit," was the first thing Trina said. So much for her not noticing what had just happened.

"What?" Aubrey asked, all feigned innocence as she picked up her white wine and took a too large gulp of it.

"Oh, don't even. You know exactly what." Trina made a circle in the air with her forefinger and pointed it at Aubrey. "Spill."

Aubrey flopped into her chair. "There's nothing to"—she made the same circling gesture back at Trina—"spill." Of course there was. There was quite a lot to spill. But Aubrey had zero handle on any of it, so she wasn't about to give it life by speaking about it out loud. She even managed not to squirm under the suspicious gaze Trina lasered her with.

After a long moment of staring, Trina finally gave up. "You'll tell me when you're ready," she said, which was likely true, though Aubrey hoped she was well on her way to there not being anything to tell. She lifted one shoulder to show just how not big a deal it all was. "Tell you what, though." Trina pointed at her again, then shifted and pointed in the direction of the open bar, where Monica stood talking to a guy Aubrey didn't recognize. "You two looked fucking hot together. No joke."

Aubrey scoffed. "Please."

"I'm not the only one who thought so. I've been hearing it all night."

An eye roll seemed to be the best response here. She and Monica, hot together? People noticing? Ridiculous. Preposterous. Ludicrous.

This was so, so bad.

❖

What time should we head to the airport?

It was a text. From Monica.

God, Aubrey's head was pounding. Even after a shower, a handful of Tylenol, and some room service breakfast, it still felt like she was wearing a headband that was too tight. She'd overdone the wine last night in a pretty big way, but it was the only thing keeping her central nervous system from completely short-circuiting from all the surprise and confusion, not to mention the fucking *arousal*. By the time she'd made it back to her room, her panties had been soaked and she couldn't get that tropical coconut scent of Monica out of her nose.

She couldn't wait to get home. Back to normal life where she wasn't walking around about ten seconds from a spontaneous orgasm caused by somebody she'd spent the majority of the time they'd known each other angry with.

And two-plus hours in a car with Monica today? Nope. Terrible idea. Terrible, horrible idea. She'd known that even last night, in her inebriated state, when she'd asked Trina and Jeff if she could ride with them.

"Shit," she muttered as she realized she'd never told Monica. She typed, deleted, typed again, deleted again, before settling on the best wording she could come up with.

Oh, I snagged a ride with Trina and Jeff. I knew your flight wasn't until later and didn't want to rush you so you could sit in the airport for hours. Thanks for thinking of me, though!

Yeah, the exclamation point was too much, as were the two smiley emoji. She knew for certain she'd hurt Monica's feelings when her response came.

OK.

Aubrey sighed. She didn't like hurting people's feelings. She avoided it whenever possible, but it just wasn't possible here. If she was trapped in a car with Monica for two hours, she'd lose her mind. It was that simple.

All she wanted was to get home, drop her bags, and sink down into a bubble bath in her big tub. Why couldn't she blink her eyes or snap her fingers and make that happen? Of all the times to not have magic powers…

She somehow managed to pack her things, FaceTime with Emma and her parents to give them details on her flight, get herself down to the lobby, say good-bye to the few guests who were still milling around waiting on Ubers or taxis, and get into Jeff's rental, all without running into Monica.

Thank fucking Christ.

She would've had no idea what to say, it would've been awkward, and she'd have laid eyes on her…yeah, so there was that. She admitted it to herself as she sat in the back seat behind Trina. She didn't actually want to even *see* Monica today because she didn't want to deal with her body's horrendously confusing reaction. She didn't have the energy.

Trina and Jeff were clearly as tired as she was. They'd been up late, had had a lot to drink, and danced their butts off. They drove in silence for the first twenty minutes. Apparently, that's as long as Trina could last.

"Okay," she said as she turned in her seat so she could see Aubrey's face. "What was going on with you and Mon last night?"

Emotions zipped through her at the words. Surprise. Irritation. Dread. Exhaustion. She finally settled on resignation and let out a long, slow breath. "I honestly don't know," she said, being completely truthful with her bestie. She shook her head slowly as she gazed out the window, not really seeing anything. "It was so weird, Tree. I've never thought of her like that. I've never had these weird feelings around her. For fuck's sake, I don't even like the woman."

"Like her or not, you guys looked incredible together." Jeff met her gaze in the rearview mirror. "Like, seriously hot, like you were meant to be dancing with each other."

"Here, lemme get that drool running down your chin," Trina said, reaching for his face with a laugh. Turning back to Aubrey, she said, "Sarah said the same thing. So did Kyle." She rattled off another three or four names, all of whom had apparently been watching the two of them last night.

"All I can tell you is that it was confusing as hell, and I'm glad it's over and I don't have to see her again."

"Until June."

"June?"

"Um, hello?" She held up her left hand and wiggled her fingers, her engagement ring sparkling in the Sunday morning sunshine.

"Oh, right. *Your* wedding."

"How is that date not seared into your brain?" Trina asked,

feigning disbelief. "It should be tattooed on your body somewhere. Because you love me that much, and of all the nine million weddings we have to go to this year, mine is the most important."

Aubrey was laughing openly by the time she finished. "Yes, yes. You're right. And I have it tattooed on my boob. Over my heart."

"Can I see?" Jeff asked.

Trina slapped his arm with a gasp that turned into laughter. "No, you cannot." She looked back at Aubrey. "You're in the bridal party and she's just a guest, so there will be no forced proximity. And you have a little over two months to pull yourself together. So do that. Please."

More than two months. More than eight weeks. That was enough time, right? She nodded. "Okay. Good. That's enough time for me get my head on straight. Hell, maybe I'll even find myself a date by then."

Trina tipped her head to the side. "And how would that happen? By magic? You're not on any dating apps. You don't go out to bars. Do you think some woman will just materialize on your doorstep and offer to take you to dinner?"

Aubrey wrinkled her nose. "Not helping."

"I have told you a million times, I would love to help. Let's set you up a profile, put your picture out there, and see what happens. Yeah?"

In the past, Aubrey had always shut her down immediately. The idea of online dating terrified her. Plus, she had Emma, so there were extra steps to be taken. But after last night, maybe it was time. Time to open her life up a bit, time to think about maybe letting somebody else into it. And time to put all the confusion of last night behind her.

Because that needed to happen.

Like, immediately.

WEDDINGS DOWN: 2
SUCCESS IN AVOIDING MONICA WALLACE: 0 AGAIN

Part Three

Trina and Jeff
June 24, 2024
Traditional Nondenominational Wedding

Aubrey McFadden is never getting married.

Reason #4
Vulnerability makes you weak.

W ill you excuse me for a minute?" Phoebe looked at her, all big blue eyes and shy smile.

"Of course," Aubrey said and watched as her date headed for the ladies' room. When she was completely out of sight, Aubrey picked up her phone and texted Trina.

So far, so good. She's nice. A decent conversationalist.

The dots bounced, telling her Trina was typing. *As pretty as her profile pic?*

Yes, she typed back. This was the third date she'd been on since Trina made her set up a dating profile on Strike a Match, and she almost didn't agree to this one. Two disappointments—one male and one female—might not seem like much to most people, but it was more than enough to make Aubrey want to delete her profile altogether. Trina had talked her into giving it one more shot, reminding her that lots of people went on *lots* of dates before they found somebody who fit.

"That's just it," Aubrey had said, trying and failing to keep the whine out of her voice. "I don't *want* to go on lots of dates."

"I know, I know, you just want Mr. or Ms. Right to pop up before your eyes and be everything you're looking for."

"I really don't think that's a lot to ask," she'd deadpanned. And now, here she was, having coffee with a woman named Phoebe Hardigan, who was a librarian and who seemed very kind and who was quite pretty, and she was waiting for the other shoe to drop. She gazed out the window, questions spinning around in her brain, wondering what that other shoe might be. Would she end up being super clingy? Would she be too aloof? Did she keep women prisoner in her basement? Was she escaping out the bathroom window right now because she hated this date?

"I'm back."

Aubrey turned and tried to hide the slight surprise. "Hi."

"Hi." Phoebe had a nice smile. Straight teeth. Full lips. Faint dimples.

"How was your trip?"

"Well, Aubrey, it's quite a decent ladies' room, as ladies' rooms go. A lovely beige with what I think are granite counters and Dyson hand dryers. Quiet but effective." She grinned and held up her hands to show proof of their dryness.

"Good to know." Aubrey grinned back.

"Were you worried I was jumping out the window?"

"Were you worried you'd come back to the table and I'd have bounced?"

They laughed together, and Aubrey felt herself loosening up for the first time since she'd taken a seat. Maybe this wasn't so bad after all.

"So," Phoebe said, moving her spoon through what was left of her mocha latte. "You have a daughter. And…how did she come about?" Then she blinked at Aubrey once. Twice. Then burst into laughter. "How did she come about? Dear God, what kind of ridiculous question is that?"

Aubrey laughed with her, and loosened up some more. "Luckily, I knew what you meant. My daughter, Emma, *came about* the old-fashioned way, by my college boyfriend."

"Ah, got it. And that didn't work, I take it."

"He dumped me on our wedding day." She didn't tell tons of people that little tidbit, mostly because it was horrifyingly embarrassing, but she felt comfortable with Phoebe—who gasped and brought her fingers to her mouth.

"*Nooooo.* You were left at the altar? I didn't think that actually happened in real life."

"Well, not *right at* the altar, but at the church. In my wedding dress. So. Yeah."

"Wow. I'm so sorry. That sucks in a big way." She took a sip of her latte. "I take it Emma was already on the way?"

Aubrey nodded. "The wedding was called off. Cody took a gap year and fled to Europe to backpack, like, two days later, and I grew a baby from scratch." She sensed things veering in the direction of heavy talk and didn't want to go there on their first date, so she steered things back to fun. "But I ended up with the coolest kid ever, so I win."

Phoebe's smile lit up her eyes. Aubrey could tell the moment she'd relaxed a bit because her smile became genuine, like it was now. "I love kids. Hope to have some of my own one day. How old is Emma?"

"She's almost ten going on almost thirty."

"Oh, I bet."

They chatted a bit more, but it was clear the date was wrapping up. Aubrey had chosen coffee during the day on a Saturday on purpose. People had things to do on Saturday afternoons. Especially her. She had a child, and she didn't want to be away from her longer than she needed to on a Saturday, which Phoebe seemed to understand. They stood up by unspoken agreement, gathered their purses, and pushed their chairs in.

"This was nice," Phoebe said. "I'm glad we did it."

"Me too."

Then Phoebe surprised her by wrapping her in a hug. She didn't linger or overstay the welcome, and Aubrey hugged her back. She smelled nice. Like the faint scent of a flower she couldn't put her finger on...hyacinth? Lilac?

"Have a great rest of your Saturday with your daughter, okay?" Phoebe said as they exited the coffee shop and prepared to walk in opposite directions.

"Thanks. Enjoy your day, too."

And that was it.

What did it mean?

She pulled her phone out as she walked to her car, the late-May weather warm and sunny.

Done. She sent the text to Trina, then added another. *Is it bad that she didn't ask to see me again?*

The dots bounced. Aubrey got into her car, which was toasty inside from sitting in the sunshine.

Not necessarily, came Trina's response. *Did YOU ask to see her again?*

She wrinkled her nose. *No?* She purposely made it a question. A line of about fifteen eye-rolling emoji came next, so many it made her laugh out loud in her car. *I know!* she sent back. *I panicked.* Her phone rang in her hand, and she laughed some more as she answered it.

Trina didn't even wait for her to say hello. "Of all the stupid-ass things to panic about." But there was affectionate humor in her tone.

"I can't help it," Aubrey all but wailed. "This is what happens."

"Okay, well, first things first. Do you *want* to see her again?"

"Hmm." She made herself think about it. Really think about it. Phoebe seemed really nice. They had things in common. She was polite to the barista—people who were rude to service people were big red flags for her. She seemed to pay attention, to really listen when Aubrey talked. She'd made a couple of small jokes, so there was a sense of humor in there. Lots of positives. What she couldn't come up with was a reason *not* to see Phoebe again. "You know what? I think I do."

"Excellent." The relief in Trina's voice was clear, but Aubrey let it slide. "That's fantastic. So, you have two options. You can text her right now and admit that you panicked like the big weirdo you are and ask if she'd like to get together again. Or you can wait a bit, acting just the slightest bit aloof—which can be cool, but don't overdo it or you'll come off like an asshole—and ask her out then."

"Wait a bit like later today? Or wait a bit like a few days?"

"Oh God, no, don't let it go a few days. Like later today or tomorrow."

"Okay. Got it."

"There's always the chance that she'll contact you first."

"You think?"

"Maybe she panicked, too."

Aubrey drove home with that thought in her head. What if Phoebe had, in fact, panicked, too, but really did want to see her again? She found herself smiling in her driver's seat at the idea that maybe somebody found her interesting. Funny. Attractive. A little sexy, even.

Yeah, she liked that thought. It had been a long time.

She was turning into her driveway when a text popped up on her phone, showing on the screen on her dashboard. She nibbled her bottom lip when she saw Phoebe's name. She parked the car and opened the text.

Probs should've said something when we left, but I was nervous...

Aubrey smiled and continued reading the next text.

I had fun with you today, and I'd love to see you again. If you want to. If you don't, totally fine, no hard feelings.

Phoebe had taken the stress of what to do right off her shoulders, and the relief was palpable. She typed.

Love to.

❖

"What do you think?" Aubrey stood in the living room of her house and turned first one way, then the other, modeling the maid of honor dress she'd be wearing to Trina's wedding tomorrow. Phoebe's eyes went a little wide, just for a second, and then they darkened, got slightly hooded. A very good sign, Aubrey decided.

"Wow." Phoebe stared, then wet her lips. "Just...wow. You look incredible." Her eyes roamed over Aubrey's body like they were her hands, and Aubrey swore she could almost feel them.

"My mom hates that it's black. *You don't wear black at a wedding!*" She did a pretty spot-on impression of her mother, if she did say so.

Phoebe was shaking her head. "Black is very trendy for bridal parties right now." She stood up and walked around Aubrey, checking out the dress from all angles. Aubrey stood a little straighter, enjoying being looked at. It had been a long time since somebody looked at her with that sparkle of desire that glittered in Phoebe's eye right now. "And I wouldn't change the color of this one for the world. You look drop-dead gorgeous, not to mention super sexy." Phoebe dropped a kiss onto Aubrey's bare shoulder, then trailed up her neck and spent some time on her mouth. When they parted, Phoebe was breathing a little bit heavier.

"You're sure you don't mind coming to the wedding?" Aubrey asked, wrapping a lock of Phoebe's chestnut hair around her finger. "I have to sit with the bridal party, so you'll be at a table with some of our college friends. You won't know a soul. I won't be mad if you bow out."

"And miss you walking down the aisle and dancing around later in this dress? No way. I may be a librarian, but I know how to make small talk. Don't you worry about me. I'll be fine." She gave her another quick kiss, then pulled back and said, "I gotta go. My mom hates when I'm late." She gathered her bag and slipped into her shoes and, with a little wave, was out the door. "See you there tomorrow, babe."

Aubrey stood at the storm door and watched Phoebe back her Civic out of the driveway. She gave a little toot of the horn, and Aubrey waved as she drove out of sight, then stayed standing there for a few more moments. She still wasn't sure inviting Phoebe to Trina's wedding had been smart. They'd only been dating a few weeks, but Trina had insisted.

"It'll be good for you to have somebody there as sort of a home base, you know?" Before Aubrey could argue any kind of protest, Trina added, "Anybody who's willing to attend a wedding where they won't know anybody just to be there for you is a keeper, don't you think?"

Yes. The answer to that question was a resounding yes. Duh.

Wasn't it?

Phoebe was great. They'd had several dates. They'd done a movie out, dinner a couple times, they'd gone to the museum so

Phoebe could introduce Aubrey to the works of her favorite artist, they'd done a movie at home on Phoebe's couch. They'd made out a lot, but hadn't gone any farther than that. Phoebe said she preferred to take things slowly, and Aubrey didn't argue with her because it felt right to take their time...something she'd never said or thought about any relationship in her entire life, not that there were many. It wasn't like she'd jumped straight into bed with every person she'd dated, but she also hadn't dated very many people. Phoebe was attractive. She had lots of great qualities. Aubrey was lucky to be dating her. She knew that. She knew all of that. So, she didn't get all pleasantly nervous or get those flutters in her body when they were kissing. So what? Maybe that just meant she was an adult and not some sex-starved, lovesick teenager. It could just be that. It was absolutely probably that. All she needed to do was be patient. These things took time. They developed slowly.

She climbed the stairs back to her bedroom to take off the dress but gave herself a little longer to look at her reflection in the full-length mirror. She looked damn good, and she didn't often think that about herself. Trina had picked a gorgeous sheath dress, with a ruched, sleeveless V-neck top. It tapered at the waist, then flowed down in a gorgeous cascade of soft black material. Not one to avoid a little sex appeal, Trina had made sure there was a slit all the way up one side. It just so happened that Aubrey's shape was perfect for such a dress, and Phoebe wasn't wrong—she looked great. The other bridesmaids were also in black, but their dresses had halter tops, making them slightly different than Aubrey's. "I want you to stand out from the others," Trina had told her. "'Cause you're special." It had been one of the sweetest things she'd ever said to her.

A glance at the clock told her she needed to go pick Emma up from her playdate in thirty minutes, so she carefully took off the dress and hung it back up. She'd drop Emma at her parents' later for the weekend while she attended the rehearsal dinner that night. Then there would be hair and makeup first thing tomorrow, and then she'd watch her best friend in the world get married.

It was bittersweet, and she could admit that. On that fateful day almost ten years ago, Cody had ensured that, from that moment on, weddings would always be just a little bit hard for her, even the one of her very best friend in the world. But she'd be okay. Because this was Trina. And Jeff. If anybody belonged together forever, it was them. She could set aside her own baggage to celebrate with them. To celebrate them.

Her phone pinged an incoming text, and as if she'd conjured her, it was from Trina.

911! Can you get here early? Big Yikes alert…

Aubrey laughed because *Big Yikes* was the code name Trina had given her future mother-in-law, who was endlessly, but subtly, critical of Trina, the only person on earth that Trina couldn't seem to make like her.

Lemme get Emma to my mom's and I'll be right there. DO NOT KILL HER. She followed that up with three laughing emoji and a knife emoji. She grinned as she pulled on the simple green dress she'd bought last month for the rehearsal dinner. This weekend was going to be fun. A lot of it.

And this time, she'd have a date.

❖

"She's never going to like me, is she?" Trina's voice was a hushed whisper as she leaned close to Aubrey. Wine had been consumed, and Aubrey could smell it as Trina breathed out her words. "I will never, ever be good enough for her." She didn't seem terribly upset by it, though. More resigned. Trina was like that. She didn't fight if she couldn't win.

"It's her loss. She clearly can't see how awesome you are." Aubrey wrapped her arms around Trina and squeezed tight. "Lucky for you, I can. And so can Jeff."

Across the restaurant, Jeff stood with his brother and father. His gaze met Trina's, and he lifted his glass in a silent salute.

"See?" Aubrey said and squeezed her again.

"He is a snack, isn't he?"

"I can agree with that."

Trina was slightly intoxicated. Aubrey could only tell because they'd known each other so long, and she recognized the slightly glassy look in her eyes. "I'm so glad you're here."

"Uh-oh, are you gonna get all mushy on me now?"

"I mean, I won't have time tomorrow. I'll be too busy being mind-blowingly gorgeous."

Aubrey nodded as she picked up her glass and sipped her Manhattan. "Valid."

"Look at you, being all bougie with the fancy cocktail." Aubrey handed it to Trina without waiting for her to ask for a sip. "Oh, that's yummy."

They sat quietly for several moments, just looking around at the other guests. The restaurant was small, and Jeff's parents knew the owner, so they'd rented it out for the evening. Dinner had already been served and enjoyed, and now folks were mingling, chatting, sipping drinks, and anxiously anticipating tomorrow. The rest of the bridal party, both sets of parents, and grandparents—a small group. Trina had decided on only three bridesmaids, including Aubrey. She had no siblings, and Jeff just had his brother.

"I kinda like the coziness of your wedding," Aubrey said.

"Well, you know, I don't have many friends, so…"

Aubrey laughed and bumped her with a shoulder. "Please. You know *everybody*. Probably in the world." Only a slight exaggeration. Trina was fun and extroverted and people naturally gravitated to her. Except for Jeff's mom.

"Can you keep a secret?" Trina asked.

"Can I keep a secret." Aubrey snorted. "I still haven't told anybody about that time at Kappa Kappa Omega when you—" Trina slapped a hand over her mouth with a gasp.

"And you *never* will."

Aubrey shook her head, laughing under Trina's hand.

Trina was laughing, too, and finally took her hand away. "My secret is the only person I care about sharing tomorrow with, aside from him"—she gestured toward Jeff with her chin—"is you."

Things went from humor to emotion in two seconds flat. "Tree." Aubrey felt her eyes well up.

"It's true. You're my bestie forever, Aubs. I'm so glad you're going to be standing next to me up there tomorrow."

This time, their hug was genuine, firm, and filled with love. Then they each wiped their eyes and sat back with their drinks in hand, silently watching the rest of the room.

"I'm nervous," Trina said after a moment.

Aubrey turned to her. "Yeah?"

Trina nodded, her eyes slightly wide.

"I think that's normal, don't you? Big day and all?"

"I guess?"

Aubrey sat up and turned her body so her knees were touching Trina's thigh. "You're not, like, getting cold feet or second-guessing or anything...?"

"Oh God, no. No way. I've never been so sure of anything in my life. I actually don't know why I'm nervous. I just am."

"Well, sure or not, it's a huge deal. Enormous. You're getting married. That's the biggest thing in your life. Like, ever."

"For now," Trina said with a twinkle in her eye.

"For now," Aubrey agreed. "Until the babies start coming."

"Oh, wow, that really is the next step, isn't it?"

"Kinda the order of things," Aubrey said.

"Life, man." They sat back again. Got quiet again. But in a good way. In the best of ways. Just two best friends, sitting side by side, enjoying each other's presence.

Aubrey could only come up with a few times in her life when she'd been this content, and one had been when she'd given birth to Emma. The aftermath. Cody had been there, of course, in the waiting room. Her mom was there as well. But the other person who'd been there through the whole thing was Trina. All of Aubrey's important moments in life since the time she was nineteen had included Trina.

She turned her head to look at her best friend. "I love you," she said quietly.

Trina met her gaze and smiled her big gorgeous smile. She always complained that her mouth and teeth were too big, said she had a horse face. But Aubrey thought her bestie was beautiful. Trina reached for her hand, clasped it, squeezed. "I love you, too."

Tomorrow was going to be incredible.

❖

The wedding was beautiful in every sense of the word.

Jeff cried when he saw Trina in her wedding dress coming down the aisle to him.

Trina cried when reading her self-written vows.

Aubrey cried through all of it and tried to remember the last time she was so happy for someone she loved.

She stood up with Jeff's older brother, Jonathan, who was gay and handsome and polite. He made sure her hand was tucked securely in his elbow when they headed back down the aisle at the end of the ceremony. He held doors for her and made sure she was comfortable. There was something to be said for a gentleman. Aubrey always hoped if she ever had a son, she'd raise him to be one.

Once photos had been taken—a million of them, it felt like— and they were in the reception hall waiting to sit for dinner, there was time to mingle. Jonathan's new boyfriend and Phoebe had been seated together at the same table, both of them being last-minute additions, so Aubrey and Jonathan searched together for table twelve.

"There," Jonathan said, pointing, and he led Aubrey through the maze of round tables to number twelve, and there sat Phoebe.

Right next to Monica.

She must've done a little stutter step because Jonathan stopped walking and looked at her. "You okay?"

"Yeah. Yeah. Fine. Thanks." She let go of his arm, and he walked around the table to a very handsome man Aubrey put in his late forties, looking very put together in a navy-blue suit and striped tie.

Phoebe stood up and walked right up to her, then wrapped her in a hug. "You look so beautiful," she said, and Aubrey heard the words, even as she made eye contact with Monica over her shoulder, who gave her a smile that didn't quite reach her eyes. She remembered that their last contact had been when she blew Monica off to ride to the airport with Trina and Jeff. Because she was too much of a wuss to face what she'd been feeling. *Typical Aubrey behavior*, her brain screamed at her.

"Thanks," Aubrey said, trying to be subtle about shrugging out of Phoebe's grasp, suddenly feeling itchy, like she wanted to crawl out of her own skin. What was that about? And who was the woman sitting next to Monica? The one whose chair had Monica's arm draped across the back. And why did it make Aubrey feel weird and stomach-churny? "You know what?" she said to Phoebe. "I'll be right back." And she gathered up her dress so she could walk without falling on her ass—which really would be icing on the cake of this weirdly uncomfortable moment—and made for the ladies' room as fast as she could in her heels.

Once inside, she shut herself inside a stall and took a moment to just breathe. What in the world was wrong with her? She'd known Monica was going to be here, so seeing her shouldn't have been a surprise. She hadn't realized she'd be at the same table with Phoebe, but she'd decided at the very last minute to bring a date, so she couldn't complain about where Trina—or more likely, Trina's mother—had seated her. Nothing was a shock here, so why was she feeling so goddamn *weird*?

No sooner had she gotten her breath under control, than the door opened and she heard Phoebe's voice.

"Aubrey? You in here?"

Damn it. She cleared her throat. "Yeah. Be right out." She made a show of flushing the toilet and swishing her dress around to make noise that simulated getting herself together. Then she opened the stall door to a smiling Phoebe leaning back against the sinks. She looked very pretty in a floral print dress with capped sleeves and a V that plunged low enough to draw the eye. Her hair was pulled back off her face, and her cheeks were slightly pink with a touch of blush. She looked fantastic. Aubrey wished she wasn't there.

"You okay?" Phoebe's voice went soft, and she walked into Aubrey's space. "You're a little flushed." She laid the back of her hand on Aubrey's forehead, then her cheeks, like she was checking for a fever or something. Aubrey fought the urge to smack her hand away. "You're a little warm."

"I'm fine. Just a lot going on." She stepped around her to the sink and washed her hands.

"Well, this place is gorgeous, and I'm really enjoying meeting your college friends."

Aubrey nodded, not meeting Phoebe's eyes in the mirror. "Good. I'm glad." She could feel Phoebe's eyes on her, and she continued not to look.

"You sure you're okay?" Aubrey nodded again and that seemed to bring relief. Which meant Phoebe talked some more. "Here's something fun. The one sitting next to me? The gorgeous blonde? She and the girl she's with have been dating almost exactly as long as you and me. Isn't that a weird coincidence? I told her we should double-date sometime."

Oh God. This was it. She was going to die right here in the ladies' room of the reception hall, wasn't she?

The door of the restroom pushed open, and one of the other bridesmaids peeked her head in. "There you are," she said, her eyes landing on Aubrey. "We're sitting for dinner. Trina needs you."

Perfect. It was exactly the excuse she needed. "On my way." She gave Phoebe a half shrug. Nothing she could do if the bride was requesting her presence, right? She was the maid of honor, after all. Phoebe smiled at her and stroked down her arm, and Aubrey escaped the restroom that suddenly felt way too small.

"You okay?" Trina asked her as she sat next to her at the bridal party table. "Your face looks weird."

"Gee, thanks."

Trina barked a laugh. "No, not like that. You just look... worried." Trina's eyes were soft, and her expression showed concern, and Aubrey was suddenly so fucking annoyed with herself, she could barely stand it. She needed to shake this off. This was

Trina's big day, and Aubrey's ridiculous, inexplicable anxieties had no place here. She took a deep breath and forced herself to push it all aside and smile, be there for her best friend.

"I'm totally fine," she said. "And if I haven't told you already, you are stunning." She grasped Trina's hand in hers and squeezed, and she watched Trina's eyes well up. "No, no. Don't cry. Your makeup has held up this long. Let's not test it again."

"I love you, Aubs," Trina said, just as the servers arrived with plates and set them in front of each person at the table.

The emotional moment passed as dinner was served and Aubrey was able to shelve the confusion of earlier. She couldn't really see table twelve well from her seat, and for that she was grateful, because this day wasn't about her or them. It was about Trina and Jeff. She ate her chicken marsala and paced herself on the drinks and tested Trina's makeup one more time with her maid of honor speech, and the evening flew by. When everything scheduled was done and all that was left was the dancing, she felt a weight lift off her shoulders. Only a couple hours left to go, and she could head home. Trina and Jeff had left to change clothes because they were headed off to the Bahamas for their honeymoon, and once they said their good-byes, she'd be free to leave.

"There you are." Phoebe was at her side, arm around her waist, and kissed her cheek. "I've been waiting for your duties to be over. Wanna dance?" She still looked great, but now her cheeks were flushed a bit and her eyes had a slightly glassy look to them. As if reading her mind, Phoebe added, "Did you taste the signature cocktail? It's a little strong." Then she laughed, and it was louder than her usual laugh, and yeah, Phoebe was drunk.

"No, I don't like whiskey. Did you drive?"

Phoebe gave a scoff that would've been cute if she'd been sober. Instead, it was a little sloppy. "Nope. Ubered."

Thank God.

"But I thought maybe I could go home with you tonight." As she said it, she leaned into Aubrey until she was holding way more of Phoebe's weight than she should've been, and it was clear she was going for sexy, rather than what she'd actually hit, which was messy and intoxicated, and there was no way in hell this was going to be their first time together.

"Actually, let's make it another night when I'm not so tired, okay?"

Phoebe didn't answer, and Aubrey wasn't sure if she was angry that she'd been turned down or starting to realize just how drunk she was. She didn't ask, she just helped her find her bag and her phone, ordered her an Uber, then waited with her in the lobby area of the reception hall.

"Thanks for taking care of me," Phoebe said, leaning in close to kiss Aubrey on the cheek.

"You're welcome," she said. "You'll be okay, right? I just can't leave yet."

Phoebe waved a hand, and it suddenly started to seem like shame was setting in. As if she'd realized she'd overdone it and was embarrassed. Her face had gone from an inebriated attempt at sexy to sheepish in only a moment or two. "I'll be fine. I'm so sorry, Aubrey."

"For what?" Aubrey asked, her own emotions changing quickly from irritation to sympathy. She didn't want to be annoyed with Phoebe. She'd come to a wedding of people she didn't know, and she'd sat with people she didn't know just to support Aubrey. So, she'd been overserved. So what?

"For having a bit too much to drink. I wanted to dance with you and maybe go home with you, and I blew it." The sheepishness stepped aside to make way for embarrassed sorrow as Phoebe's eyes welled up.

Okay, Aubrey was veering back toward annoyed, and she didn't want that. Thank God, the Uber pulled up then. She led Phoebe out to the car, checked the plate against the app, and opened the door for her. "Don't worry about it. Let me know you're home, okay?"

Phoebe nodded and made no attempts at another kiss, and Aubrey was thankful for that...which made her feel like shit as she watched the Uber pull away and disappear into the night.

"She seemed fun."

Aubrey knew the voice. Oh yes, she knew that voice, and she

gave herself a beat before she turned to meet those cool blue eyes. She wasn't sure what to say. Was Phoebe fun? Kinda, yeah. She was nice, which was more important. She was—

"I'm teasing." Monica waved a dismissive hand. "I sent mine home, too."

"Drunk?"

"Texting her ex all evening."

"Ouch."

"Right?"

They stood side by side in the lovely night air. The cicadas were singing, and there was a slight breeze that tickled the hem of Aubrey's dress and wafted through Monica's hair at the same time as she looked off into the thick trees across the parking lot. She was gorgeous—like, when was she not, but still—in a light blue dress that made her eyes pop and heels that had her slightly taller than Aubrey in *her* heels, and suddenly Aubrey's heart was pounding so heavily in her chest, she was surprised Monica couldn't hear it.

"I'm sorry your date was texting her ex all night," she said softly.

Monica turned to her, something in her eyes that Aubrey didn't want to dwell on. "I'm sorry your date had too much to drink."

They stood smiling at each other, and Aubrey reached for some levity. "Weddings, man."

"They really suck, don't they?" Monica asked.

"So much."

"One more drink?" Monica asked. "My treat."

"Why not?"

They headed into the reception hall together, Monica holding the door for Aubrey.

❖

Trina and Jeff reappeared just after Monica and Aubrey got their drinks. Trina was dressed in a cute little flowery sundress and shades, clearly reminding them she was off to the beach. Jeff had board shorts and a tank top on, with flip-flops on his feet and Ray-Bans on his face.

They looked stupidly happy.

Trina found her from across the room and ran to her. She threw herself into Aubrey's arms and hugged her tightly. Her lips next to Aubrey's ear, she said, "I love you so much. Thank you for being my maid of honor. I'll call you when we get back. And I still say you guys are ridiculously hot together." Then she planted a sloppy kiss on Aubrey's cheek and seemed to float out the door on the sound of the remaining guests waving and calling out their good-byes and well-wishes.

"You two have such a great connection," Monica said once the bride and groom were gone and people were dancing again. She sipped her whiskey neat. "I have always envied it."

"Really?" Aubrey had opted for a club soda with lime, and she took a sip as she watched Monica. The openness of her face, the vulnerability, was surprising.

"I mean, I have friends. I have good friends. Great friends. But you and Trina have been BFFs for, what? Ten years? Twelve?"

"Fourteen," Aubrey said with a smile. "We were slotted as roommates our freshman year, and somehow, we were a perfect match." She grinned as she shook her head. "We got so lucky."

"You really did. My freshman roommate hung blackout curtains in our room and listened to nothing but death metal."

Aubrey barked a laugh. "So...a chill and easygoing kind of girl."

Monica gave a snort. "Not even a little."

"I think I remember her. She wore nothing but black, right? Eyebrow piercing and tongue ring? Kept black eyeliner manufacturers in business?"

"That's her. She had long, straight black hair. I was rooming with the girl from *The Ring*."

"You lasted a whole semester, though, didn't you?" Aubrey scrunched her nose as she tried to remember.

"I did, but only because I had no idea I could ask for a new roommate. And she wasn't mean. She was nice to me. I didn't want to insult her. She was just being herself."

"It wasn't her fault she got paired up with the hottest girl in the dorm." Oh God. She'd said that out loud. She looked down at her drink. It *was* club soda, right?

Monica tipped her head and smiled, studied her for a moment before saying quietly, "Thanks."

"Sure." Okay. That wasn't so bad, right?

"I didn't know you thought that," Monica said, then sipped her drink and looked off at the dance floor, as if eye contact with Aubrey was too hard. Or weird. Or dangerous.

"I mean, I didn't actually mean to *admit it*," she said, and Monica laughed.

"Of course not. That would be silly."

"So silly."

The crowd had thinned a bit, but there were still lots of people dancing. Sarah and Bailey. Kyle and Jenny. Jonathan and his boyfriend. Others that Aubrey either didn't know or vaguely recognized from Trina's or Jeff's life.

They stood and watched in silence for a few minutes before the corners of Monica's mouth turned up just a bit and she glanced down into her glass as she said, "Well, look at us. Standing next to each other. Saying nice things to each other. Not wanting to kill each other."

"Hold up," Aubrey deadpanned, looking her in the face. "I never said I didn't want to kill you. I mean, I have a reputation to uphold, you know."

"Of course. Of course. Apologies. How could I forget?" But Monica grinned, clearly getting that she was teasing. "Seriously, though." Her throat moved as she swallowed. Was she nervous? "I like us a lot better this way."

Aubrey nodded and, this time, looked her in the eye. "Me too."

Monica drained her glass. "And on that very unexpectedly pleasant note, I'm gonna go." She set it on the bar, then turned back to Aubrey. "And your date was not wrong. You looked beautiful today." And before Aubrey could even begin to comprehend what was happening, Monica leaned in and kissed her softly on the cheek. "Get home safely," she whispered, then turned and left her standing there. Shocked was an understatement. Stunned didn't even come close. And another phrase floated through her head: *turned the hell on.*

She watched as Monica headed toward their table to grab her purse, stopping here and there to say good-bye to people. Then she headed for the door where she stopped and turned to meet Aubrey's eyes across the room. She gave a small wave that seemed like it was just for her, and she was gone.

Aubrey blew out a long, slow breath because what in the kisses-from-the-enemy was that?

She turned to the bartender and ordered a shot of tequila, throwing her claim of never having shots right out the window, because her hands were shaking a little bit, and she needed to steady them. The shot came, and she downed it without preamble. Or salt or lemon. It burned her throat on the way down, which was what she wanted. Something tangible, painful, to wake her the hell up.

"What the hell was *that*?"

When she turned around, both Sarah and Bailey were standing there, eyes wide, brows raised in expectation.

"Am I drunker than I thought, or did Monica Wallace just kiss you?" Sarah blinked at her, clearly astonished by what she'd seen.

"On the cheek. Yes." Aubrey went back to her club soda.

"Told you," Bailey said to Sarah, who nodded in clear agreement.

"Told her what?" Aubrey looked from one of them to the other and back.

Sarah shook her head, but Bailey had clearly had enough alcohol to loosen her lips and tank her inhibitions, and she grasped Aubrey's forearm. She leaned close but spoke at her normal volume, which Aubrey would've found funny if not for what she said.

"We all thought Monica had a thing for you in college. Like, all of us."

Sarah gave her a slap. "Honey. Stop."

"No, no, it's okay," Aubrey said. This wasn't the first time she'd been told this, but it wasn't any less surprising. "She hated me in college."

"Did she, though?" Bailey asked as she tipped her head, her voice higher than usual, and Sarah slapped at her again.

Aubrey blinked at them, looked back and forth from one to the other, trying to absorb this—not new, but repeated—information. Was it possible? Had her friends mistaken what they'd seen, heard, felt more than ten years ago? Were they saying it was still a thing?

She gave her head a shake. No. No way. She had no idea what to do about this. About any of it. She was tired. She was tipsy. It had been an absurdly full, very emotional couple of days, and her brain just did not have the capacity to absorb any of this.

"You okay?" Sarah asked, as Bailey started moving to the next bop the DJ played.

Aubrey nodded. "Fine." She gestured at Bailey with her eyes. "You guys rent a car? You're driving, yeah?"

"Uber," Sarah said as she followed Aubrey's gaze. Her expression went soft, her eyes sparkling with clear love for her wife, and Aubrey felt a little squeeze in her chest. Envy? Longing? Probably both.

"Good. Me too, and I'm headed out."

"Okay." Sarah wrapped her in a hug. "Love you."

"Love you, too. Text me when you get back to Philly so I know you're safe."

There weren't that many people left to say good-bye to, so she was in the back of her own Uber within fifteen minutes. The car was quiet, the music some soft easy-listening, which her ears were grateful for after hours of loud dance tunes. Her feet were killing her, and much as she'd loved her dress, she was ready to get out of it.

You looked beautiful tonight.

Yeah, Monica Wallace, enemy of enemies—at least in her memory—had actually said that to her. Like, close to her. Close enough that Aubrey could see her glossy lips and smell her perfume.

She swallowed hard as she remembered.

Alone in the back seat, she gazed out the window at the night as they drove and replayed her interactions with Monica, which she fully expected would be living rent-free in her head for the next who knew how long.

I like us a lot better this way.

There was so much to unpack in those eight little words. Or was there? Was she reading into things? Was she overthinking? Because that would be unsurprising. She excelled at overthinking, was a certified pro, held titles. But it seemed all her friends thought there was something there ten years ago. And how was she just finding out about it now? And why did it make her heart race just a little? Then her brain headed down another path, one that was clearly marked *No Trespassing*, but it didn't seem to care because she wanted to know: Were her friends right? And more importantly, if they were, was it still there, after all this time? If so, how did she feel about that? And more importantly, what should she do about it? Nothing? Something? Anything?

"Oh my God," she muttered, rubbing at her forehead with her fingertips and meeting the worried eyes of the driver in the rearview mirror. "I'm okay," she assured him. "Just…a really weird night."

He returned his gaze to the road.

She sighed quietly and gazed out at the night.

❖

With the wedding excitement over and Trina off on her honeymoon, Aubrey was able to concentrate on her daughter and her job. Thank God. She was still uncomfortable, confused, aroused, and struck speechless by the whole Monica thing the previous weekend, and having other things to put her focus on was a huge help. By the time she got to Wednesday, she felt like a regular human being again. Making lunches for Emma. De-escalating escalated phone calls. Sexy blond women who smelled like heaven and kissed her cheek were tucked away into a deep, dark, secret corner.

Of course, it was about to be all stirred up again because there was another wedding on the way.

"Mom—Dad and Kimmy are here!" At nearly ten years old,

everything Emma said seemed to have an exclamation point after it, whether she was ecstatic or completely moody and pissed off. This was the former, which was no surprise, as Emma was pretty much always ecstatic when it came to her dad. And no, Aubrey wasn't jealous. Much. Emma zipped by her in a blur of little girl and opened the front door. "Daddy!" She threw herself into Cody's arms, and he swooped her up like any good superhero would.

She watched from a little ways back into the living room. She always gave Cody his space with Emma. Emma didn't see him all that often—he'd been out of state during Trina's wedding last weekend but had been invited just the same—so despite her pangs of envy, it did make her happy to see Emma so thrilled to see him. And vice versa.

"Hey, Aubs." He smiled at her as he and Kimmy stepped into the house and closed the door behind them. His dark hair was floppy and too long. He was tanned deeply, the lines at the corners of his eyes white from squinting. He looked good. Happy. It was the thing she'd noticed most immediately about him the first time she'd seen him after their catastrophic wedding day. He'd taken a gap year before law school and done some traveling and backpacking, but he'd come back for Emma's birth. He'd visited often. But then he got the opportunity to backpack through Europe a second, longer time, and he'd jumped at it. He was gone for nearly four months that time. He'd finally returned, and as luck would have it, Aubrey had run into him at the grocery store of all places, and the very first thing she'd noticed was how happy he was. His face was relaxed. There was an easiness, a comfort to the way he carried himself that she'd never seen before. It made her happy for him…and a little sad for herself, knowing she'd never been able to make him look like that. But Kimmy clearly could.

"Hey, you," she said, shifting her face into happy-to-see-you mode. "Kimmy," she said to the tall, kind-looking woman next to him. "How are you?"

"I'm good," Kimmy said as Emma wrapped her arms around her soon-to-be stepmother's waist. "Real good." Aubrey guessed it was that look of kindness that lulled Kimmy's competition into a false sense of security. She was a prosecutor, and her record was beyond impressive. Aubrey wondered if defense attorneys took one look at her soft blond bob, her long legs, and her gorgeous green eyes and figured they had the win all sewn up.

They would be wrong.

"We wanted to go over a few wedding details, if that's okay," Cody said, "since this little Minion is gonna be in it."

"Of course. Come in and sit down. Give me a second and I'll be right out." She disappeared into the kitchen to grab the hors d'oeuvres she'd put together and pour the wine that had been breathing on the counter—a nice one, not the eight ninety-nine bottle she usually had in the fridge. She didn't want Kimmy thinking she was cheap.

When she returned to the living room and set the charcuterie in the center of the coffee table, the other three were laughing and joking about something she wasn't in on. Emma's giggle was probably Aubrey's favorite sound in the world, and she smiled as she returned to the kitchen to get the wine, and a beer for Cody.

Emma, Kimmy, and Cody were all seated on the worn microfiber couch, so she took a seat on the ottoman that matched the oversized blue chair.

"This looks great," Kimmy said, helping herself to a cracker with brie. She had such an interesting face. Her mouth was slightly too wide and her eyes were set a bit too far apart, but together, it worked. "Thank you so much."

Aubrey nodded and took a sip of her own wine. Oh, wow, that was good. Clearly, the pricier wine was pricier for a reason.

"So, we just wanted to iron out some of the details of the wedding." Cody glanced at Kimmy with a tender smile. "It's coming up fast."

"I can't believe you're doing a camping wedding," Emma said, practically bouncing in her seat on the couch. "It's gonna be so cool."

"It's really just a small gathering." Kimmy took up the story. "We have the campground booked, invites have gone out—did you get yours?"

Aubrey nodded. "I was…surprised, to say the least." She kept it light, made sure to smile.

Kimmy smiled right back, and hers seemed genuine. "We want you there. You're Emma's mom, and you're important to Cody."

"But if it's too weird for you…" Cody let his words trail off.

She gave him a look. "It's been ten years. Safe to say, I'm over you."

He laughed at that. "Good. Good. Okay, so, like we said. Small. Kimmy's sisters are both going to stand up with her. I have Monica and Emma. My parents. Her parents. And just a handful of friends."

"Can I sleep in a tent, Mom? Please?"

Aubrey glanced at Cody with a question in her eyes. Tent?

"Oh, right. Most people will be at the hotel down the street from the campground, but a few wanted to set up tents. We'll have one, Kimmy's sister and brother-in-law have one. And just last week, the kids—her sisters' kids—decided they all want to be in one. It's just three kids. A boy and twin girls. Eight and ten. They asked if Emma could bunk with them, make a big slumber party out of it." Aubrey must've made a face because he rushed on. "They'll be right with us, right in our campsite. We'll put their tent between ours and we'll keep an eye on them. I mean, I'm kinda hoping most people will sit around the fire for a while after the ceremony, you know? Have a few beers. Make s'mores."

Goddamn, he was so charming. Even now, even after everything they'd been through, even though he had hurt her more than any person on the planet, he could still charm her. She still had a love for him. She knew that. It wasn't sexual any longer. It wasn't a yearning. It was simply love. He'd made terrible decisions, yes. He'd practically destroyed her, true. But he was the father of her child, and he was a good man with a good heart, and she knew that in her bones.

"Kimmy's parents will be there in their RV, so if the tent isn't working, there will be an actual bed inside that we could move her to." His face was open and expectant as Kimmy nodded next to him with a hopeful smile on hers.

"That sounds great," Aubrey said, shifting her gaze to her daughter. "You will behave yourself, yes?"

"I promise!" Emma shouted and threw herself into her mother's arms. Her happiness almost made her vibrate, and Aubrey squeezed her tight, holding on as long as she could because these moments of physical affection were starting to wane. Her mother had prepared her for this. Emma would be ten in the fall. She was beginning to find her own way, to assert her independence, to grow the hell up, and hugging her mother wasn't as high on her list of awesome things as it used to be. Aubrey breathed in quietly, took in the scent of her child—sugar and crayons and nail polish, combined with her strawberry shampoo. Her baby.

"Perfect," Kimmy said, then took a sip of her wine and set it down. "I'm so glad we got that settled. My nieces and nephew are good kids, I promise you. You have nothing to worry about. They'll have fun, and we'll keep an eye on things, as will my parents."

"I trust you," Aubrey said with a nod and was surprised to realize it was true. Not just Cody. Of course she trusted him with his daughter. But her. Kimmy. The woman who was about to become her daughter's stepmom. She was good people. Aubrey had met her several times, and while some childish part of her expected—hoped?—Cody would end up with somebody shallow and maybe not the sharpest tool in the shed, she'd always gotten nothing but good vibes from Kimmy. She was funny, successful, and kind, and if she was about to be a permanent part of her child's life, those were key descriptors.

"We'd like the people standing up with us to be dressed the same," Kimmy went on. "Don't worry, no gowns. Or even dresses. I wasn't sure I wanted to wear one, so I don't expect my bridal party to either if they don't want to."

"No dresses?" Aubrey asked.

Kimmy's small laugh was soft. "Nope. You sound surprised."

Aubrey shrugged. "I am. I mean, you're always in a suit of some kind. Skirts. Heels. I just assumed…"

"That those are my preference? Hell, no. Those are for work.

My personal life rarely includes a dress or heels of any kind. I mean, I do have a dress for the ceremony, but it's sporty." She turned her gaze to Cody, and the love Aubrey could see was palpable. "And we're getting married barefoot."

Cody turned to Aubrey, his eyes slightly wide. "We'll be putting a blanket or something down." Aubrey laughed at his clear dislike of this plan.

"So, we'd like Emma to wear black on the bottom and white on the top. Shorts. Pants. Skirt. Whatever she wants."

"Blech. No skirts." Emma made a face like she'd tasted something sour.

"There's the tomboy I know and love," Cody said with a grin, giving Emma a playful tickle.

"Okay," Aubrey said. "We can handle that. Can't we, kiddo?"

"Yes!" Emma drew the *S* out like she was a snake, then snuggled into Cody's side.

The topic of discussion shifted to Emma's school, her homework, how she was struggling a bit with math, but how she excelled at science, and they vowed to help more with homework, which Aubrey took with a grain of salt because Cody always *said* he'd help, but he traveled so much that he was rarely around enough to *actually* help. About twenty minutes later, she poured a second glass of wine for Kimmy and herself. Cody waved away the offer of another beer, saying he was driving. Then he and Kimmy exchanged a look that Aubrey caught.

"Hey, Emma, wanna show me your room?" Kimmy asked.

Not one to ever miss an opportunity to show off her stuff, Emma jumped up from the couch with an exuberant yes, grabbed Kimmy by the hand, and led her to the stairs.

"Well, that was cryptic," Aubrey said, once they were gone.

Cody smiled. "Yeah, I just wanted to have a moment, just you and me."

"Oh." What was happening? Was there bad news? "Should I be bracing myself?"

"What? Oh no. Of course not." Cody scooted forward on the couch so he was balanced on the edge of the cushion. His forearms on the knees of his jeans, he clasped his hands in front of him and seemed to stare at his shoes for a moment. When he finally looked up, his dark eyes had gone soft, and there was a tender smile on his face. "I owe you an apology."

Not at all words she expected to hear, and it took her a moment to absorb them. "For?" she finally managed.

"Everything. For the way things went ten years ago—God, can you believe it's been ten years? For leaving you to do the hard stuff with an infant all by yourself. I know I sent child support. I also know it was barely anything. What I did..." She watched his Adam's apple move as he swallowed. "It was the best thing for me at the time, but I know it sucked for you. I'm so sorry about that, Aubrey."

Why couldn't she see? Why was her vision all blurry? She sniffled quietly. "Thank you," she said, and it sounded like a croak. She cleared her throat. "I appreciate that."

"Kimmy's work is here. Her office is here. And while my job takes me on a lot of travels, my plan is to be here in town much more often. So, I'd like to be a better dad. A more present dad."

She was quiet for a long time, and she peered at him. Finally, she asked, "Who are you, and what have you done with Cody?"

The tension in the room broke with her words as they both started to laugh.

"Just a guy who realized how much he misses his kid." Cody shrugged again.

"I gotta tell you," she said, "this was not at all how I saw tonight going. This is...unexpected."

"Well," Cody said, lifting his shoulders in a shrug, "it's been a long time coming. I'm sorry about that as well."

"Wow." She looked at him, and suddenly, her mind took her back almost ten years. There sat the boy she'd loved with all her heart, the boy she was certain she'd spend the rest of her life with. Yes, he'd aged. He had a few lines on his face now. His shoulders were broader, and his limbs were no longer gangly. But he was that same boy and the father of her child, and much as she hated to admit it, he would have a place in her heart forever. "I like Kimmy," she heard herself say before she even realized she was going to say it. "She's good for you."

Cody nodded, and—

"Oh my God, are you *blushing*?" she asked, laughing.

"Yeah, probably," he said, and his cheeks went a deeper pink. "I do that now when it comes to her. I'm a blusher."

They sat there, looking at each other, tandem smiles on their faces, and who would've ever thought this was where they'd be?

"I'm happy for you," she whispered, and it was the truth.

"Thanks, Aubrey. That means more than you know."

They stood, and he came around the coffee table and hugged her. It was the first time they'd actually touched each other in almost ten years, she realized, tightening her hold, just for a second or two.

"I'm so glad you're going to be at the wedding," he said, his lips close to her ear. "I wasn't sure if you'd want to."

"Well," she said as they let go of one another, "I am planning on talking Kimmy out of marrying you. But not until the morning of the wedding. So, enjoy the next couple of weeks while you can."

A flash of panic zipped across Cody's face before he realized she was kidding, and he laughed.

"Had you for a second there, didn't I?" she asked with an eyebrow waggle.

"You did. Christ." He chuckled, looked at his shoes for a second, then met her gaze. "I heard you and Monica are actually being nice to each other."

"You heard correctly." She'd done her best not to think about Monica, but the second her name was mentioned, the image of her came screeching into Aubrey's brain, all blond and pretty and smelling lovely and softly kissing her cheek.

"I'm really glad to hear that. She's always liked you, you know." He shook his head and blew out a breath as she absorbed those words. Then he chuckled. "Man, life is weird, huh?"

"God. So weird."

They didn't have a chance to talk any more about that subject, as Kimmy and Emma returned to the living room then. Kimmy sat on the couch, and Emma sat between them, and things felt...

different somehow. Lighter. Easier. Kimmy and Cody exchanged another look, in which he clearly let her know things had gone well, and she seemed relieved. It was interesting to watch, this man she'd loved with all her heart having silent conversations with a new person, a person he fit better with. And she was okay with that. In fact, she was happy about it. They were good together, Cody and Kimmy. They were excellent together.

She watched them as they listened to Emma tell a joke she'd learned in school that week. They paid close attention and laughed at the punch line and held hands and it was nice. Sweet. And she wasn't jealous. At all, and that was new. She was, however, envious, and for the first time, she really understood the difference.

She wanted that. Not Cody. But what he had. Not Kimmy, but a relationship like theirs, where the love and the trust was so deep that anybody looking at them could see it. She wanted that.

Maybe it was time she started looking for her own *excellent together* person.

WEDDINGS DOWN: 3
SUCCESS IN AVOIDING MONICA WALLACE: 0 DAMMIT

Part Four

CODY AND KIMMY
AUGUST 10, 2024
CAMPGROUND WEDDING

Aubrey McFadden is never getting married.

Reason #5
She can take care of herself.

I t was so fucking hot out. Holy crap.

Aubrey had chosen a cute sundress with spaghetti straps. It was light and airy, white with pink flowers, as summery as any dress could possibly be, yet she was sweating like she'd just worked out at the gym, then run a marathon, then put on jeans and a heavy coat. August could get rough in the Northeast, a fact most of the rest of the country didn't believe. The humidity was so thick, it felt like she could grab it with her hands and wring it out in front of her. That is, if she had the energy to move her arms. Which she probably didn't.

Things were going to be pretty informal. The attendees were all here and numbered somewhere around twenty-five. Kimmy's friend from law school had gotten herself ordained online and was going to perform the ceremony. At least they were under cover of some trees and not standing in the blazing sun. It was a beautiful August day... for floating in a pool or sitting on the dock of a lake with your feet in the water and a cold drink in your hand. Not so much for standing around in nice clothes in a place where the air didn't move. At all.

Cody and Kimmy and their respective wedding party members were all tucked into an RV parked about fifty yards away in another campsite. It belonged to Kimmy's parents and that's where they were getting ready. They'd eschewed traditional superstition, not caring that they were seeing each other before the ceremony, and part of Aubrey admired that.

Emma was in there with them.

So was Monica.

Aubrey hadn't seen her since Trina and Jeff's wedding reception. Since Monica's line about liking them better when they were being nice to each other. Since the infamous cheek kiss.

She hadn't seen her or talked to her, but she'd gotten an earful from Trina the second she'd returned from the Bahamas.

"Monica *kissed* you?" she screeched through the phone without even saying hello or letting Aubrey know she was back.

"On the cheek, weirdo," she'd replied. "Take several seats, ma'am." Then she'd told her how it had all happened.

"I told you," Trina had said. "I told you she has a thing for you."

Aubrey had sighed. "She doesn't have a thing for me. We're just…adults now. Grown-ups—"

"*Kissing* grown-ups," Trina had teased, and the conversation devolved from there.

She smiled now as she recalled that phone call. Trina and Jeff had been invited—they couldn't make the ceremony but would be there later to help their friends celebrate. She hoped they were someplace inside with air-conditioning.

Just as she felt a bead of sweat running down the center of her back, the door to the RV opened, and a tall, fit woman in her fifties or sixties hurried across the campground to where the guests stood. She had short, blond hair the same shade as Kimmy's and wore a lovely mint-green sundress. Her face was flushed and her hands sort of flitted around a bit like she was nervous. But her smile was big and contagious.

"Okay, I think we're good to go," she said as she waved her arms like she was parting the Red Sea. "If we could just make a path here…" She successfully split the guests into two even groups on either side so there was now a walkway between them. Aubrey stood toward the front and close to the pathway, so in case Emma got a case of the nerves, she'd see her mom.

The woman moved to the front of the pathway she'd created. She waited until she had everybody's attention, her smile still wide. Even never having met the woman, Aubrey could still tell she was incredibly happy. She clapped her hands once and kept them clasped in front of her.

"Thank you all so much for being here. For those of you I haven't met yet, I'm Catherine Whitford, Kimmy's mom, and I am over the moon today because my daughter is about to marry the most wonderful man. Kimmy and Cody have so much in common— first and foremost, a love of nature and of camping, which is why we're all standing out here sweating our behinds off." Chuckles rumbled through the small gathering. "The ceremony will be quick. Afterward, we've rented the community room over that way." She gestured vaguely off toward her right. "There will be food and drink and restrooms. In the community building, we'll have dancing and an open bar. There will be a food truck in the parking lot from Athena's Greek restaurant. When it cools down—assuming it cools down—we'll have a fire going over that way." She indicated to her left this time. "We've rented all the surrounding campsites, so feel free to set up your tent and hang with us, toast marshmallows, make s'mores, all that good stuff. And now, without further ado, let's have a wedding!"

The crowd broke into applause. Catherine moved aside and stood next to a handsome man in khaki shorts and a white button-down shirt who must've come from the RV while the guests were focused on her.

The door to the RV opened again and out came Emma and a woman that, if Aubrey hadn't already known she was one of Kimmy's two sisters, she'd have guessed it simply by the way she was built just like Kimmy, tall and lean, with the same blond hair and a very similar smile. Both she and Emma wore black shorts and white tank tops. She held out her hand, and Emma's smile was so big, it brought tears to Aubrey's eyes. As she got closer, Aubrey could see the subtle hints of makeup on her face. A little mascara, a little lip gloss. Kimmy had asked permission, and of course, Aubrey gave it, and now her heart did a little skip in her chest because here was a tiny glimpse of what grown-up Emma would look like, and oh, wow, she was beautiful.

Emma glanced at her and gave her a huge smile as she walked

past, gave her hand a quick squeeze, and Aubrey had to work hard to swallow down the lump that had suddenly lodged itself in her throat. Emma and the sister—what was her name again?—took their places on either side of the officiant, Emma still beaming. Then the crowd turned collectively to see the next two wedding party members.

Kimmy's other sister, who wasn't as tall but was just as blond and had the same wide smile, was one. She crooked her elbow and laughed softly as if it was an inside joke, and Monica tucked her hand into it and grinned back at her.

Good God.

How was this possible? More importantly, how was it fair?

How could a woman wear black shorts and a sleeveless white button-down shirt and look that fucking hot? How? How was it possible? And why? Why was that all Aubrey could see? The long, tanned legs—somebody had clearly been lying out by a pool all summer—the sandy blond hair that had more golden highlights in it since the last time Aubrey had seen her, probably also thanks to the summer sun. They walked down the aisle arm in arm, and how was Monica the only person in the whole group who looked completely unaffected by the humidity? As the pair passed by her, Monica caught her eye and—Was that a wink? Did she actually wink at her? Aubrey felt herself blush. Yeah, that's all she needed was more body heat because she wasn't already sweating like a farm animal.

They took their places on either side of the officiant, Monica standing next to Emma, who looked up at her with what Aubrey could only describe as happy admiration. She felt the rest of the crowd turn to look at the RV again, but Monica had captured her gaze, and pulling away from that was harder than she imagined. Aubrey finally gave a small smile, then turned to see the bride and groom coming out of the RV. Cody held his hand out for Kimmy to grasp, and they hadn't been kidding about being barefoot. Kimmy wore a flowing gauzy white dress that made her look like she'd stepped out of a dream. Cody wore black shorts and a white polo shirt. He'd gotten a haircut since she'd seen him last. He looked handsome and tidy.

And happy.

He looked so indescribably happy that Aubrey felt her eyes well up yet again. And this time, it wasn't out of envy or regret or anything at all negative. Her tears were purely of happiness for somebody who was important to her. Despite everything they'd been through, she still cared about Cody, and seeing him this happy made her happy, too.

They really had grown up, hadn't they?

Both the bride and the groom smiled at people and grabbed hands to squeeze as they walked toward the front of the gathering. Cody bent down to kiss Emma, then leaned over her and kissed Monica as well. She must've been feeling like Aubrey was, the expression on her face registering such pure joy that Aubrey felt like she could almost reach out and touch it.

As promised, the ceremony went quickly. It was nontraditional. Cody and Kimmy had written their own vows. Emma had the rings in her pocket, and her face was so serious when she pulled them out that Aubrey almost laughed. It was her most important job, as she'd told Aubrey a few days earlier. And no sooner had things started than the officiant was telling them they could kiss, and then the crowd broke into applause, and then everybody beelined for the building they prayed had air-conditioning. And cold drinks.

"Did you see me, Mom? Did you?" Emma was pretty much bouncing next to her, face flushed.

"I did. You were great."

"I'm gonna go catch up with Dad." She gave Aubrey a quick hug, then darted ahead with Aubrey shouting for her to drink some water when she got inside. She laughed and shook her head. It was Cody's day, and his daughter should be with him.

"She is nine going on about thirty," a voice said from behind her.

She knew who it was, and a slight shiver ran up her spine, like featherlight fingertips. And shivering was so weird, given how hot it was, but she felt goose bumps on her arms, just for a second or two. She turned and met those blue eyes. "That is a very accurate assessment of my kid."

"Seriously. She's great."

"Thanks. I think so, too." She let her eyes roam quickly over Monica before asking, "Why are you the only one not melting? Unfair."

"Are you kidding? I'm dying. I'm pretty sure, any minute, I'm gonna just puddle into the ground like I'm made of wax."

"Well, you don't look it."

Monica smiled as she watched the ground while they walked. "Thank you. You look pretty great, by the way."

"Oh, this old thing?" she asked, and they smiled at each other.

"Yeah. That old thing. You're like the epitome of what summer should look like."

"Complete with buckets of sweat."

"No." Monica put a hand on her arm and stopped their progress. "No, I mean it. You look beautiful." Monica's gaze landed on her hand on Aubrey's arm and she removed it with a half shrug. "I just thought you should know."

The eye contact right then? It did things to Aubrey. Things she didn't expect. Sensual things. Sexy things. A little flutter began low in her belly. Her palms itched. She wet her lips, and when she spoke, her voice was a hoarse whisper. "Thank you."

"You're welcome." Another second locked on those eyes and then Monica smiled and used her head to gesture toward the building where the rest of the wedding guests had gone inside. "Let's get a drink, yeah?"

"Yes, please."

❖

For a community building on a campground, it was a pretty nice setup—clean bathrooms, plenty of chairs, but also a cleared space for a small dance floor. Somebody's speaker was mounted up high, and a playlist of fun dance music was playing. There was an open bar in the corner with two bartenders. And air-conditioning. Blessed air-conditioning.

The first thing she did was hit the ladies' room, which was apparently what every other woman there had in mind because there was a line. With a sigh, she took her place behind a woman wearing a black dress and way too much perfume. She was wondering how the woman hadn't spontaneously combusted wearing black in this heat when Monica was suddenly by her side. She held out a clear plastic cup of white wine.

"Sauv blanc. I took a guess." Her smile wavered slightly, like she was uncertain.

"Bless you," Aubrey said and took a sip. The wine was icy with a sharp tang. Perfect. Between the cold wine and the AC, she began to feel human again.

Next to her, Monica turned toward the woman in the black dress, then immediately turned back to Aubrey, eyes wide, face a grimace of distaste. Aubrey held back a laugh, and the two of them had an entire silent conversation about how much perfume the woman must've put on that morning, and how she'd better stay inside or the bugs would eat her alive. It was interesting, wasn't it? The fact that she knew exactly what Monica was thinking and that Monica seemed to know exactly what she was thinking, though neither of them said a word?

The bathroom had exactly three stalls, so it took a while to get in, but before long, the two of them were at the sinks, washing hands, checking makeup and hair.

"Yeah, I was afraid of this," Aubrey said, trying to tame her hair.

"Of what?" Monica asked, reaching for a paper towel.

"The humidity always frizzes me out." She had a small bottle of hair spray in her purse. It wouldn't do much, but it might help a little.

"You're not frizzy. You look terrific."

"Says the woman who always looks like she just stepped off the runway of *America's Next Top Model*." She snapped her mouth shut, because yeah, she'd said that out loud. Their eyes met in the mirror. Other women milled in and out, but she hardly noticed them. It was like everything around them blurred, and time stopped.

Monica's face broke into a soft smile, and when she said thank you, it was just above a whisper. Did her cheeks tint a slight pink as well? Had she made the unflappable Monica Wallace blush? Because that earned her points as far as she was concerned. Points for what, she didn't know. But points. Definite points.

Feeling emboldened now, she shot her a grin, then focused on reapplying her lip gloss. She'd only looked forward to today for Emma's sake, to see her stand up with her father. With one last glance in the mirror, she snapped her purse shut and exited the restroom.

"Mom!" Emma was suddenly there as if she'd materialized out of thin air, like she'd been beamed there.

"Emma!" She used the same inflection in response.

"I was wondering where you were."

"I'm right here."

"Well, I know that *now*." Emma put her hand in Aubrey's. "I'm hungry."

She didn't realize Monica had passed by her until she belatedly registered the hand that briefly swept across her shoulders, and then she could see her from behind...the golden hair, the sway of the hips. She was seeing Monica Wallace in an entirely new light lately, and right now, she was painfully aware of it.

Forcing her attention back to her daughter, she said, "Okay. Let's go see what the food truck has."

Emma had always been an adventurous eater, something Aubrey was eternally thankful for, especially after hearing horror stories from friends whose kids ate nothing but chicken nuggets. There were few foods Emma didn't like, so the fact that the food truck was serving Greek food didn't worry Aubrey in the slightest. Before long, they were sitting at a picnic table in the shade of a maple tree, eating gyros that were some of the best she'd ever had. Emma insisted on baklava for dessert, and Aubrey couldn't blame her. It looked delicious and smelled even better.

Half an hour after they'd come outside, Emma was scooting back in, wanting to check in on her dad and play with Kimmy's nieces and nephew, the ones she'd be in a tent with that night. Aubrey sat there for a few moments longer, watching her daughter and feeling that familiar mixture of love for her kid and worry that time was moving way too fast for her liking.

"Next thing you know, it'll be the prom," said a familiar voice. "Then college. Boyfriends—or girlfriends. No preference here."

Aubrey laughed and spun around on the bench to see Trina and Jeff behind her. "You stop that. It's already happening too fast. I don't need you speeding it along." She stood up and hugged her, then Jeff.

"How was the ceremony?" Trina asked as Aubrey cleaned up her garbage. They headed toward the community center.

"Sweaty, but really nice. Short and sweet. And Emma was adorable."

"Duh. Of course she was."

A short time later, she was sipping a glass of wine as she stood at a bistro table in a corner, listening to Trina tell a story about trying to explain TikTok to one of her bosses.

"He's, like, in his seventies and doesn't understand that TikTok is not the same as Netflix. He's all *But you watch videos in both places, right?* And I do my best not to get impatient, because I know he doesn't understand and I just need to explain it better to him, but for fuck's sake, man, it's the twenty-first century. Come join us!"

Aubrey laughed at the sheer indignation on Trina's face. Jeff shook his head because he'd probably heard the story a dozen times. He and Aubrey made eye contact over Trina's head and then laughed louder.

"Here's where all the action is," Cody said as he walked up to them, bobbing his head to the hip-hop tune playing over the speaker. He held Kimmy's hand. Monica came up behind them. "Gang's all here." He hugged Trina and then Jeff.

"I mean, like, half the gang," Trina said, then grinned to show she was teasing.

"Yeah, turns out people are busy in August. Who knew?" He lifted one shoulder. "And I missed a couple weddings, so I can't be butthurt if some people miss mine, right?"

Aubrey met Monica's gaze as the others chatted. How was it Aubrey still felt like a wilted flower left in a vase with no water while Monica still looked—sticking with the flower analogy—fresh as a daisy, as her grandma would say. Monica tilted her head to the side, looking inquisitive, and Aubrey realized she'd been staring. When she shook herself back to the conversation, Trina was looking at her, one eyebrow arched in question. She gave her head a subtle shake, silently telling her ex-roommate that it was nothing. Everything was fine.

A slow song came on over the speaker, and Cody turned to his new bride. "Care to dance, my love?"

Kimmy sighed comically. "If I have to."

Cody led her out onto the small dance floor, and they were followed closely by Trina and Jeff. Which left Monica and Aubrey standing alone together to watch.

"This is the part that's always a little hard when you're single at a wedding," Monica said, then sipped what looked like an old-fashioned to Aubrey.

"What happened to your last wedding date? The one who was texting her ex the whole time?"

Monica shrugged, keeping her eyes on the dancers. "She's back with her ex."

Aubrey snort-laughed before she could stop herself, then clamped a hand over her mouth and looked, chagrined, at Monica. "Oh God, I'm so sorry. That was so rude of me."

But Monica was grinning. "No, don't apologize. It's funny, right?"

"It's not, though."

"What about your last wedding date? Drunky McDrunkerson, wasn't that her name?"

"*D* for short. No idea. I haven't seen her since that last wedding. She called it off."

"I'm sorry. I didn't know that."

"Don't be. It was the right thing to do. I was relieved."

"Yeah?"

Aubrey nodded. "Yeah."

The slow song ended but led into a second one. A moment passed before Monica spoke again, but when she did, it was surprising. "I don't think we should be the only ones from our college friends to not be dancing. Do you?"

Aubrey met those blue eyes with her own, and whatever was in them, it made her feel strangely brave. "Are you asking me to dance?"

"I am." And there was Monica's hand, held out for the taking. "I mean, what's there to lose, right? It's just a dance."

It's just a dance.

Without waiting for a chance to talk herself out of it, she set her wineglass down, put her hand in Monica's, and let herself be led onto the dance floor. She ignored the wide-eyed look from Trina as well as the surprise on Cody's face. Instead, she focused on the warm softness of Monica's hand in hers. And then they were facing each other. Monica's other hand slid around and settled on the small of her back. Aubrey lifted her arm, let her hand rest on Monica's shoulder, as she was subtly pulled closer.

The lengths of their bodies touched, and what in the inappropriate responses was happening to her nerve endings? It felt like every single one of them had been awoken. She could feel everything. *Everything.* Monica's body heat. The way her muscles moved under Aubrey's hand. How she gently flexed her fingers against Aubrey's back. The rise and fall of her chest—of her breasts—as she breathed. She was just a little bit taller than Aubrey, and if Aubrey tilted her head up just the smallest bit, their lips would meet. That's how close they were. She swallowed.

Things blurred. The music...what song was on? She couldn't remember. Who else was here? She was drawing a blank. All she could see, all she could focus on were the shiny lips so close to hers and the body pressed all along her own. There was nothing else in the world. Not a thing.

"Mom."

The voice registered somewhere in the back of her mind.

"*Mom.*"

She blinked as though she'd been in a trance, and when she looked down, Emma was tugging at the side of her dress. The world came crashing back in, all bright colors and too loud music. She stepped out of Monica's space, ignoring the near shriek of protest from her body. "What do you need, honey?"

"Those guys are going out to the campfire. Can I go? Other people are out there. Kimmy's dad and stuff. Can I? Please?"

Aubrey loved that Emma took the time to ask. "Honey, as long as you're staying with your dad's family, you're fine. You don't have to ask my permission."

"And Kimmy is dad's family now." It was an astute observation for a nine-year-old, and Aubrey nodded.

"She is."

"Okay. Thanks, Mom. Hi, Aunt Monica. Bye, Aunt Monica." And she was gone, sprinting toward the entrance where Kimmy's nieces and nephew were clearly waiting for her, and then the four of them were out the door and visible through the window running toward where Kimmy's father was poking at an impressive campfire.

"Looks good for toasting marshmallows." Monica's voice was low and close to her ear.

Aubrey nodded, then turned to meet her gaze. What was it about those eyes? She had to make a conscious effort to look away from them, so she followed the line down the side of her neck to her shoulder and down her arm. It was only in that moment she realized they still held hands. When she looked back up at Monica, she was also looking at their hands, and then very subtly, she let go. Aubrey couldn't read her expression.

"I'm gonna…" She jerked a thumb over her shoulder.

"Yeah. Yeah. Sure." Monica nodded, her eyes darting.

The two of them walked in opposite directions.

❖

Much of the humidity disappeared with the sun, and for that, Aubrey was grateful. Leaving the comforts of the air-conditioning in the community building didn't feel like she was walking into a wall of moisture anymore, and she breathed a sigh of relief as she crossed the threshold into the evening and headed for the campfire. She'd snagged a bottle of water on her way out, and she cracked it open to take a healthy slug.

Her head was a bit of a swirly mess, and she knew it but had no idea how to sort it out, especially not right now. She was slightly tipsy. She was having a better time than she expected to. And she wanted to be in the vicinity of Emma. At least for a little while. Her daughter was the steady factor in her life, and whenever she started to feel adrift in any way, she found Emma and used her as a sort of touchstone. She was what was important. She was what mattered. Everything else was excess.

Kimmy's dad, who Aubrey had learned was named John, was a pro at the fire, and he clearly took it as his job. He stayed close to it with a large stick in his hand that he used to prod logs and embers in various spots, poking them into just the right positions for maximum burnage, it seemed.

"You're good at that," she said, after she stood watching for a while.

He looked up at her and smiled, and she immediately saw how Kimmy had gotten her wide mouth. "Thanks. Years of practice." He seemed to study her for a moment. "You're Emma's mom?"

"I am. Aubrey."

"I've heard a lot about you."

"I bet."

John laughed good-naturedly. "All good. Promise." He poked a spot with his stick, then added a log. The fire was blazing hot, and she took a small step back just as Emma and another girl ran by.

"Hi, Mom," she called with a laugh and kept on running.

Aubrey grinned and shook her head as John spoke. "She's a good kid, that one. Polite. Kind. You raised her well."

The fact that he'd said she raised Emma well and not she and Cody told her all she needed to know about Mr. John Whitford.

"Thank you. I appreciate that. I'm pretty proud of her."

"You should be."

Little by little, more people started trickling out from the building and pulling up chairs or coolers or whatever else they could sit on around the fire.

"Eighty-two degrees and we're sitting around a raging fire," somebody commented with a laugh.

"Can't have s'mores without a fire," said Catherine Whitford, who'd just come out of the RV with an armload of marshmallow bags, Hershey bars, and a box of graham crackers. As if she was a bug light and the kids were flies, they suddenly appeared from everywhere. Tents, the woods, the RV. "Everybody got sticks?"

Aubrey had brought a chair and was now simply sitting and watching the evening play out before her. She settled into her buzz, sipped her water, and people watched. While she knew many of the attendees, there seemed to be more she didn't know, so she watched. It was almost as if she was there, but not.

On the other side of the fire, she saw Cody's parents. They'd been polite and had said hi to her, but that was it. They were Emma's grandparents and were always good to Emma, but they seemed to only tolerate Aubrey. It had bothered her for a long time, but in recent years, she'd learned to let it go.

"Is this patch of grass taken?" Trina dropped a folding chair next to her and sat. "Holy crap, it's been a long day." She had a plastic cup of red wine in one hand and two long, sharp sticks in the other.

"Planning on stabbing somebody?"

"Yes, a marshmallow." She sought out the bag near Kimmy's mom and grabbed a couple, then slid them both onto her stick at once and shoved them directly into the flames.

"How did I not know you're one of *those* people?" Aubrey asked, mock horror on her face.

"One of what people?"

"The people who turn their marshmallows into charcoal."

"Listen, there is no other way to eat them."

"I beg to differ." Aubrey took Trina's other stick, found herself a marshmallow, and proceeded to toast it gently, just slightly above the lick of flame. "It's done like this."

"Please." Trina had a mouthful of blackened marshmallow. "I can eat seven of mine by the time you finish toasting one your way."

"Yes, but mine will be perfectly golden, not made of ashes."

"Gotta say, I'm with Aubrey on this one." Monica set a chair down on the other side of Aubrey.

Without saying a word and with her eyes on Trina, Aubrey

swung her stick so the marshmallow—toasted to, yes, a perfect golden brown now—was right in front of Monica. She happily pulled it off with her fingers and popped it into her mouth with a smile.

"Oh, you're a team now, I see. Fine." Trina speared another marshmallow and shoved it right into the flames again. "More marshmallows for me."

Aubrey wanted to think about how weird it was to be sitting there between the two most important women from her senior year at college, her best friend and her archnemesis at the time. Now? Now, instead of weird, it was…interesting. Intriguing. A little confusing, if she was being honest. Now they were her best friend and…What was Monica exactly? Aubrey didn't think of her as an enemy any longer. She'd grown up. She'd moved on. And being around her more often this year than she had in the past ten was…eye-opening? Was that the right word? She felt like Monica had gone from a flat, one-note person to a fully-fledged, three-dimensional human with intelligence and a sense of humor and a magnetic pull of some kind that Aubrey didn't want to dwell on but also couldn't deny.

She gave her head a little shake. She didn't want to be thinking about this, and as if sensing exactly that, Emma appeared out of the growing darkness with the makings of a s'more. She pushed her way between Aubrey's knees and leaned back against her.

"Mom, can you do my marshmallow?" she asked in a slightly pouty voice. "Every time I try, it catches on fire."

"That's the way you should do it," Trina said, trying again to win folks to Team Charco-mallow.

"Then it's all burned and gross," Emma said with perfect reason in her tone, an unspoken *duh*.

"Exactly," Trina said.

Emma rolled her eyes. "Mom. Can you do it how I like them?"

"I'd be happy to," Aubrey said, then stuck her tongue out at Trina. She speared a marshmallow and did her thing, her arms around Emma, patiently rolling the stick gently to toast all sides evenly. "Got your cracker and chocolate ready?"

"Uh-huh."

"Okay, here we go." She set the marshmallow on the square of chocolate and helped Emma remove it from the stick without making too much of a mess. The entire time they worked together, she could feel Monica's eyes on them. On her. Watching. It made that flutter in her belly, which had been there since they danced, kick it up a notch. Or two. Or seventeen.

Emma took a bite. "Mmm. Perfect." She shot a look to Trina, who laughed. "Thanks, Mom." And she was off to find her new friends again, Aubrey assumed.

"That kid is sassy. I love that about her," Trina said.

"Me too."

"Gotta hit the ladies' room, b-r-b."

Aubrey watched Trina go, then turned back to her stick.

"So, could you toast me two while I go get the rest of the makings?" The firelight cast Monica's face in an orange glow that looked amazing on her.

"Sure." Aubrey put two marshmallows on her stick and went back to work, turning the stick slowly as she gazed into the flames. While she was not a fan of camping at all, she was a big fan of campfires. They had so many great qualities. They were warm. They kept the mosquitoes away. They hid faces a bit so they weren't so easily read by others. She hoped that last one was true because she didn't want anybody to see what she was pretty sure was written in her eyes: arousal. She didn't quite understand what was happening to her when it came to Monica. Well, she did understand that it was physical attraction, that it was enormously unexpected, but that it was there. She couldn't deny it. She'd tried. It just came back stronger the next time, like it was toying with her. Teasing her.

As if to demonstrate how closely her body was paying attention, she knew Monica was back without looking because she actually felt her. She felt her presence from behind and then next to her. A hard swallow, and then she asked, "Ready?"

"Yes." Monica said it like a small child about to get some candy, and when Aubrey turned toward her with her excellently toasted marshmallows, there were two squares of chocolate on two crackers. Monica picked up the first one.

"Double fisting, are you?" Aubrey asked on a grin.

"No, one is for you."

Aubrey set the first marshmallow on the chocolate square but stopped for a second and met Monica's gaze. "Really?"

"Of course. What, I'm gonna make you do all the work for me but get no reward out of it? Please." Monica scoffed as if that was the most ridiculous thing she'd ever heard. "My mama raised me better than that." They made two s'mores like they were choreographed. The sweet little sandwiches came out perfectly, melty chocolate and all. Monica held hers toward Aubrey. "Cheers."

Aubrey touched her sandwich to Monica's and they each took a bite. The marshmallow stretched and made a line of white on Monica's chin. Without thinking about it, Aubrey reached up and wiped it off with her thumb, which she then put in her mouth. Monica's eyes hooded, and Aubrey realized what she'd done. But instead of being mortified or embarrassed or yanking her thumb out of her mouth, she took her time getting all the marshmallow off, pretending not to notice Monica's stare, but being absolutely aware of it.

Oh, this was fun.

When was the last time she'd felt her power as a woman? When was the last time she'd turned somebody on and *known it*? God, it was exhilarating.

Monica swallowed the bite in her mouth, and it seemed to take some effort on her part to look away. Was she feeling it, too? She had to be. The way her eyes went all glassy and dark? She had to be. And for that, Aubrey was grateful. She didn't want to be the only passenger on the inappropriate-desire train.

They ate their s'mores in silence. There were many others around the fire, but they all seemed to be talking amongst themselves. The kids were playing near the RV—Aubrey could hear them. Cody and Kimmy looked like they might be making rounds. They were on the other side of the fire, talking to a couple Aubrey didn't know.

"Got you a refill." Trina sat back down in her chair next to Aubrey, carrying two plastic cups of wine. Then she looked past Aubrey at Monica. "I didn't think to ask you what you were drinking. I'm sorry."

"No worries." Monica had to clear her throat and say it a second time, which Aubrey found interesting. And fun. "I need to stretch my legs anyway. I'll get something." Without looking at Aubrey, she pushed to her feet and headed not toward the community building, but toward the wooded path that led to the lake.

"Was it something I said?" Trina asked, then shrugged and grabbed for the bag of marshmallows.

Staring after Monica would be too obvious, so Aubrey forced herself to focus on toasting another marshmallow, her gaze glued to the flames of the campfire. She managed to sit there with her stick for several minutes before handing it to Trina and muttering something about needing to find Emma. She went around the fire toward the RV, and when she was sure she was out of Trina's sight, she headed for the woods.

❖

This had been the weirdest damn day.

The thought ran through Aubrey's head over and over as she trudged into the woods. She was at her ex's wedding. The same ex who had left her the day *they* were to get married. And she understood why she'd been invited, but why had she accepted? And more importantly, why was she still here? That was the real question, wasn't it? Emma was fine. She was with her father and her father's family, new and old. She was fine. She didn't need her mother hovering over her. While it was true that Cody had invited her, had welcomed her to the festivities, she could've gone home right after the ceremony. Or at least a short while into the reception. People who knew who she was had to be wondering why she was still hanging around.

So, why was she?

The mind was a funny thing, and the heart was even funnier.

And funnier than both of them? Instinct. Instinct was hilarious, and not in a ha-ha kind of way. Instinct drove her now, and somewhere in the dark recesses of her brain, she knew it. Didn't stop her, though.

She didn't know exactly where she was going, but she knew the general direction, part of her hoping her target had already gone inside. Or better yet, gone home. She was just thinking maybe that's exactly what had happened and the relief was just starting to trickle in, when her eyes caught a glimpse of a white shirt, practically glowing in the moonlight. Monica stood there, leaning with her back against a tree, gazing out onto the still water of the small lake that belonged to the campground.

Stopping in her tracks would've been the best idea for Aubrey right then. *Just...stop walking. Stand there for a minute. Be still. Let her see you. Get a handle on what she might be feeling by taking a moment to look at her face, to gauge, to assess.*

She did none of those things.

Instead, she kept walking. Monica turned to her, let her gaze rest on her. She didn't look the least bit surprised by Aubrey's sudden presence. She didn't look the least bit uncomfortable. In fact, rather than fold her arms over her chest or look away or do something to indicate that she preferred to be alone, she did the opposite. She stood up straighter. She maintained solid eye contact, and when Aubrey got close, she opened her arms.

Aubrey didn't stop at all. She walked right into Monica's open arms, directly into her personal space, and their mouths crashed together. No preamble, no intro announcing her intentions. Right to the kissing.

And for the love of God, what kissing it was.

Though kissing was probably the wrong word. They went straight to making out. A full-on make-out session, complete with tongues and wandering hands and gasping breaths. Monica released a small *oof* as Aubrey pushed her hard up against the tree trunk, her tongue deep in Monica's mouth.

Not to be outdone, apparently, Monica gave back as good as she got. Her hands were suddenly everywhere, making Aubrey question if she might actually have more than two. Fingertips tickled along her bare shoulders and against the skin on her back that her dress didn't cover. Her left ass cheek was definitely cradled. Her hips, her face, her hair...Monica's hands were everywhere and it was shocking and surprising and so damn *good*. When was the last time she'd been kissed like this? Deeply. Thoroughly. As if her mouth was the only thing in the world that existed.

Never.

That was the answer. She had *never* been kissed like this before, and her body knew it and reacted accordingly. Her skin tingled and her nerves stood at attention, as though a gentle buzz of electricity was running through her system. And the wetness! God, her panties were soaked in a matter of seconds, her body preparing itself for more. She tried to slow down her body's reactions by focusing on what she could feel with her own hands. Monica's body was taut, which came as no surprise. She'd always been in great shape, you could tell just by looking at her. But feeling her? A whole different story. Wow. Monica's arms were strong as they held Aubrey, her hands sure and firm on her waist, in her hair, the muscles under her clothes smooth and solid.

And holy crap, could she kiss.

The sound of a moan filled the air, and Aubrey wasn't sure which of them it had come from. She didn't care. She doubled down, pulled Monica impossibly closer, and pushed her tongue into her mouth more deeply. She tasted so good, the flavors of her s'more still lingering in her mouth, the sweetness of marshmallows and chocolate, and Aubrey knew she'd never look at s'mores the same way again.

Lost.

That's how she felt. Lost, but in the best of ways. It was dark. They were alone. And somehow, she felt safe. But...with this woman? How? How was that possible? Doubt tried to worm its way into the situation, to make her analyze, and she fought it off, kept it at bay. She honestly wanted to keep everything at bay and live right here, in these woods, kissing this woman, for the remainder of time.

The sound of a twig snapping registered somewhere in the

back of her mind, even as Monica's hand tugged her head back to expose her throat. And then her hot mouth was on Aubrey's neck, finding the exact spot near her shoulder that drove her absolutely wild. Another twig snapped and then…a voice.

"Oh my God. Oh God, we're so sorry. We didn't…"

Aubrey's entire body flinched at the sound, and she took a step back from Monica, whose face registered equal surprise. Even in the dim light of the moon, Monica's face was flushed, her lips swollen from kissing, and her top four buttons were unfastened, though Aubrey had no recollection of actually unbuttoning them. They turned their heads at the same time to see Cody and Kimmy standing not five feet away. Kimmy hid a smile, not well, and Cody looked utterly shell-shocked.

"You two?" he asked, the disbelief crystal clear in his tone. "I mean, like, when? How? I—you two? I'm so confused right now."

Kimmy tugged at his hand. "Let's talk about it later, okay?" She waited until he met her gaze, and they seemed to have a silent discussion before he nodded.

"Okay. Yeah."

"We're so sorry we interrupted you," Kimmy said, still smiling. As she led Cody away, Aubrey heard her stage-whisper to him, "They are *so* hot together. Just sayin'."

She and Monica watched the couple walk away until they could no longer see them, until the dark of the woods seemed to absorb them completely.

"Oh my God," Aubrey finally whispered. "I…what…oh my God."

Monica didn't seem nearly as…God, what was Aubrey? A blend of confused, surprised, and completely turned the hell on, at least on the surface. If she dived deeper—which she should, but didn't want to—there was a whole mess of other crap, both good and bad. And yet Monica just stood there, looking calm, a gentle smile on her face.

"Why are you smiling?" Aubrey demanded. "What is there to smile about?"

Monica had the good sense to look somewhat embarrassed, and she glanced down at her feet before reaching out to run her fingers down Aubrey's bare arm. "I'm just happy. That's all."

"You are?"

A slight lift of one shoulder, almost imperceptible in the dark. "Just something I've always wanted to do."

Aubrey blinked at the words. "Kiss me?"

"Kiss you. Yeah."

"Oh. I..." Aubrey shook her head. "I didn't know."

"I know you didn't. I didn't want you to."

She glanced off at the lake, stunning in the moonlight now. "Why now?" she asked softly.

Monica studied her for a moment, that slight smile still playing at her lips. "I'm sorry, did I come walking right up to you and kiss your face off? Oh no, wait. That was you." She poked her gently in the chest with a finger.

Her go-to emotion when it came to Monica Wallace was always either irritation or anger. But this time, she surprised herself by smiling. And then that smile grew and a little bubble of laughter escaped from her throat. "That *was* me, wasn't it?"

"It really was. And wow."

"Yeah?"

"Oh yeah. You're, like, a really good kisser."

Aubrey laughed softly. "Right back atcha." And they stood there, glancing at each other, but also away from each other, as they each seemed to absorb what had just happened between them. Monica reached out again, ran her fingertips down her arm again but, this time, entwined their fingers together and held her hand. She tugged Aubrey closer, brought her hand up between them, and kissed her knuckles.

"I don't know what this is," Aubrey whispered. "And I'm maybe not ready to analyze it."

Another half shrug. "Totally fine. It doesn't have to be anything, you know." Monica held her gaze for a beat before adding, "Or it could be something."

They headed back to the campfire. Monica stopped there and

helped herself to a beer from a cooler. Aubrey searched for her daughter, gave her a kiss and a hug, and told her to be good. Then she escaped.

She Ubered home, sitting in the back seat in the dark, seeing nothing out her window because her mind kept playing back the last two hours. Her own determination, how she'd walked right up to Monica, no words, only action. And the kissing.

God. The kissing.

And while the kissing played on a loop in her brain, Monica's words echoed through her head.

It doesn't have to be anything, you know.

That was true. It really didn't. She could chalk it up as a silly, spontaneous moment, a reckless move on her part that ended up being, well, kind of fun. Nothing wrong with that. Nothing at all.

Or it could be something.

Yeah. That's the line that stuck with her. The one that poked at her the entire ride home. The one that followed her to bed and then parked on the pillow next to her and whispered in her ear all night, tickling and teasing, sending her mental replays of Monica's mouth on hers, her hands all over Aubrey's body, her skin under Aubrey's fingertips. She tossed and turned and dreamed of trees and moonlight and her fingers digging into soft blond hair and Monica's fingers drifting across her skin. She woke up several times in the night, flushed and throbbing and wanting.

Or it could be something.

❖

Only two more weeks.

Two more weeks until school started, and Aubrey couldn't wait. She loved her daughter more than life itself, would do anything for her, would take a bullet to save her life. But if she heard Emma say one more time that she was bored when she lived in a house full of toys and games and electronics, Aubrey might have to jump off a roof.

It had been almost two weeks since Cody's wedding. He and

Kimmy had headed off to Colorado on their honeymoon to hike and camp but would be back Thursday and planned to take Emma for the weekend. She laughed a bit to herself about how it was probably good she and Cody hadn't ended up married, given how much she did not enjoy camping and how much he did. She was also glad he was gone because she'd managed to avoid talking about anything but Emma before he left, much as he'd tried to steer the conversation toward…other things. She'd have to talk to him when he got back, though.

Her phone buzzed in her back pocket, and she slid it out, then smiled at the text. *Just saying hi. Was thinking about you this morning.*

This was new, texts from Monica. She wouldn't call them regular, but they'd been showing up here and there since the wedding. Just like this one, telling her she'd been on her mind or asking a question like did she like dark chocolate or milk or what was her favorite shade of jeans, super dark, just dark, faded, washed?

Oh yeah? she texted back. *What exactly were you thinking about?* No, it wasn't exactly flirty, but it had all the elements of leading them in that direction, and she was very aware of that.

A lady never gossips, came the reply, followed by a wink emoji and an emoji with a zipper mouth.

Aubrey grinned and typed back, *I see no ladies here…*

"Em," she called up the stairs, just as Monica's reply of *GASP!* came through and she laughed. "Ready?"

As she headed back into the kitchen, a herd of elephants came tromping down the stairs, which was surprising since Emma was the only one who ended up next to her. She shook her head as her daughter threw her a salute.

"Ready. Let's go buy all the stuff."

"How about we go buy *some of* the stuff?"

Emma groaned and rolled her eyes. "Ugh. *Fine.*" And the word fine had about sixteen syllables.

Aubrey had taken the day off from work. It was something she did every August, took a day off so she and Emma could go school shopping, have lunch together, get pedicures. Just a fun mommy-daughter day. She hoped they'd continue to do this each summer, even once Emma became a teenager who would probably hate her. While she liked to think she and Emma had a different relationship, she wasn't naive. The stories she'd heard about teenage girls battling their moms came from somewhere. Even her own mother had stories about Aubrey when she was in high school. "Teenage girls are not for the faint of heart," she'd said.

But the day went well. They'd hit the mall first, found some good sales, grabbed Emma a couple outfits as well as new jeans and two new pairs of shoes. Aubrey tried not to cry when she realized that Emma had gone up a size in everything. They'd be shopping for bras soon, and she hoped she didn't burst into tears right there in the lingerie section when that time came.

"Happy Crab?" she asked as they dumped their bags in the trunk of the car.

"Yes!" Emma said, excited for sushi at their favorite restaurant. They buckled themselves into their seats, and when Aubrey glanced at Emma, she was looking at her intently. "Thanks, Mom," she said quietly and reached out for a hug.

These were the best moments—when her child surprised her with a sign of affection. An unexpected *thank you* or *I love you* or a hug like this one. Aubrey's eyes filled, but she squeezed them shut even as she squeezed her daughter tightly, willing the tears back. "You're welcome," she said, then pressed a kiss to Emma's forehead and sat back. "Ready? Those spicy tuna rolls are not gonna eat themselves."

Emma pointed at the windshield. "Onward," she ordered.

"Yes, ma'am."

The Happy Crab had been their place for three years now, ever since she'd had sushi delivered after a particularly rough day of work and Emma had eaten almost Aubrey's entire Philadelphia roll on her own. A seven-year-old who enjoyed sushi was nearly unheard of among her friends and family—and most of her friends and family weren't fans—so it became their thing, whether they were celebrating or mourning. Emma got an A-plus on her math test? The Happy Crab. Aubrey got a promotion? The Happy Crab. Emma's parakeet died? The Happy Crab.

And it was a busy place for lunch, the clientele a mix of folks having business lunches, girls' day lunches, and couples grabbing a quick moment from their jobs to spend an hour together. The owner was a lovely Japanese American man who recognized them, greeted them with a warm welcome, and seated them at a corner table for two.

They started with an appetizer of edamame and an order of fries. Of course. Always fries, they were Emma's go-to, no matter where they ate. At the Happy Crab, she'd eat both raw and cooked rolls, so they ordered the Philadelphia roll with raw salmon, the spicy tuna roll with raw tuna, and then the California roll, the Louisiana roll, and the cinema roll, all with cooked seafood inside. The dishes came out, the presentation pristine as always, with pieces arranged artistically on each plate, and they ooed and aahed as they always did before they dug in. It always looked like so much food, but Aubrey knew from experience that the chances of them eating pretty much every last bite were high.

"So, how are you feeling about fifth grade?" Aubrey asked, then used her chopsticks to dip some California roll into her soy sauce.

Emma chewed and sort of bobbed her head as she seemed to look for words. "I'm feeling pretty good about it, actually." And she sounded so incredibly grown up that Aubrey had to stifle a surprised laugh. "I got a good feeling."

"Well, I'm glad to hear that."

"I'm glad Sierra will be in my class." Emma's BFF since kindergarten. Aubrey kept waiting for the two of them to find different interests or new friends and split, as so often happened at this age. But so far, they'd stayed tight.

"Me too." She was about to float the idea of maybe making some other friends, just because you couldn't have too many friends, right?

And then somebody was standing next to their table and a

familiar voice said, "I thought that was you two," and it crawled right into Aubrey's ear and shot through her body until it sat right between her legs, gently throbbing.

"Aunt Monica," Emma said excitedly, sliding out of her chair and wrapping her arms around Monica's business-suit-clad waist. "What are you doing here?"

"I'm just finishing up lunch with some clients," she said, jerking a thumb over her shoulder at a table of men in jackets and ties, as her eyes snagged Aubrey's and held. "Hi."

"Hi," Aubrey said, and her voice was soft, as was everything about her body in that moment.

"It's good to see you," Monica said. "You having a girls' day?"

Emma nodded with enthusiasm as she returned to her chair and picked up her chopsticks. "We got some school stuff, new clothes, we're having sushi, and then we're getting pedicures."

"That sounds like a fantastic day."

"How's your day?" Emma asked.

"Well, as soon as I finish up with my clients, my day is over, so that's kinda nice." Monica reached out and snagged a piece of the California roll and popped it into her mouth, then grinned.

"Hey, you should come get a pedicure with us," Emma said, her voice tinted with excitement at the idea as she looked from Monica to Aubrey and back again. "Right, Mom?"

And instead of flinching or feeling herself fill with dread, she heard herself say, "Absolutely. You're welcome to join us. The more girls the better on girls' day."

Monica looked from Emma to Aubrey. "I mean, I could use a pedicure. If you're sure I'm not stepping in on your time together."

Their gazes held, and Aubrey could've sworn there was a sizzle that ran between them like an electric current. They hadn't seen each other since the wedding reception, and Aubrey's brain chose this exact moment to toss her an image of Monica, backed against a tree, Aubrey's tongue in her mouth. She had a fleeting moment where she wondered if she shouldn't have said anything, if Monica coming with them was a bad idea, but then she thought, Why? Emma adored her. It would be good for both of them. A pause, then, *It'll be good for all three of us.* And the next thing she knew, she was giving Monica directions to the nail salon where they were going, and Monica told them she'd meet them as soon as she could, to save her a chair.

Half an hour later, they were checking into their appointment. Aubrey told the clerk there was one more coming, and he said he'd reserve the chair on the other side of Emma.

As they sat and rolled up their pants legs, Emma glanced at her, a worried expression on her young face. "Mom?"

"Hmm?"

"Is it okay that I invited Aunt Monica? It kinda slipped out, and I didn't think about how you might feel like I ruined our girls' day."

Her heart. Oh, how her heart swelled. She reached out a hand and grasped Emma's smaller one in her own. "Sweetie, you didn't ruin anything. Honestly? I think it was really nice that you invited her."

"Okay. Good." They let go of each other. "She's just alone a lot, and I sometimes feel bad for her."

"You do?"

"Yeah. I mean, you're alone, too, but you have me. She's *all* alone."

She didn't know how she had managed to raise such an empathetic kid, but she felt her pride grow in her chest. "You're really sweet, you know that?"

Emma shrugged, and before they could say any more, Monica was walking toward them, a pair of flip-flops on her feet in place of her earlier heels. They were adorably wrong for the business suit, and Aubrey found herself grinning over that. Emma indicated the seat next to her. Monica smiled at Aubrey, and she blinked slowly before she sat, and there was something about that...something sensual.

"What color are you going with?" Monica asked Emma.

"Cotton Candy," Emma said happily, holding up the bottle of polish she'd chosen on the way in.

"And you?" Those blue eyes met hers over Emma's seat.

Aubrey held up her own bottle. "Plumthing to Talk About," she said with a grin.

Monica held up an identical bottle. "Great minds, I guess."

"Seems so." And that delicious eye contact held for several seconds. Delicious. It was the only way to describe it, as far as Aubrey was concerned. Finally breaking it, she glanced at her daughter, wondering if she was at all aware of any kind of tension between them, sexual or otherwise, but she was busy splashing her feet in her tub, trying to squish the bubbles with her toes. And as Aubrey watched her, she had a flash of something she couldn't quite put a finger on. Monica and her, sitting here in this nail salon—side by side, though, no Emma between them. They were laughing and talking while their toes were done, and they both looked indescribably happy.

Just like that, the vision left her.

"You okay?" Monica asked, and Emma looked her way as well. "You seemed to go somewhere else there for a second."

She gave her head a subtle shake and smiled. "All good. Just daydreaming for a second."

For the next hour, the most prominent thought in Aubrey's mind was how she could possibly be turned on by somebody's feet. How? Who looked at feet? And more than that, who looked at feet and thought they were sexy? How had this happened? What was wrong with her? Monica Wallace had always been a person Aubrey avoided, rolled her eyes about, and carried an intense dislike of. How had it turned around so quickly after literal years of the first three things?

But it had. Clearly. She understood that now—well, that it had happened, but not the why or the how of it. Because here she was, sitting in her comfy chair, watching the nail tech paint plum polish on Monica's toes, and having a sexual fantasy about her while three feet away from her ten-year-old daughter. Oh yeah, she was a disaster, all right.

"Right, Mom?"

Emma's voice jerked her back to the present, and when she tore her gaze from Monica's feet, God help her, they were both looking at her. "I'm sorry, what?"

"Grandma and Grandpa and Dad and Kimmy are taking me to a baseball game this weekend."

"Oh. Yes. That's right. They are." She glanced at Monica, whose expression seemed almost knowing, and that made Aubrey give herself a mental shake. "I'm sure they've missed you while they were away."

"I mean, duh," Emma said. "Of course they did."

"You going for the weekend?" Monica asked. "Or longer?"

"The weekend," Emma said, watching as her nail tech stroked a topcoat over her bright pink toes. "I think they get home tomorrow. Then Dad's gonna get me on Friday and I'm staying until Sunday. I don't usually stay longer than that at Dad's."

"Oh." Monica looked a bit taken aback by Emma's words, which Aubrey found interesting, and their eyes met over the top of Emma's head. They had a quick, silent conversation where Monica raised her eyes, clearly asking *Really?* and Aubrey shrugged with a frown that said *Life with Cody as a father.*

When they'd finished and Monica had paid for all three pedicures, despite Aubrey's arguing, they headed out into the heat of the August afternoon. Emma immediately spotted the ice cream truck parked at the end of the lawn and turned to her with pleading puppy dog eyes.

Aubrey laughed. "Aren't you still full from lunch? You ate your weight in sushi."

"Mom. There's always room for ice cream." Emma looked to Monica for confirmation.

"I mean, the kid's not wrong." Monica shrugged.

Shaking her head, Aubrey laughed again and fished a five dollar bill out of her purse. Then Emma ran off ahead of them to get herself some ice cream.

"So, Cody doesn't ever take her for longer than a weekend?" Monica asked quietly, her eyes on Emma as she jogged away. She was clearly still stuck on that fact, which was apparently news to her.

Aubrey shook her head as she also watched Emma at the ice cream truck. "No. He said many years ago that he needed to do small bites until he got a handle on things, and"—she shrugged again—"that just never changed."

Monica frowned, and Aubrey could almost hear the gears in her head grinding. "I mean, it doesn't matter if you need to *get a handle on things*." She made air quotes, but kept her voice low, presumably so Emma didn't hear. "You're her dad. Spend some fucking time with her." The passion and vehemence in her tone surprised Aubrey. When their gazes met, Monica looked slightly sheepish and said, "Sorry. I had an absent dad, so I'm a little sensitive about the subject."

"I'm sorry to hear that," Aubrey said.

"It must be hard for you to watch."

"It is. She's a great kid, and I just don't understand why he wouldn't want to spend as much time as possible with her. You know? And she's gotten pretty used to it, but once in a while I'll see the disappointment on her face and it just kills me." She rubbed at her heart with her fingertips.

"I had no idea," Monica said. "Truly. I've gone to his place many times over the years—when he's not off gallivanting around the globe—and I've seen Emma there. I guess I just never realized he didn't take her for weeks at a time. I mean, not even in the summer? When she's off from school?"

Aubrey shook her head. "I mean, she goes back to school in two weeks, so summer's pretty much over for her. He's had her for a few weekends. His parents take her for a weekend here and there as well."

"Does she end up at his parents' when she spends the weekend with him?"

Aubrey met Monica's gaze. "Wow, you're good. Yeah, she has a few times."

"I've just been there is all. I've been her."

Emma came trotting back to them, carrying a cone of soft serve ice cream, vanilla and chocolate swirl.

"Good?" Aubrey asked.

"Meh," Emma said, which made her laugh. "It's fine. There wasn't much to choose from."

"I know a great ice cream shop," Monica said. "They have a ton of flavors, and they make it right there every day." She glanced at Aubrey as she said, "We should all go sometime."

"Cool," Emma said, as Aubrey did her best to not look surprised at the suggestion.

"Okay, well." Monica held her hands out. "Thanks for letting me crash your girls' day and get my toes done." She wiggled them to punctuate.

"Good thing you had flip-flops in your car," Emma pointed out.

"Right?" Monica turned to Aubrey. "I'll text you later. See if maybe you want some company this weekend, since you'll probably just be crying without Emma home."

Emma busted out laughing and pointed her cone at Aubrey. "She probs just sits in a corner and rocks until I come back again."

"You two are hilarious," Aubrey said, but when her eyes met Monica's, there was that electric sizzle again. She didn't have to say any words to know she'd totally given Monica the go-ahead to text her later.

Monica gave Emma a one-armed hug to avoid getting ice cream on her suit. "Catch ya later," she said, then gave Aubrey a cute little wave and headed off to her car, the flip-flops with her suit still looking nothing less than adorkable.

Emma's words pulled her attention back. "This was a great day, Mom."

Aubrey smiled down at her daughter, then draped an arm over her shoulders. "It really was." She dropped a kiss on her head. "Let's go home."

❖

Aubrey always felt like she got a lot done when Emma was away. Laundry, clean sheets on the beds, dust and vacuum, she was a cleaning whirlwind when she had access to every room and no ten-year-old whining about how she was touching her stuff or there was nothing to eat in the house or that she didn't want to strip her bed right now.

At the same time, she missed Emma terribly and counted the minutes until she was home again. Strange how both those feelings could exist within her simultaneously.

Cody's mother had picked Emma up yesterday afternoon, and while Aubrey was irritated that he'd sent somebody else to do his job—which wasn't unusual, to be honest—she was also relieved not to have to deal with him directly because the third degree about what he'd walked up on in the woods on the day of his wedding still hadn't been addressed. She knew it wasn't something he'd just forget about, just let slide by, but she appreciated the extra time because she had no idea how she'd explain it to him.

She, however, was at a point where she needed to talk some things through. She sent a text to Trina.

Got a minute?

Before she could count to ten, the phone rang in her hand. "I always have at least sixty seconds for you," Trina said. "Everything okay?"

Aubrey dropped into a chair because, yeah, she needed to sit down for this. "I need to talk to you about something, and I need you to promise not to freak out on me."

"In my experience, when somebody says they need you not to freak out, they're about to tell you something that is definitely going to make you freak out. That being said, I'll do my best to remain calm." As if punctuating her words, Aubrey could hear her blow out a long breath, like she was practicing a yoga position.

"Okay, so, something happened the night of Cody's wedding."

"What? Cody's wedding was nearly two weeks ago," Trina said, the pitch of her voice going up. "You're just telling me now?"

"And what did we say about freaking out?"

"Okay. Okay. Right." Another long breath. "I'm good. Go."

"I kissed Monica."

Silence.

Aubrey waited. In fact, she waited so long that she wondered if the call had been dropped. "Tree? You still there? Did you hear me?"

"Sorry! I had to mute the phone so I could *freak the fuck out*, because I might be mistaken, but I'm pretty sure I heard my best friend tell me she locked lips with her archnemesis *almost two weeks ago* and didn't tell me. Is that what I heard?"

"Yeah. Pretty much."

There was a beat, seemingly for Trina to get her bearings. "Okay. All right. We're going to set aside the amount of time that's passed, but don't think we're not revisiting that for sure. But oh my God. Seriously, how did this happen? Because oh my God."

It was Aubrey's turn to blow out a long, slow, steadying breath, and in doing so, she realized that her entire body had been waiting to tell the story to somebody. "I'm honestly not even sure, Tree. It was the weirdest thing."

"Kinda seems like you've been leading up to it, right? With the ride from the airport in North Carolina. And the dancing at Cody's wedding. And the marshmallows."

"I know, right? I guess when I look back, you're right. But why her? Of all the people in the world, men and women, this is the one I choose to make out with?"

"Oh, whoa, hang on there, Charlie. You said you kissed her. Now you're saying you made out with her?"

Aubrey cleared her throat. "Same thing."

"Oh, I beg to differ. So *not* the same thing. Which was it? Were tongues involved?"

Yeah, she'd opened this can of worms. Now she had to deal with all the wriggling. With a sigh, she said, "They were. Yes."

"Oh my God, you totally made out with her. Who made the first move?"

This is where things got dicey, and Aubrey knew it. "I did."

"*What?*" Trina practically shouted the word through the phone. And was she laughing now?

The story came spilling out. She couldn't stop it even if she'd wanted to. "She went for a walk in the woods, and I have no idea why, but I decided to follow her. I'd had a few drinks. I wasn't drunk, but I was feeling…less cautious than normal? So, I followed her, and I found her leaning with her back against a tree trunk, and my God, Trina, she looked so beautiful. My feet never stopped. I didn't falter once, I just walked right up into her space, took her face in my hands, and kissed her face off."

"God, that is so romantic," Trina said, her voice a little dreamy. "Wow."

"Yeah." She remembered the softness of Monica's lips, the sweet taste of the chocolate and marshmallow on her tongue. Her body started that subtle throbbing that seemed to be a thing now.

"And then what happened?"

"And then Cody and Kimmy caught us."

"*No!*" Trina said, drawing the word out with her disbelief.

Aubrey couldn't help but laugh softly at the absurdity of it all. "Yeah. And then he went off on his honeymoon, so there's been no fallout."

"Yet."

"Exactly."

"And have you talked to her since?"

"She texts me every so often. Emma and I were having girls' day on Wednesday and ended up running into her at lunch. Emma invited her to get pedicures with us."

Trina winced. "Was that awkward for you?"

"Not even a little bit. And that's why I'm calling you. What is happening right now? I'm so confused."

"It's definitely unexpected, and also not."

"What do you mean?"

Trina sighed softly. "I mean, I told you some of us thought she had a thing for you back in college. Looks like we were right, except maybe you had a thing for her, too."

"I didn't, though," Aubrey said, and she was sure of it. "I mean, I knew I was bi, but I loved Cody with my whole heart."

She could almost see Trina shrug as she said, "Maybe it's about timing, then. You know? Maybe now, you're ready for her."

"Huh."

The conversation ended not long after that, but Trina's words remained like an echo in Aubrey's brain.

Maybe now, you're ready for her.

She gazed out the front window of her house, watched a man walk his golden retriever, noticed the letter carrier on the other side of the street, people just going about their Saturday like they didn't have a care in the world. Meanwhile, she sat there, contemplating every single thing she'd thought she'd known about herself since college, and coming up with zero answers to ease her racing mind.

Maybe now, you're ready for her.

As if somehow privy to those words bouncing around in her skull, her phone pinged a text notification and there was Monica. Because, of course.

Hey, I know you're Emma-less tonight. You busy?

She was typing her answer, trying to figure out what to say, when the phone rang in her hand.

"I thought I'd just call," Monica said. "Hi." And how was it that her voice was like honey? Warm and thick and soothing.

"Hi," she said back, her own voice going soft.

"Have you cleaned your entire house yet?"

Aubrey barked a laugh. "Just about. How did you know?"

"My mother used to tell me that on those rare occasions I did spend time with my dad, she missed me so much that she had to keep herself busy until I got back. The house was always sparkling clean and smelled like Pine-Sol every time I got home."

Aubrey glanced around. "It's pretty shiny here, not gonna lie." They each laughed softly, and Aubrey could sense an element of... what was it? Awkward? Nerves? Hesitation? Something. And then Monica spoke.

"So," she said quietly. "Are you busy tonight?"

Aubrey didn't even hesitate. Her voice just as soft as Monica's, she said, "I am decidedly *not* busy tonight. No."

"Could I take you to dinner?"

"Would this be a date?" Oh God, she'd said it. Out loud. With words. Actual words. Swallowing hard did nothing to get rid of the lump that was suddenly in her throat.

"Well," Monica said. A second or two went by, as if she was debating her words but then thought, fuck it, just gonna say them. "You've already had your tongue in my mouth, so I think the least I can do is take you to dinner."

A laugh shot out of her like a small explosion. "That's true," she said, because it absolutely was. "A little bit backward, huh?"

"Only a little." There was a moment of silence. Aubrey could hear Monica's breathing, even as her own breaths sounded into the phone. "What do you think?" Monica finally prompted. "Will you have dinner with me?"

"I would love to have dinner with you."

Also one hundred percent true.

❖

Help! Fashion 911!

That was the text she'd sent to Trina not three seconds after hanging up with Monica. Because what the hell was she supposed to wear? And Trina, being a true best friend, dropped everything she was doing and drove her ass to Aubrey's house in less than an hour.

Now, they sat in Aubrey's bedroom, her closet doors gaping open as Trina perused what was available.

"What kind of date is this gonna be?" she asked Aubrey.

"What do you mean?"

Trina took a breath and then sat next to her, looking like she was trying to find the best way to say what she was about to. "I mean…what do you want this date to be? Is it just dinner with a friend? Is it you trying to figure out intentions and such? Is it going to lead to something more?" Trina studied her face as she waited for an answer.

"I honestly don't know," she said. "That's the truth."

"You want to know what I think?"

"Yes. *Please* tell me." She needed somebody else's thoughts, opinions, observations on the whole thing because she felt like she was floundering.

"I think you should talk to her tonight."

Aubrey tilted her head. "Talk to her? That's your plan?"

"Talk to her about this," Trina clarified. "Ask her what she's thinking, so you can see if you're on the same page. Or if you even want to be on the same page. You know?"

Okay, well, Trina's simple advice actually did make sense. How many books had she read or rom-coms had she seen where the couple was kept apart because of a lack of communication? So many. "Yeah. Okay. I can do that."

"Also..." Trina got that mischievous glint in her eye. "Make sure you shave. Like, everything."

Aubrey gave her a playful shove. "Find me something to wear, damn it."

Once Trina had helped her pick out what to wear, Aubrey had a couple hours to kill, and in any other circumstances, she'd use that time to clean. Since she'd already done that, she decided to take advantage of her extra time and sit outside with a book. She poured herself a glass of iced tea, grabbed both the romance novel and the nonfiction book on customer service, and took them out back, not sure which one she was in the mood for.

Turned out, she wasn't in the mood for either because as soon as she sat down in her lounge chair, her consciousness was filled with visions of a gorgeous blonde with big blue eyes, a soft, sexy smile, and a voice that did things to Aubrey's body. Sensual things.

She shook her head and inhaled deeply. A bright red cardinal landed on the bird feeder she and Emma had hung from the maple tree, then flew away, probably in a huff because it was empty. She pushed to her feet and went to the small shed in the back corner of the yard where she kept the seed, as well as her yard tools and lawn mower. She found the plastic container of birdseed and filled the feeder. The cardinal must've been watching because as soon as she hung the feeder back up and stepped away, he was back.

"You're welcome," she said. He ignored her and kept eating.

It was so weirdly different to have somebody on her mind this much, and she was having trouble understanding it. She'd dated a bit here and there—though, honestly, raising a child pretty much by herself knocked dating pretty far down on her priority list. She'd seen a woman when Emma was not quite three, and then there'd been a guy about two years ago. Neither lasted, and she hadn't exactly been searching. And all of a sudden, bam! There was Monica—archnemesis, person she'd known for over a decade, the one who shouldered as much blame for her wedding day disaster as her actual fiancé—suddenly a player. Suddenly a suitor. A possibility. How? *How?* How had that happened? She didn't understand any of this, and she realized Trina was right. The only thing that was going to help was if she talked to Monica, openly and honestly.

"What a novel concept," she said out loud to the empty yard, then laughed through her nose as she dropped back into a chair, sipped her iced tea, and picked up the nonfiction book.

Romance was the last thing she needed to be reading about right now.

❖

Trina had chosen well.

Aubrey had no idea where Monica was taking her for dinner, whether she should dress up, go casual, or something in between. Trina had decided on something in between, choosing a simple sundress in a muted yellow the color of spicy brown mustard with big, cream polka dots. Not a lot of women could pull off that color, but because Aubrey had a healthy tan from summer, it worked perfectly with her skin tone. It had been a toss-up between an updo or leaving her dark wavy hair down, and they'd opted for door number two. Down and loose. The dress was a faux wrap and showed an amount of cleavage that was far from scandalous, but also far from prudish. She added a simple gold necklace with a heart that Emma had given her for Christmas last year, a pair of wedged espadrilles, and a spritz of perfume, and she was ready.

If Monica's reaction was any indication, Trina deserved a hefty tip. "Wow." It was the only word she'd said when Aubrey opened the front door, but her eyes roamed over her, pausing at various places—most notably on that cleavage—then working her way back up to Aubrey's face. "Hi. You look incredible."

She felt her cheeks warm at the compliment. "Thank you. And might I add, right back atcha." Not to be outdone, Monica looked fabulous in wide-leg black pants and a snug-fitting sleeveless ivory top that hugged every curve of her torso like a lover. The neckline was high, so no cleavage, but her breasts were clearly outlined, and Aubrey had trouble not ogling them. *Don't be a creep, don't be a creep, don't be a creep...*

"Shall we?" Monica held her elbow out, and Aubrey took it.

Once they were in Monica's SUV and buckled up, and Monica had started the drive, Aubrey asked where they were going.

"I thought we'd eat by the lake tonight. It's so nice out. Is that okay?"

"That sounds great." And it did. The humidity had broken a few days ago. It was still very warm out, but not stifling. Sitting by the water would be lovely.

The ride was quiet, oddly so, and it made Aubrey wonder if Monica was nervous. Reservations had been made, and it wasn't until they were seated at their very romantic table for two and each had a glass of wine that she decided to just jump into the deep end. She leaned her elbows on the table, wineglass in hand, and went for it.

"So, what's happening here, exactly? Do you know?" She took a sip of her wine and watched as something that looked a lot like relief washed over Monica's pretty face.

"It's so weird, right?" Monica said with a soft laugh.

"It really, really is."

"But...in a good way? 'Cause it feels good to me." And then Monica mimicked her position and they were both sitting elbows on the table, wineglasses in hand, faces only a few inches apart. "And let's remember that *you* are the one who kissed *me* in the woods. So if either of us should have to answer what's happening here, it should be you." Her sexy smile took any sting or accusation out of her words. Plus, she wasn't wrong.

Aubrey nodded. "I did. That's true." She sipped her wine. "And you're the one who set up our first date."

"Also true." Monica sat back and waved her glass as she asked, "So? What do we do?"

"What do you mean?"

"I mean, do we analyze and critique and beat things to death? Or do we lean in to being on a date, enjoy dinner and each other's company, and, for lack of something less cliché, see what happens?"

Aubrey indicated her with her wineglass. "That's not a bad plan, gotta say."

"Perfect. Let's do that, then."

The waitress showed up then to take their orders, and that gave Aubrey a little time to get her bearings. Things had shifted, she felt it. It was like they'd each taken a big, deep, cleansing breath and let it out slowly. Not a fresh start exactly, but something akin to one. Interesting.

"So, how many weddings are left this year?" Monica asked. "Is it just Brad and Kara and then we're done?"

"Yes, thank God," Aubrey said with an eye roll. "In October. Seriously, how did everybody decide to get married in the same year?"

"It's a little ridiculous."

"I'm so glad I'm not in this one. My bank account can't take any more."

"Being a bridesmaid—or a groomswoman—is *expensive*."

"I mean, unless the bride and groom get married at a campground and you wear shorts and a top." Aubrey shot Monica a half grin to show she was teasing.

"Valid." Monica held up her glass. "To one last wedding."

"I will definitely drink to that." They clinked glasses and sipped, and the waiter brought their dinners.

"So, maybe a touchy subject, coming from me," Monica asked once they'd both taken bites of their food and made the proper humming sounds of approval, "but do *you* want to get married? I know weddings aren't your favorite things."

Aubrey chewed a bite of her scallop. "Honestly? I do. But I wouldn't do it in June this time. Not just because of bad memories, and not because June is the most popular wedding month. But because I have always thought a Christmas wedding would be gorgeous."

"Really?"

"Yup. Not on Christmas. That'd be a little obnoxious. But maybe in early or mid-December, so all the decor could be Christmassy. Twinkle lights and mistletoe and garland and red and green and silver and white. A crackling fire." She was gazing off into the middle distance, visualizing the kind of wedding that had sat in the back of her mind for a few years now. Then she blinked rapidly, clearing her vision, and met Monica's gaze. She was smiling at her. "What?"

Monica shook her head and took a bite of her risotto. "Nothing. Just watching you talk about something important to you. You got passionate."

"Did I?"

A nod. "It was fun to watch." There was a beat where their gazes held before Monica spoke again. "A Christmas wedding. That would be pretty."

"Right?" The waiter stopped by to check on their food and ask if they wanted more wine. Monica declined, as she was driving, but encouraged Aubrey to have another glass. Once he'd left to get her a refill, she asked, "What about you? You want a wedding?"

"I do," Monica said without hesitation. "I'm a traditional kind of girl. I want to buy a gorgeous wedding dress. I want my dad to walk me down the aisle to the traditional wedding march. I want a tiered cake and a wedding party and a first dance with my wife." Her voice had gone soft, a little dreamy, and watching her talk about it did sexy things to Aubrey.

She cleared her throat. "You're passionate about it, too."

"I guess I am."

"That's a good list for a wedding. I like tradition, too. And"— Aubrey raised her glass for yet another toast—"here's to nobody even *thinking* about talking your bride-to-be out of marrying you."

Another laugh shot out of Monica, and Aubrey decided she liked making her laugh. "Amen to that." They touched glasses, sipped, and then Monica's expression grew serious. "You know that wasn't selfish, right?"

Aubrey lifted a shoulder, feeling like they were straying into dangerous territory. The night had been going so well, and heading into this subject could very well ruin things completely. Maybe if she acted nonchalant about it, they'd veer in another direction. "Hey, you were just trying to save your best friend from doing something stupid. I get it. You were protecting him."

"No." Monica reached across the table and closed her hand over Aubrey's forearm. Tightly. Her grip almost hurt, and she held it until Aubrey met her gaze. "I wasn't protecting him. I was protecting *you.*"

Aubrey blinked in surprise, Monica's words seemingly knocking all of her own out of her head. All she could do was look at Monica and wait for her to say more.

"I knew he'd be a disaster of a husband. He wasn't ready. I'd talked to him a dozen times about figuring out if he was sure. And I didn't even know about Emma at the time. If I had, I think I might've pushed him even harder." She let go of Aubrey's arm and took hers back, but her eye contact was so intense, Aubrey wouldn't have been able to look away, even if she'd wanted to. "I wasn't trying to hurt you. I was trying to *save you* from hurt."

Wait, what?

Aubrey felt like her world was turning over, like everything she'd known was wrong. Up was down. Right was left. Black was white. She sat there quietly, staring at Monica as she took in the words, let them absorb.

Monica sat back in her chair and let go of a quiet laugh. "I can see by the stricken look on your face that was not what you expected to hear." She picked up her water, took a sip, and seemed to wait for Aubrey to collect herself.

Which was easier said than done. "I..." She shook her head, swallowed, then reached for her own glass, thanking sweet baby Jesus she'd ordered a second glass of wine, and took a healthy slug of it. "I"—she tried again—"I didn't know."

Monica nodded slowly. "Yeah, I knew if I managed to get Cody to be honest with himself, you'd likely hate me. I accepted that, but wow, did it suck."

Aubrey tipped her head, waiting for her to go on.

"I liked you a lot. I just…I couldn't stand the thought of him tying you down and then making your life miserable. Which is exactly what would have happened. I worried you'd get pregnant, which would've made him hang out a bit longer, but eventually, he'd have felt trapped, and he would've found a way to escape, leaving you a heartbroken single mother."

"Which I ended up being anyway," Aubrey said, the irony not lost on her. Their eyes met and held for a beat before they both snorted in laughter. Soon, they were both cracking up, trying to be quiet so as not to disturb the other diners, but it was hard. Aubrey wiped tears from her eyes as they finally calmed down.

"So, all my emotional turmoil and heart-wrenching decisions were for nothing," Monica said, still chuckling. "Things are the same as they would've been if I'd just shut the hell up."

"No." Aubrey studied her face. The smooth, creamy complexion, the golden hair that hung in light waves along her shoulders and collarbone, those expressive blue eyes. For the first time, she realized that everything she might want to know was reflected in Monica's eyes. And right now, she saw slight worry, a bit of hesitation, and desire. "We wouldn't be sitting here now. On a date." She saw Monica's throat move as she swallowed. "And I sure as hell wouldn't have thrown myself at you in the woods. That is *so* not me."

"No?" Monica asked. "'Cause you seemed pretty sure of yourself."

Was it hot in here? Aubrey touched a hand to her face and looked around, wondering if anybody else was suddenly stiflingly warm.

"It's just you," Monica said, a knowing tone to her voice. "Don't worry. I know how we can cool you off."

❖

A Second Scoop Artisan Ice Cream and Dessert Experience was a stand-alone building just outside Jefferson Square. Aubrey had passed it many times but had never stopped in, and now she was kicking herself for that very egregious oversight.

"Oh my God," she said for probably the fifteenth time as she scooped a spoon of a very subtle honey ice cream called Baby Bear into her mouth. "I could live on this. Eat it every day. Bathe in it. I want to bathe in it."

"That sounds cold," Monica said with a grin. She'd ordered herself Berry Blast ice cream in a waffle cone, and watching her lick it was swirling Aubrey's insides around in a very sexy way.

"That's a valid point. Okay, maybe not bathe in it. But I want to eat it for every meal."

"What about the other flavors? They'll be sad if you don't even try them."

Aubrey sighed. "Another valid point. You are certainly full of them tonight." The little shop was bustling, but they'd managed to snag a table for two in the corner, the air-conditioning keeping them inside. A redheaded woman and a college-age boy were behind the counter taking care of customers. Aubrey could see a tall, attractive brunette in the back. She pointed toward her with her spoon. "Do you think she's the *artisan*?" She made the air quotes.

"I don't think. I know. That's Adley Purcell, one of the owners and a friend of mine. She creates all the ice cream flavors and makes them right back there by hand. The other owner is her wife, Sabrina, who's probably back there in her office."

"It's women-owned as well as frigging delicious? Sold. I will never go anywhere else for ice cream ever again."

"My friends will appreciate that."

Aubrey paused a moment mentally and took stock of everything around her, everything they'd done, and how she was feeling. It was still weird to be on an actual date with Monica, but things were shifting. That was the right word. "Do you feel the shift?" she asked, then went to elaborate because Monica was not in her head, but Monica spoke before she could.

"Around us, you mean?" She nodded and smiled and licked some more of her ice cream. Aubrey couldn't pull her eyes away, and she was pretty sure Monica knew it. "I do. It's still a little strange, but that's fading by the minute."

"Exactly." Their eye contact held for a beat or two before she added, "I like it."

"Same."

A few minutes later, they were done with their ice cream. Monica tossed a wave toward the back where the tall brunette waved back, then held the door for Aubrey.

Things were different now. That thought ping-ponged through Aubrey's head as she sat in Monica's car and she started the engine. Ever since Monica had explained that she hadn't been trying to hurt Aubrey, she'd been trying to protect her, it felt like her whole world had altered. Just a little, but noticeably. Like a cloud had drifted a bit farther off the sun, letting in more light and more warmth.

She liked it.

"Where to now?" Monica asked quietly. It had gone almost dark, and a glance at the dashboard told Aubrey it was nearing nine. Monica's expression was open, waiting. Aubrey didn't hesitate.

"My place."

With one nod, Monica put the car in gear and headed them home.

❖

Aubrey hadn't been drunk at the restaurant. Maybe a little tipsy, but the hour at the ice cream shop had sobered her up. She unlocked her front door and let Monica in behind her. "Wine? Something else?"

"I'll have a little wine. Thanks."

Her house was small, but the first floor was mostly open concept, and she watched as Monica wandered slowly around, looking at books and knickknacks and framed photos.

"This is a great little house," she said, setting a photo of Emma back down on an end table.

"Thanks. It's pretty small, but we like it." She returned to the living room with two glasses of merlot, and they settled on the couch. Aubrey sat with one leg tucked under her, facing Monica, her arm across the back. God, Monica was pretty. She hadn't ever really let herself look at her, had never really just…stared. Or felt like she could. Her skin was porcelain smooth, and Aubrey wondered if it was as soft as she suspected. The blue of her eyes this close up was like the deep shade of the summer sky, her hair golden like the sun. She realized then that the word *pretty* didn't do her justice. She was beyond pretty. She was stunning. Aubrey held up her glass. "To our first date."

"I hope there's another," Monica said with a grin, and they touched glasses.

"Me too."

Their gazes held as they sipped, and it suddenly felt like the room was charged, like the air held static electricity, making everything crackle. Monica seemed to notice it as well, shifting slightly in her seat, and her throat moved as she swallowed. Just as Aubrey felt the throbbing between her legs intensify, Monica cleared her throat.

"So, what do you normally do at night when Emma's not here?"

It was an odd question, and Monica picked at a piece of lint on the couch as she waited for an answer.

"I take a bubble bath," Aubrey answered with a laugh. "That's how exciting I am. I soak myself."

"Oh, bubble baths are awesome." Monica sat up straighter. "I love them. A little candlelight. A little wine. Some soft music…" Her voice drifted off as they stared at each other.

"Wanna take a bubble bath with me?" Aubrey asked softly and without one iota of hesitation.

"I really, really do."

Aubrey stood, wineglass in one hand, and held out the other to Monica, whose smile was dazzling as she took it. "Come with me."

Aubrey's house was small, but the en suite bathroom was her favorite place. Her escape. Her sanctuary. Nobody used it but her. Nobody had ever stepped into the small shower stall but her.

Nobody had ever been in the bathtub but her. Emma had her own smaller bathroom down the hall.

Oh God, what was she doing?

"This is beautiful," Monica said, her voice almost a whisper. Aubrey tried to see it through the eyes of somebody new, seeing it for the first time. The textured beige ceramic tile, the sage-green walls, the big garden tub in the corner, the hanging plant that looked so real, she often had to touch the leaves to remind herself it wasn't. "This tub is huge."

"It was a prerequisite when I was house hunting. It was the only prerequisite, really. I take a bath almost every night before I go to bed. One of my guilty pleasures."

"Me too," Monica said with a smile. "But I just have a regular tub. It's extra deep, but not nearly as roomy as this one."

Aubrey opened a cabinet to reveal an array of bubble bath bottles. "Okay, what do you prefer? Soft scents? Floral? Food-like?" She lit several candles while her guest made a decision.

Monica chose a bottle of Black Cherry and Cashmere. "I have no idea what cashmere smells like, but I like black cherries."

"A fine choice, madame." Aubrey turned on the water, adjusted the temperature, then poured in a generous amount of the bubble bath. Then she used her long lighter and lit the candles around the tub, creating the most delicious ambiance. With that done, she set the lighter down, stood, and put her hands on her hips. When she turned to Monica, her breath hitched at the clear desire in those blue eyes.

"Hi," Monica said softly and closed the short distance between them. She took Aubrey's face gently in her hands, brought their faces close together, and took her damn sweet time just moving her face in small increments, touching their noses, swiping a cheek, before she finally let her lips touch Aubrey's.

Aubrey moaned in relief, and her body sank against Monica's, and she grasped at Monica's top, needing something for purchase because she was worried she'd explode from the buildup of sexual tension she'd been feeling all night and be shot off into oblivion.

They kissed. And kissed.

Deeply. Slowly. Thoroughly. Aubrey couldn't remember the last time she'd been kissed so deliberately, and it was delicious. There was a gentle humming sound in the bathroom, barely audible above the running water, and she finally realized it was her. She was making that noise, oh yes. Because holy make-outs in the bathroom, Batman, Monica could *kiss*.

Before she could even register the exact source of the sensation, Monica had unzipped her dress in the back and pulled the straps off Aubrey's shoulders and let it go. It dropped to the floor, pooled at Aubrey's feet, and suddenly, she was standing in front of Monica Wallace in only her mint-green bra and underwear. The strangest thing happened then. Instead of falling back on modesty or, worse, embarrassment and shame, she stood up taller and owned her body. Somehow, Monica made her feel brave and proud and confident, and she reached around behind and unclasped her own bra, letting it fall at her feet with the dress. The small hitch in Monica's breath was immensely satisfying. She stepped out of her underwear and that was it. Monica was fully dressed, and Aubrey was completely naked, and they stood there, staring at each other, arousal painted all over Monica's face and rushing through Aubrey's bloodstream.

"You are fucking gorgeous," Monica said softly, then held out her hand and helped Aubrey step into the tub, now filled with fluffy white bubbles.

Aubrey turned the water off but didn't sit. Instead, she waved a finger up and down in front of Monica. "You're wearing too many clothes for the tub. Off." God, where had this assertiveness come from? It wasn't like her, which was the same thing she'd said about kissing Monica in the woods. She watched, eyes hooded, as Monica quickly undressed, then she held up a hand, stopping her from stepping into the tub. "I want to look. Just let me look."

Monica swallowed, and her cheeks went slightly pink, but she stood quietly and let Aubrey run her gaze all over her. God, she was beautiful. Rounded hips and smooth skin and breasts that were a bit larger than she'd expected, and suddenly, Aubrey's mouth was watering. It was her turn to hold out a hand, and Monica stepped in next to her. Together, they slowly sat, facing each other, the water just hot enough to make Monica clench her teeth.

"So, where was *take a bubble bath with Monica* on your bingo card?" Monica asked once they'd both relaxed in the water.

Aubrey laughed softly. "Yeah, nowhere. Not on my bingo card or anywhere in the vicinity of my bingo card." She watched Monica sip her wine, her gaze never leaving Aubrey's. Her voice went very quiet as she said, "You've been...a surprise."

"A good one, I hope."

"An unexpected one. And a good one, I think."

"You think?"

Aubrey sat back against the tub, and her foot rubbed along Monica's thigh. "I'm still unraveling some things, still rolling them around in my head. But yeah, a good one."

Monica nodded slowly. "Makes sense."

"How long ago was your last relationship?" Aubrey asked, slightly startled by her own words because she'd only been thinking them. Wondering. And then her mouth just blurted them out.

Monica broke eye contact, her gaze shifting to her hand as she played with the bubbles in front of her stomach. "Define *relationship*."

"What do you mean, define relationship? Somebody you were with for more than a few weeks, I guess?"

"I see. Okay."

"Somebody you'd planned some kind of future with, however basic."

"Oh. Wait."

Aubrey squinted at her. "It's a simple question."

At that, Monica shifted a bit as she continued to play with the bubbles. Her nipple was visible through them and made Aubrey swallow hard. "I haven't really had anything long-term," Monica said quietly. "I think my longest was about six months, but it was more of a casual dating scenario than a relationship."

"*Oh.*" She drew the word out, kept her voice soft. "How...? I mean..."

Monica must've understood her confusion because she lifted one shoulder, still not looking at her, and said on a whisper, "My heart has always been with somebody else."

"Oh," she said again. A few seconds went by before she asked, "Don't you get lonely?"

"Sure, but…" And here, Monica met her gaze and held it for a beat before saying, "I'm not lonely now."

Aubrey couldn't wait any longer. She'd been pretty certain where they were headed from the moment Monica had asked her to dinner. She just hadn't wanted to admit it to herself. But now? With a very naked, very sexy Monica in her bathtub, all she wanted was to move them along to their ultimate destination. Not *too* fast, but not so slowly either. She shifted herself so she was on her knees, then moved closer, between Monica's legs and into her space, until their noses almost touched. "Let's keep it that way," she whispered before crushing her mouth to Monica's.

Had she ever wanted somebody this badly?

The question ran through her head as they kissed, and it was about the only coherent thing, and it was gone before she could even attempt to focus on it, because suddenly, everything was simply *sensation*. The heat of the water, the tickle of the bubbles, the tang of wine and leftover sweetness of ice cream still clinging to Monica's tongue as she pushed it into Aubrey's mouth, the slippery wet skin under her hands as she attempted to touch Monica while also not slipping face-first into the water.

"Turn around," Monica's voice whispered from somewhere that seemed really far away, and Aubrey complied. And then there were new sensations—Monica's breasts against her back, Monica's hands sliding around to her stomach and up to cup her breasts, Monica's lips, teeth, tongue on her neck, her shoulders, Monica's thighs slick against hers.

And then Monica's hand dipped lower, and there was nothing but that. Monica's fingers at her center, pressing, stroking, searching for just the right places to touch her. And God, did she find them. All the right places. All of them. She felt like magic, like she knew every spot that would make Aubrey gasp, moan, whimper. And she did all those things. She gripped Monica's thighs, tightening her fingers at each new sensation, which Monica clearly used as a gauge for whether she was touching the right spot, applying the right pressure, if and when she should press inside. She finally did, and Aubrey arched slightly to give her better access, as a soft cry tore from her throat. Monica was using both hands now, pulling Aubrey against her more tightly as she stroked with one hand and slid in and out with the other, and Aubrey's breath caught as she pressed her head back onto Monica's shoulder, turned enough to meet Monica's gaze, then her mouth. They kissed hard, passionately, tongues in a battle for dominance, until Aubrey's orgasm crested, and her entire body went rigid. She wrenched her mouth from Monica's and arched her neck, her back, squeezed Monica's thighs, while colors exploded behind her eyelids and she moaned out a sound she'd never heard herself make. Monica stopped moving her hands and just pressed, the fingers of one hand against her flesh, the fingers of the other tucked snugly inside her body.

"Oh God," she uttered. She might have said it more than once, she wasn't sure. The world was nothing but color and physical touch. She could rattle off every part of Monica's body that was touching hers but couldn't come up with her own name if her life had depended on it.

Monica pressed a kiss to her temple, and Aubrey slowly came down. Her eyes were still shut, but little by little, her body relaxed and her breaths came slower. The water in the tub had gone tepid, and most of the bubbles were gone now, leaving their bodies visible, which she saw when she finally opened her eyes. Something about the sight of Monica's strong arms around her middle made her center clench, which Monica must've felt because she wiggled the fingers that were still sheathed in her body. A tickle of arousal came with that, and Aubrey reached down and slowly removed Monica's fingers from the spots where they could wreak more bodily havoc. Then she held her hands tightly, feeling the rise and fall of Monica's chest as she lay against her.

With no idea how much time had gone by, she finally said, "I think we should move things to the bedroom before we both become prunes." She sat up, away from Monica's body, and her skin seemed to cry out in protest at the loss of contact, the loss of heat. She met Monica's eyes, dark now, hooded with desire, and that look—the one that said she wanted her—was something Aubrey wanted to file away and keep forever. "Okay?"

Monica nodded once. "I didn't want to assume."

Aubrey narrowed her eyes. "You didn't want to assume... what?"

Monica's gaze went to the water, and Aubrey was surprised. She'd known Monica for a long time, and she'd always thought of her as confident to a fault, a control freak of sorts, a woman who got what she wanted and took shit from nobody. But now, she seemed uncertain, hesitant. It was so not her.

Aubrey turned on her knees so she was facing Monica, reached out, and lifted her chin with a finger. "Did you really think I'd be okay with things being one-sided? No reciprocation?"

Monica's mouth opened, then shut. She made a face that seemed to be a half frown, half grimace and shook her head.

"Well, I'm not. If you think I'm going to let you be in my house, in my bathtub, in all your gorgeous naked glory and not have my way with you? You'd better think again." She pressed her lips to Monica's, and she could almost taste the relief there. Making a mental note to circle back to this, she wrenched her mouth away and stood, reaching for a big fluffy white towel. She stepped out of the tub onto the thick mat on the floor, held her arms open with the towel, and ordered, "Come here."

God, who was she? All this assertion—she wasn't gonna lie—felt really good, really right. Turned out, power was every bit the aphrodisiac she'd heard it was.

Whatever hesitation and uncertainty Monica had had, it was gone now. She stepped out of the bath and into Aubrey's arms and let herself be toweled. Aubrey let her hands wander as she did the drying, taking special care on certain body parts—nipples and the apex of her thighs. Once they were both dry, they stood in the middle of the bathroom kissing for what might have been a few minutes or a few hours, Aubrey wasn't sure, because kissing Monica was like losing all sense of time and space. Nothing else existed but their mouths, their lips, their tongues.

Finally managing to extricate herself, she spoke on ragged breaths. "Come with me. Now. I don't want to do this on the bathroom floor, but I'm about six seconds away from exactly that." She grabbed Monica's hand and tugged her toward the door.

"We'll leave that for another time," Monica said with a sexy grin.

"God," Aubrey said, once they'd reached the bedroom. She stopped and searched those blue eyes. "Where did you come from?"

Monica lifted her hand to Aubrey's face and stroked her cheek with the backs of her fingers. "I've been right here the whole time," she whispered.

Being with Monica Wallace was…it was so many things. It was hot. It was balanced. It was sensual. And did she mention hot? So fucking hot. God, Monica had the most gorgeous body, and Aubrey wasted no time telling her so, which made Monica laugh softly.

"Thank you," she said as Aubrey kissed her neck. "I don't think I compare to you, but I'll take the compliment."

Aubrey stopped her neck worship to look at Monica's face. "Seriously? Do they not have mirrors where you live? You're fucking beautiful. I've always thought so."

That seemed to get Monica's attention, if the rising of her eyebrows was any indication. "You have?"

Aubrey tipped her head. "Being angry with you didn't render me blind."

"You weren't angry with me. You *hated* me. *Hated.*"

She inhaled and let it out slowly. "That's true. I did. For a little while, I did. Because I wasn't ready to admit my own part in that whole situation. It was easier to blame you."

"Makes sense."

"I'm sorry. For what it's worth." She pushed herself to her knees between Monica's legs, her hands on Monica's thighs, and gazed at her.

"No need. You did nothing wrong."

And suddenly, like she was in a movie, memories flooded her. Monica had always been part of her friend circle, if only on the periphery due to their past. But they shared the same college friends, so any gatherings included them both—they lived in the same town, after all. The difference now was that there were so many of those gatherings in the same year. They'd gone from seeing each other here and there on occasion to seeing each other every other month or so, and every time, Monica had been on her own. She'd never brought a date, aside from the one she'd brought to Trina and Jeff's wedding—the one she'd just met who ended up texting her ex all night. She'd seemed perpetually single. But now? Now Aubrey's head was replaying all those times that Monica arrived alone, how more than one of her friends had told her they thought Monica had a thing for her back then, and Monica's own words earlier in the tub. Her voice was barely above a whisper when she asked, "Who has your heart been with?"

Monica didn't move. Didn't blink. She did swallow, however, and it was loud, but she didn't answer.

"Monica? You said earlier that your heart has always been with somebody else. Who?"

"Shh," Monica said softly as she sat up. "Busy here." Her blue eyes glistened in the candlelight before she moved her head to Aubrey's neck and tasted it.

Deciding her questions could wait, she dropped her head back and gave Monica full access before pulling away to look at her gorgeous face. God, had she ever seen a more beautiful woman in her life? She practically dived at her, at her mouth, and kissed her hard. Possessively. Her fingers slid into the blond hair and gave it a tug, and then she was all about Monica's neck again, something Monica very much enjoyed if the sounds she was making were any indication.

She wanted to take her time. She wanted to go slowly. To tease, to torture in the best of ways, to explore and learn and file away. But her own body wouldn't let her. Her hands and mouth wouldn't listen when her brain ordered them to slow down. They were too far gone, which was understandable because Monica's body was a wonderland, with curves and dips and mounds and valleys. Her skin was like velvet, soft and warm, and the sounds she made— little hums and moans, soft and sexy—might have been the biggest turn-on of all for Aubrey. She kissed and nipped and bit and licked every inch on her way down Monica's body until she'd settled between her legs. She looked up, along her stomach, until they locked eyes. Monica was up on her elbows, and her eyes had gone so dark, so hooded, her arousal as clear as if she'd held a sign that read *I am so turned on right now!* Not breaking their eye contact, Aubrey lowered her head just a little and took the first swipe with her tongue. Monica's head dropped back, and a long moan came from her throat.

Aubrey went to work.

Monica was beyond soaked, and Aubrey tasted every drop, learning where to press, where to stroke, and how much pressure Monica liked. Again, she wanted to go slow but couldn't keep from chasing the sounds Monica made, and within minutes, Aubrey felt a hand in her hair, gripping tightly, as Monica's hips came up off the bed, the moan going longer and getting louder. A hand slammed flat against the headboard, and Aubrey did her best to hold on, to watch the whole show without removing her tongue from the warm wetness.

Time seemed to stand still.

Finally…finally…Monica's hips lowered slowly to the bed. Her hand was still in Aubrey's hair, not gripping as tightly, but now stroking gently, scratching her scalp, which felt wonderful and sent a pleasant shiver down her spine. Aubrey gently reclaimed her tongue, a little sad to leave such a sensual place.

"Holy shit." Monica's voice was a hoarse whisper, ragged, as she threw an arm over her eyes and said it again. "Holy shit."

Aubrey stayed where she was, simply enjoying the ability to stare at Monica's naked body uninterrupted. She had tan lines near the apex of her thighs, but her stomach was tan, and the sudden image of Monica in a bikini materialized in her head, sending a surge of arousal straight down between her legs. God, was she ready to go again? When was the last time that had happened? When was the last time it hadn't been one and done, because sex had always been fine, but never spectacular.

Sex with Monica Wallace was nothing short of spectacular.

"Hey," Monica whispered, tugging Aubrey out of her whirling thoughts. "Come up here."

Aubrey crawled up Monica's body, kissing different spots as she went, until she'd settled against Monica's side, her head tucked under Monica's chin, her leg thrown over Monica's, and yeah, they absolutely did fit together like two puzzle pieces. It was cliché, and it was eye roll-inducing, and it was perfect.

Holy unexpected complications, Batman, she was in trouble.

And then Monica was rolling over on top of her, and their mouths met, and Aubrey's body told her that yes, in fact, she was ready to go again, and then there were no more coherent thoughts.

Only Monica's mouth.

Only Monica's hands.

Only Monica.

❖

What was buzzing?

Was there a fly in her room?

Aubrey cracked one eye open. It was about all she could manage. She was so tired, she felt drugged, her limbs filled with water, so that moving them took extra effort.

The buzz sounded again, and she realized it was her phone telling her from the nightstand that someone was texting. The question was who? Who would be texting her so early?

The bright sunshine streaming through her bedroom window should've been a clue, but she grabbed the phone, and that's when she realized it *wasn't* early. It was after ten on Sunday morning, and Emma would be home by eleven.

"Shit," she muttered, sitting up. Emma always sent a text in the morning when she spent the night away from home. Aubrey texted back, told her good morning, said she couldn't wait to see her because she'd missed her too much, and then she tossed her phone back onto the nightstand and turned to shake Monica awake.

And she stopped.

And she just looked.

And she smiled.

Monica was sound asleep on her stomach. Her arms were tucked up under her pillow, one leg was out from under the covers and bent, and Aubrey let her eyes roam over the foot with its plum-polished toes, the shapely calf, the smooth thigh that she remembered kissing, tasting. She reached for the covers and slowly dragged them, revealing the rest of Monica's naked body like she was a prize, a reward unveiled for the winner, which was Aubrey, of course. Then she simply stared, wet her lips, and stared some more.

Maybe she could feel the weight of Aubrey's stare or maybe she just got chilly. Either way, Monica woke up slowly, her eyes opening, blinking into focus, meeting Aubrey's, and she smiled.

"Good morning," Aubrey said softly.

Monica slid her hand along the mattress until she hit Aubrey's leg, and she squeezed it. "Hi."

With a frown, Aubrey took a deep breath and let it out, a big sigh. "I hate to shove you out the door, but…"

Monica lifted her head. "Emma's coming home."

A nod. "I'm sorry. It's just—"

"Don't be." Monica was up and out of the bed in two seconds flat, looking for her clothes. "I get it. She doesn't need to know about…this." She moved a finger in the space between the two of them.

Aubrey watched her as she frantically looked around for her bra. She wanted to take a moment to look, to admire the literally naked beauty before her eyes, but Monica's scrambling around made her get up and cross the room to her. Monica bent over to grab her underwear, and Aubrey put a hand on her back. "Hey." Monica stood up, panties in hand, and Aubrey waited until she met her gaze. "If it wasn't for my child coming home, I'd be making us breakfast."

"Yeah?"

"I mean…" She let her eyes roam over Monica's skin. "I'd

probably keep us in bed awhile longer. And then I'd make us breakfast." She pushed to her toes and kissed Monica softly on the mouth, then said, "So stop running around here like a cartoon character. I'm not shoving you out the door. I'm not done with you." They kissed again, and this time, it went deeper. Mouths opened, tongues entered the game, and Aubrey was wet and throbbing in a matter of seconds. Jesus, this woman. She gave her a little push on her chest and wrenched her mouth away. "God," she said, breathless. "Get dressed before I drag you back to bed."

Monica laughed softly, but nodded. "Yes, ma'am."

While Monica dressed, Aubrey threw on some boxer shorts and a T-shirt and headed down to the kitchen to make coffee. The least she could do after their amazing night was send Monica away with a travel mug full of caffeine.

"Text you later," Monica said at the doorway as Aubrey pushed the mug into her hands. They kissed softly. Then Monica gave herself a full-body shake that made Aubrey smile, and she was off.

Aubrey stayed in the doorway, door open, until Monica had driven out of sight. And then she stood there a bit longer, reliving the night before until a red SUV pulled into the driveway, Cody in the driver's seat.

"God, that was close," she muttered under her breath, and then Emma jumped out of the car and ran toward her.

"Hi, Mom," she said, wrapping Aubrey in a hug. Emma might be ten and she might be growing up way too fast, but when she was away, she was always very much a hugger upon her return. Aubrey squeezed her tight.

"Oh, I missed you." She dropped a kiss on top of Emma's head.

Emma looked up at her, chin pressing into Aubrey's sternum. "Can I watch TV?"

Aubrey nodded as Cody approached the door, Emma's bag in hand. Aubrey caught a glimpse of the black wedding band. "Hey, married guy."

"Hi," he said with a grin and a little pink in his cheeks. "You got coffee in there?"

"Always. Come on in."

A few minutes later, they each had a mug in hand. Cody glanced into the living room of the small house, where Emma lay sprawled on the couch watching a show. He seemed to hesitate, then said, "Wanna go outside? It's not brutally hot yet."

Once they were on the deck and the sliding glass door closed tightly behind them, he turned to look at her, and she knew exactly what was coming just from the slightly wide-eyed look on his face.

"So?" he asked.

"So…what?" Yeah, she was going to make him spell it out. She sipped her coffee and waited.

"You and Monica, that's what!" Self-consciously, he glanced at the door, then lowered his voice. "You were making out in the woods. What the actual fuck was that about?"

She shrugged. "We made out in the woods."

He clearly didn't appreciate her teasing because he tipped his head to one side and sighed loudly at her. "Come on, Aubs. I saw you."

"Yes, I remember that." She ran her tongue around her teeth and then took another sip of coffee.

"So? What's going on? Are you guys a thing? 'Cause you should be careful of her."

Oh, now that was interesting. "Why? Isn't she your best friend? What should I be careful of?"

Cody seemed to realize what he'd said, and it felt like he dialed his concern back several notches. "I know. I know. I guess…" He looked off into her small backyard as if searching for the right words to say what he was trying to say. "It's just that she never seems to have a girlfriend for very long. You know? I mean, she dates. She's seen people. But they never last." He looked down at his feet and toed the edge of a board on her deck that had warped over time.

She had no idea what to say to that. Zero. She nodded so he knew she'd been listening, but she couldn't think of the right words to reply. She certainly wasn't ready to tell him Monica had spent the night.

"Just be careful." He grimaced. "That's all I'm saying. She's kind of a player."

Monica's voice echoed through her head then. *My heart has always been with someone else.* And what she wanted to do most was to defend her. Defend her to Cody. Tell him he was wrong and out of line and how could he say such a thing about his best friend. But something stopped her. It wasn't that she thought he was right—was he?—but what if he was? He knew Monica way better than Aubrey did. She'd been avoiding the woman for a decade. He saw her all the time.

"I appreciate the concern," she said and winced internally at how impersonal she sounded.

Cody studied her for a moment, then gave one nod. "Okay. I just don't want to see you get hurt is all."

"Thanks."

It was a little awkward now, and he felt it as much as she did. She could tell by how he sort of squirmed in place. God, she knew him well. Even after all this time, even after he'd gotten married to somebody else, she could still read him like a book. That's how she knew his concern was genuine.

And that's why it worried her.

❖

For the next two weeks, Aubrey and Monica texted daily. Sometimes, they were flirty. Sometimes, they were downright sexting. Aubrey couldn't remember the last time—or ever—she'd been so excited-thrilled-flattered-turned on by simply typing words on a phone to somebody.

They also talked on the phone, but not terribly often. They both worked during the day, and school had started up again. In the evenings, Emma sometimes needed help with her schoolwork. And the house was small. She didn't trust she wouldn't be heard through the thin walls by overly curious ten-year-old ears.

But they were making it work. What *it* was, she wasn't sure. Were they dating? It seemed like it. They hadn't talked about exclusivity. And they hadn't been together again since the first time. Not for a lack of want. Because want, they did.

What are you wearing? Was the first text Monica sent that day, and it had devolved after that.

Aubrey waited until she knew Monica was in a meeting. Then she tugged her shirt off her shoulder and took a photo of her bare skin with her lavender bra strap showing and sent it.

Monica's response was a series of emoji, from the wide-eyed one to the heart eyes one to the one with its tongue out. They made Aubrey laugh. It was coming up on lunch, so she set the phone down and went back to work for a few minutes, thinking she'd take her lunch break soon.

She'd worked for about thirty minutes when her doorbell rang.

"Why is the Amazon guy ringing the bell," she wondered aloud as she took off her headset and headed to the front door.

She only had time to open it and register that there was a wildly attractive blond woman on her front step, before Monica pushed her way in, grabbed Aubrey's face with both hands, and kissed her senseless. Lips, teeth, tongue, everything was involved, and the rest of the world went hazy and fell away.

Did time stop? She had no idea. It felt like it might have. After who knew how long, the kiss slowed and stopped and then Monica pressed her forehead to Aubrey's and let out a long breath. "Sorry," she whispered. "I couldn't wait."

Aubrey nodded and swallowed and took much longer than it should have to find her voice. "I…yeah…s'okay," was all she could manage to stutter out.

That made Monica laugh softly. "Okay, gotta go back to work." She kissed Aubrey one more time, then turned around and headed out to her car, which Aubrey realized only then was still running.

"The Kissing Bandit," she said quietly as she waved to Monica backing out of the driveway. Nobody had ever left in the middle of their workday to find Aubrey and to kiss her face off simply because she couldn't wait to do so. Nobody. She walked slowly back to her desk and flopped back into her chair. Her body was on fire now, just from that one kiss. Monica had more sexual power over her than she cared to admit.

A glance at her computer screen told her there was nothing

pressing at the moment, so she signed herself out on break, went upstairs to her bedroom, found her vibrator, and finished what Monica had started.

It took less than three minutes.

❖

A week later, Aubrey and Trina were sitting at a two-top table in Martini's. Aubrey sipped an old-fashioned and Trina had gone meta by ordering a martini.

"I can't believe I haven't seen you since Cody's wedding," Trina said, a slight edge in her voice. "And you've become terrible at texting. What's going on with you?"

She'd known she couldn't avoid giving Trina details for very long. It was the reason she'd set up tonight: she wanted—needed—to talk to her friend about what was happening. Finding someplace to begin, however, was hard, and she stared into her drink as she worked out the words.

"Okay, now you're scaring me," Trina said, reaching across the table to close her hand over Aubrey's forearm. "Is everything okay? Is Emma okay? You're not sick, are you?" The worry on her face was so clear and so palpable that Aubrey felt instantly guilty.

"Everything is fine Emma is fine I'm fine I slept with Monica." What should've been four separate statements came out as one as she rambled through them.

Trina blinked at her for a moment before saying, "I'm sorry, you did who to the what now?"

Aubrey blew out a breath. "I slept with Monica. We're kind of...seeing each other. I think."

Another moment of blinking went by before Trina seemed to find herself again and began to shake her head. "Wait, wait, wait. Back the truck up for a minute. You slept with Monica?" Aubrey nodded. "You're kind of seeing each other? You *think*? What the fuck, Aubs?"

Aubrey groaned and let her head drop backward, noticing for the first time the black tin ceiling. "I know!" She looked back down at her drink and poked at the dark burgundy cherry with her swizzle stick. "Gah. I know. I…" She shrugged. "I have no idea what I'm doing, but…" She met Trina's gaze again and couldn't keep the corners of her mouth from turning up even a little bit.

Trina gasped. "Oh my God, you *like* her."

Aubrey nodded slowly as the smile bloomed wider. "I do. I can't help it."

"But…but…we're talking about Monica. Monica Wallace? Woman who single-handedly destroyed your wedding day?"

"I mean, she didn't *destroy* it exactly."

"Woman you've spent a decade hating?"

"Hate is a strong word."

"Aubrey!"

Aubrey grimaced. "I know. I know. I have no idea what's happening. But…" She relayed the story of Monica showing up out of the blue in the middle of the workday just to kiss her. "She makes me feel…" She squinted off into the distance, looking for the right words. "She makes me feel beautiful. And wanted. And sexy. And I haven't felt those things in a really long time."

Trina sighed. "Listen, you deserve to feel all those things. I don't have a problem with that. It's just…it's Monica."

Aubrey laughed at Trina's wide eyes. "It is Monica." She leaned over the table so their faces were close and whispered, "And she's goddamn incredible in bed."

"Oh my God," Trina said, her eyebrows rising toward her hairline. "I knew she had a thing for you. I told you so." She tipped her head. "Good in bed? Really?"

"I'm totally serious. Best sex I've ever had. Hands down."

"Wow." Trina sipped her martini, then lifted it in a salute. "Go, Monica." They touched glasses and both sipped. "When will you see her again?"

"Emma's at my parents' this weekend, so probably tomorrow."

"Does Cody know?" Aubrey nodded, and Trina grimaced. "And? How did he take it?"

She waited a beat before she answered. There was still an

element of uncertainty around what he'd said. "He told me to be careful. That she's a player."

Trina made a face. "A player? Monica? I think I've seen her with a date, like, twice since we graduated."

"I know. I thought the same thing." Monica's words about her heart belonging to someone else and the intimation that the someone else was, in fact, *her* wasn't something she was ready to talk about. Hell, she hadn't even dwelled on it herself because, well, because then it would need analyzing. And it would be real. And it would mean something. So, no, she kept that to herself. "But that's what he said. I kinda want to ask her about it, but maybe not yet."

"I think you definitely should," Trina said, pointing at her. "I don't think Cody would lie to you about that, do you?"

Aubrey tipped her head from one side to the other and back. "I honestly don't know. Monica's his best friend. On the one hand, I think he'd want to protect her, so I would expect him to be warning her off me, not the other way around. On the other hand, maybe he's jealous? Afraid I'll take up her time?" She sighed. "I don't know, I'm just thinking out loud here."

"Well, I'm glad he knows, regardless. Keeping that from him wouldn't be cool."

"I didn't really have a choice," she said with a laugh. "After he caught us in the woods, I think he's been on high alert."

They were quiet for a moment before Trina began to laugh, shaking her head. "It's all just so weirdly unexpected. I'm still wrapping my brain around it."

"You? How do you think I feel?" She laughed, too, but Trina had stopped. Now, she was just smiling as she studied Aubrey's face.

"I think you feel happy."

WEDDINGS DOWN: 4
SUCCESS IN AVOIDING MONICA WALLACE: EPIC FAIL

Part Five

Brad and Kara
October 12, 2024
Animal Shelter Wedding

Aubrey McFadden is never getting married.

Reason #6
People can't be trusted.

"You know, I kinda thought if any of us got married at an animal shelter, it would be the lesbians," Trina said with a laugh.

"Right?" Aubrey said.

"Wait...is that offensive?"

"What?"

"Did I just insult lesbians? Did I insult you? I mean, I know you're bi, but..." Trina looked genuinely concerned, which sent a little wave of love for her through Aubrey.

"I don't think that was offensive at all."

"You do love your animals."

"You are not wrong, my friend."

Aubrey pulled her car into a parking spot at the Junebug Farms animal shelter. Kara, the bride-to-be, worked there and had met Brad, the groom-to-be and fellow frat brother of Cody, when he came in to adopt a dog. It made sense that this was where they wanted to say their vows.

"Tell me again why you're here with me and not Monica," Trina said as they got out of the car. The shelter had closed early for the wedding and reception, so everybody there now was there for the nuptials.

"Because your hubby is out of town." Trina gave her a look, so she sighed and went on. "And because we're not ready for people to know." She cleared her throat. "And I'm not really sure what we are yet. I've never been in...something...like this before."

"*Something?*" Trina asked, making air quotes.

"Yeah, I…" Aubrey shook her head as she shouldered her purse and they headed toward the main building. "September was nuts. For both of us. She had two work trips, so she was gone for half the month. Emma had just started school again, and Cody was out of town almost as much as Monica was, so I've had Emma every weekend. And my job kicked things into high gear."

"Is that your way of saying you haven't had any time together?" Trina pulled the door open and held it as Aubrey walked through.

"Exactly. Which means we haven't really talked about anything in-depth because I don't want to do that in text. You know?"

"I do."

"I mean, if *I* don't even know what we are yet, I don't want other people speculating what we are. I'm not cool with that. So, we decided to come separately."

"I guess that makes sense." Trina didn't sound like she actually meant her own words, but Aubrey wasn't in the mood to defend her choices. And yes, they were *her* choices. Monica would've easily come as her date, but the conversation she'd had with Cody had stuck. It had been over a month, and his words still hung out in her brain, rent-free. *She's kind of a player.* She knew she needed to talk to Monica about them, but September really had been a ludicrously busy month. And now here she was, in the middle of October, with Halloween just around the corner and the holidays rocketing toward her after that, and she really needed to make some time to sit and talk.

Meanwhile, another fucking wedding.

The lobby of the animal shelter had been set up with rows of matching white folding chairs and a small arched arbor at the front. It was going to be very small—maybe fifty people—and the reception would take place right there as well. The front desk had been fashioned into a makeshift bar, and she could smell food coming from somewhere behind it, through the door back there maybe? The soundtrack was that of muffled barking dogs and some quiet instrumental music being piped in from…somewhere. Aubrey scanned the high-ceilinged lobby until she saw a door in the back corner with a line drawing of a dog's head on it. Dogs were back there, she suspected.

They made their way to the fourth row of chairs and took seats. Aubrey knew a handful of the attendees, a wave here, a smile there. Trina seemed to be in the same boat, leaning over occasionally to whisper about who she was seeing that she recognized, and whether they'd become bald or wore too much makeup or should've spent more time shopping for their wedding attire.

At one point, Aubrey leaned close to Trina and said quietly, "I get why they're having their wedding here and I admire that they're taking donations instead of gifts, but I have always avoided shelters."

"Yeah? How come?"

"Because they break my heart." She frowned. "I came here once when I was a teenager for a class field trip. I cried when we left. I wanted to take them all home. All of them—dogs, cats, goats, horses, sheep. All of them. I haven't been back since."

Trina frowned too and nodded. "I'm sorry." She squeezed Aubrey's hand. "You are tenderhearted, my friend."

There really was only one thing that could take Aubrey's mind off the dozens upon dozens of homeless animals on the other side of the huge wall to her left, and that one thing walked in right at that moment. Perfect timing. You had to appreciate it.

Monica's dress was royal blue, an excellent color choice for accenting the blue of her eyes. She stood in the back and scanned until her gaze landed on Aubrey's face, and a smile broke across hers.

"Oh my God, did you see her smile when she saw you?" Trina asked quietly with a shake of her head. "She's got it *bad*." She drew out the last word, then she leaned into Aubrey and bumped her with a shoulder as Aubrey felt her face heat up.

There was an empty chair next to her, and Monica claimed it, sitting down and crossing her legs, and it took every ounce of willpower Aubrey had not to stare at them. The dress hit just above her knees, so there was plenty of leg to look at, and Aubrey swallowed audibly. Which Monica apparently found amusing because she turned to look at her with a very sexy grin on her face. "Everything okay?" she asked.

"Mm-hmm," was all Aubrey could manage, and she rolled her lips in and bit down on them.

"You look fantastic," Monica said quietly as she leaned closer. "Also, hi. It's good to see your face." Then she leaned slightly forward and looked around Aubrey. "Hey, Tree," she said with a wave.

Trina gave her a little finger wave back. A few minutes later, she tipped closer to Aubrey and whispered, "Glad he could come to at least one wedding this year besides his own."

Aubrey followed Trina's gaze to see Cody and Kimmy making their way through the lobby, smiling here and waving there. They took seats directly behind them. Aubrey felt a little squeeze on her shoulder.

"Hey," Cody said.

She turned and greeted him, smiled at Kimmy.

"Hey, Mon," Cody said.

Monica turned halfway and gave him a nod, then said hello to Kimmy. There was a definite chill in the air around them, Aubrey noticed. Before she could examine it or ask anybody about it, the music changed and grew louder, the groom walked down the aisle, followed by his groomsmen, and the wedding began.

It was a lovely ceremony, short and sweet but filled with emotion. Brad had always been one of the nicer guys in their little group in college. Kind and respectful, even when he'd been overserved by his frat brothers. He began to silently cry when Kara walked down the aisle to him, and you could hear his quiet sniffles throughout the entire ceremony. So sweet. It made Aubrey mist up more than once.

Everybody and their brother decided to hit the bar the second the ceremony was over.

"I feel like I'm at a club," Trina said with a good-natured roll of her eyes as they stood four deep at the bar, bass line of the music thumping through them, waiting to place their orders.

"I need the restroom. Get me a pinot grigio?"

At Trina's nod, she made her way through the lobby where the chairs had been rearranged from rows to small seating pods along the edges of the big space. She assumed there would be dancing, and waitstaff were walking around with trays of finger foods. She saw Kimmy in a corner talking to a woman she didn't recognize and waved at her. Down a small hallway, she saw the sign for the restroom, but as she reached out to push the door open, she thought she caught a glimpse of the blue of Monica's dress as it disappeared around a corner farther down the hall. A moment later, she heard hushed voices.

Aubrey wasn't nosy. She wasn't a busybody, and she wasn't an eavesdropper. Normally. But when she thought she'd recognized the voices, even hushed, her feet carried her closer before her brain even registered she was moving.

"What do you mean what am I doing?" Monica asked, her voice low.

"It's a pretty simple question. What are you doing with her?" That was Cody, and Aubrey had an instant sickening feeling she knew exactly who *her* was.

"Well, first of all, what I do is none of your damn business. And second, I'm not *doing* anything. I like her. A lot."

"And *that* is nothing new. I mean now. What are you doing *now*? I mean, a random make-out session in the woods when you're drunk is one thing. But are you, like, dating her now?"

"We were not drunk." This line was spoken through clenched teeth. Aubrey could picture it, Monica's jaw tight. "And if I *was* dating her, let me say this once again—it would be none of your damn business."

"That's where you're wrong. She's the mother of my child, and what she does affects Emma, and that makes it my business."

"I think Aubrey would disagree with you." There was so much more in that one statement than the seven words Monica spoke, and Aubrey could hear them loud and clear.

There was a beat of silence, and she could picture Cody's angry face. His skin was fairly pale, so when he got mad, his entire face went red, even his ears. "I warned her about you, you know."

"You what?" Monica's voice was deathly quiet.

Wow, for best friends, they were doing their best to rip each other to shreds.

"Yeah. I told her how you dated a ton but never got serious with anybody. Since college. It's been like that since college. You just move on to the next unsuspecting girl. I told her to be careful."

There was a long beat of silence, and Aubrey started to think maybe she should leave before she was discovered listening in, but she couldn't make her feet move. She stood like a tree that had grown roots, anchored to the linoleum as she listened to Monica's strained voice.

"That's what you think of me? Seriously? We've been friends since we were kids. Best friends. And you decide to *warn* somebody about me?" And the way she said the word *warn* made Aubrey think she was struggling to hold back tears, the betrayal was so clear in her voice. "Good to know. Thanks for clearing that up for me." And suddenly there was the clicking of heels on the floor, and Aubrey panicked for a few seconds before realizing that the footsteps were moving away. Not wanting to be discovered eavesdropping by Cody, she hurried back the way she'd come and pushed through the bathroom door.

Once seated, she blew out a breath and tried to wrap her brain around what she'd heard. Cody was clearly bothered by the two of them together, which she didn't really get. Why did he care? He was married. And Monica seemed more upset by Cody's assessment of her than excited about being with Aubrey and telling him so. She didn't love that.

Her mind spun. Maybe this was all just a terrible idea. Maybe she and Monica together was just a mistake. Maybe everybody else would think so, too, because they'd have to tell people eventually. What if they all had the same reaction as Cody? What if he was right about Monica? But then the spinning stopped, and her brain tossed her an image of Monica's body above her, of Monica's mouth on hers, of Monica's fingers against her center. She thought about Monica's eyes, how sincere they always seemed to be. She thought about their ride together in North Carolina, how easy it had been to be with her, much as she fought it. She recalled how she had actually made the first move by kissing Monica in the woods, not that Monica had protested. Like, at all. And then her brain circled back to how incredibly, amazingly compatible they were in bed, how it had only been the one time, and how much Aubrey was looking forward to making it two times, then three, four. But Cody's words hung out in the back of her head, adding to his words from a few weeks ago, and she felt stuck. Confused. Uncertain what to do next.

She heard the door creak open just before Trina's voice called out, "Aubs, you in here?"

"Yup. Hang on." She hadn't even relieved herself. She'd simply sat on the lid of the toilet while her mind spun her in circles. With a sigh, she stood up, flushed nothing, and headed back out into the party.

❖

The reception was in full swing now. Music played, though not at too loud a volume, given all the nervous animals on the other side of the cement wall. Some guests had left, and a few new ones had arrived. Brad had Kara's hand firmly tucked in his as they wandered the large lobby, greeting their guests and chatting up old friends. Aubrey felt a pang of envy deep in her gut as she watched. She'd never really thought she might have something like that until Monica had changed roles in her life from enemy to love interest. And now? She could picture herself walking hand in hand with her. Greeting guests. Smiling like they were the most in-love people on the planet.

In love?

Hold up a second.

Was that what she wanted with Monica? Did she want to be in love with her? Or was it just that feeling you got at weddings? Everybody else seemed so in love, why shouldn't you be too? Before she could dwell any more on things that were turning her brain into mush, the music shifted, and a slow song came on.

"Terrific," she muttered under her breath, just as a hand landed softly on her shoulder.

"Hey. Wanna dance?" She turned to look into those blue eyes that were becoming more and more familiar this close up, and somehow, her body took over before her mind could recalibrate itself and make the decision.

"Absolutely."

And then they *were* hand in hand, weaving through the small crowd toward the corner of the lobby that had become a makeshift dance floor. People were looking. Even if Aubrey hadn't been able to see them, she would've felt their eyes following them as they walked, then moved close together, then began to sway. Monica's hand was warm and soft, holding Aubrey's gently. Her other hand was solid against Aubrey's back, and the unfamiliar sense of safety that Aubrey suddenly felt then was disconcerting, not to mention confusing. She'd spent ten years hating this woman, and now, she suddenly felt held and protected by her?

What the hell was happening?

She glanced up into Monica's face, looking for an answer, but was surprised by the faraway look of sadness parked there. Something about it seemed to reach into Aubrey's chest and poke at her heart.

"Hey," she said softly. "You okay?" She didn't let on that she'd overheard Monica's conversation with Cody, but it was clear that something was bothering Monica. She seemed weighed down, her shoulders slightly slumped, her usual flare of confidence nowhere to be seen.

"You know what?" Monica asked, keeping her voice as low as Aubrey's. "I'm gonna go."

"Already?" Did that sound desperate? She hoped not, but she didn't let go of Monica's hand.

"Yeah, I'm not feeling great. I'm tired, but I've got some work I need to get done for a big meeting next week."

She was lying. It surprised Aubrey how easily she could tell. Monica didn't make eye contact with her. In fact, she looked everywhere but at Aubrey. And Aubrey wanted to argue. Wanted to talk her out of leaving. Wanted to beg her to stay, to dance with her some more. But the expression on her face and the sadness in her beautiful eyes told Aubrey to let her go. That she needed to go.

"Okay. Well, I'm glad we got half a dance." She went for humor. It didn't land solidly, but it made one corner of Monica's mouth twitch up.

"Me too." Monica bent forward and kissed Aubrey's cheek. "See ya."

She headed toward the bar as she watched Monica say goodbye to Brad and Kara, then push her way out the front doors, and the disappointment felt like a too heavy blanket draped over her shoulders. She let out a quiet sigh as Trina sidled up to her.

"More cheek kissing, I see," she said with a mischievous glint in her eye.

Aubrey shook her head. "Sadly, it doesn't come close to the actual kissing. On the mouth." She left a tip for the bartender and took her wine back to a table. Trina got her drink and followed, then sat next to her.

"What's going on?" Trina asked, and the expression on her face said *And don't bother to lie to me because I know you too well.*

A sip of the mediocre wine helped grease the wheels, and before she knew it, she was telling Trina what she'd overheard. "What do you think it all means?"

Trina lifted one shoulder and gazed away at the dance floor. The music had shifted back to dancier stuff, Katy Perry was singing about California girls, and half the guests were out there bopping to the beat. "I mean, Cody isn't wrong." Trina cleared her throat. "You have always avoided Monica, and most of us don't talk about her when we're around you. But he wasn't lying. She's dated sporadically but never seems to ever have something real." She sipped her drink, then said, "Maybe that's just how she lives. No commitment. No strings." She shrugged again, as if trying to say that she didn't really know for sure, that this was just one possibility.

"Maybe." Aubrey didn't want to let Trina know how much her

assessment bothered her. She didn't want her to know how much she didn't want it to be true, how much she really wanted Monica to give them a chance. A real chance. And when that thought registered in her brain, she almost gasped from the weight of it. "But…" She let the word dangle in the air between them because going farther scared the crap out of her. Giving voice to what she was thinking would make it real. For both her and for Trina.

"But what?" Trina's eyes searched hers.

"I'd like to…" She swallowed, the lump in her throat so large she wondered for a split second what the hell she'd eaten. She cleared it, then glanced down at her hands. Trina covered them with one of hers.

"Aubs. Talk to me." And when Aubrey looked into her eyes, she saw nothing there but the love and support of her best friend.

"I like her," she whispered, barely audible. "I like her, and I'd like to try, like, seeing her." There. She'd said it out loud. There was no taking it back now. Holy shit.

"You mean, like, dating her?" Trina's surprise was clear, but there was no judgment. Surprise? Yes. Concern? Definitely. But judgment? Zero. At Aubrey's hesitant nod, "Well, okay then. You should give it a shot. If that's what you really want, you should give it a shot." She sat back and took a much larger gulp of her drink, her eyes never leaving Aubrey's. "You've been different since you started spending time with her, you know."

"I have? How?"

"You're happier." Trina's words were simple and plain. Factual. And they caused a grin Aubrey couldn't stop. "You seem lighter."

"I do?" While she'd understood that her time with Monica had had an effect, she hadn't realized others could see it.

"Hundred percent."

"Huh." There was a soft smile that she couldn't hide, and Trina pointed at her.

"See?" They laughed and then Trina seemed to sober. "But listen. Be careful. I'd say go slow, but, I mean, you've already fucked, so it's probably too late for that—" Aubrey took a playful swat at her arm. "Just be careful, okay? I'm not saying you'll get hurt, but I don't want to see you get hurt. You know?"

"I do."

Trina held up her glass, and Aubrey touched hers to it. "I love you, weirdo."

Aubrey barked a laugh. "I love you, too, but why am I a weirdo?"

"'Cause you want to date the same person you've spent a decade hating. It's weird."

She scrunched up her nose. "It kind of is, isn't it?"

"There's nothing *kind of* about it. Weirdo." But Trina's grin took away any of the sarcasm that might've laced her words. She wasn't wrong, though, was she? It *was* weird.

"I have spent my life doing the sensible thing," Aubrey said quietly. "I've taken the job I needed to. I've raised my kid mostly on my own by making the sensible choices for her. For us. And now?" She met Trina's gaze. "Now, I'm allowed to choose the weird."

"Word," Trina said with a nod, and they cheersed again.

❖

Things changed for Aubrey after Brad and Kara's wedding, though if you asked her to define how, she'd be at a loss for words. But things felt different. Maybe it was because she'd actually told somebody—speaking of, Trina was texting incessantly, asking had she and Monica gone out again, were they officially dating, had there been more sex yet?

Unfortunately, the answer to all those questions was no, because Monica was avoiding her. She was pretty sure about that.

Got time for a quick lunch?

She'd texted that around ten o'clock this morning. Monica's response didn't come until after eleven.

Sorry, can't. Meeting after meeting today.

The answer could be legit. Totally. Monica's job was busy. She was a higher-up. She had lots of meetings, that was true. But she could also be lying. She could be avoiding. She might have decided to just say no to every invitation Aubrey extended—this was the fourth one—until Aubrey gave up completely and left her alone.

"Well, that's not gonna happen," she muttered under her breath. It was Friday. Brad and Kara's wedding had been nearly two weeks ago. Halloween was next week. It was fall. There were barely two months left in the year, and she'd be damned if she was going to let another year end without taking control. She picked up her phone and texted her mom.

Hey, I know you're taking Emma overnight. Can you pick her up from school? Something's come up...

The dots bounced and then her mother came back with, *Of course. Everything okay?*

She'd never really used the *something's come up* line on her mom, so she knew that's why the question. *All good!* she sent back, purposely adding the exclamation point and three smiling emoji, which she realized after she sent them might be overkill, but it was too late at that point. She would be quizzed later. She was sure of it.

She spent the rest of the workday glancing at her phone way too many times to check the hour. She unplugged her laptop and took it upstairs with her, paying attention to her email and her staff while she changed out of her jeans and hoodie and into nicer jeans and a chocolate-brown turtleneck sweater. She pulled her hair back into a loose ponytail, touched up her makeup, and checked herself in the mirror. She added gold hoop earrings and a matching gold bracelet, then spritzed herself with her favorite scent, something warm with a bit of fall, including pumpkin, nutmeg, and sugar. She stared at her own reflection.

"Okay. You can do this. No pressure. Just talking. You need to know if she's in the same place you are. You got this." She sighed quietly. "And if she's not, at least you'll know. Right?" Her reflection didn't answer, but that was okay. Pep talk complete.

She went back downstairs and signed off her computer at four forty-five, which was earlier than usual. She normally took a break to go pick up Emma from school, then signed back on for another hour or two, rarely finishing before six. But today, she was taking a chance, and she didn't want to wait too long.

The air was brisk as she pulled on a cream down vest and headed out to her car. October in the Northeast could go either way—sometimes, kids would be trick-or-treating in shorts, sweating under their masks, and other times, they'd be battling brittle and cold winds, their costumes stretched over their winter jackets. This year, it was going to be somewhere in between, the forecast calling for temps in the low fifties for the next several days. Aubrey didn't mind the chill, though. She'd always enjoyed sweaters and fires and hot cocoa.

She found the office building easily, and she slowly drove up and down the rows in the parking lot until she found the familiar silver SUV with the *HSB* in the license plate. So what if she'd used *hot sexy blonde* to remember it? So what? There was an empty spot not far away, and she backed into it so she could keep an eye on the silver SUV. She kept her own car idling, as it was a bit too chilly to turn it off and sit there with no heat, especially considering she had no idea how long she'd be. She unbuckled her seat belt and adjusted herself more comfortably in the seat as people began to exit the building. It was nearly five thirty, which seemed to be quitting time for this building. Cars started up and pulled away a few at a time, Aubrey squinting to make sure she looked at every person coming her way.

It didn't take that long. The crowd exiting had thinned quite a bit, and a glance at her phone told her it was five forty-eight when she saw her. Her breath caught for a second, and she swallowed down the anxiety that had suddenly made itself known in her stomach, along with the pang of arousal that seemed to be a regular thing now whenever she saw the current object of her stakeout.

Monica was dressed for work, obviously, and Aubrey had always been a sucker for a woman in a suit, but this was beyond. Like, *beyond.* Monica's suit was black, pants and a blazer. Her shirt underneath was black with white pinstripes, her heels were sexy black pumps. She wore a long black coat over it all, and her hair was pulled back into a twist of some kind—Aubrey couldn't see the back. Before she could talk herself out of it or ask herself what in the actual hell she was doing, she pulled on her door handle and stepped out of her car.

"Hi," she said, and when Monica glanced up at her, the surprise was clear on her face.

"Wha—oh, hey. Hi. What are you doing here?"

Aubrey was pretty sure that underneath that surprise, there was happiness to see her. Pretty sure.

"I am here to take you out for a drink." There. She'd said it, and she hadn't even sounded weird or uncertain. *Point for me.*

"Me?"

Aubrey made a show of looking behind Monica. "I see no other attractive blond women I've been trying to get together with for nearly two weeks now, so yes. You."

Monica had the good sense to look slightly ashamed, and Aubrey knew for certain in that second that she *had* been avoiding her.

"I think we should talk," she added, keeping her voice light so she didn't sound like doom and gloom.

Monica seemed to take that in and roll it around for a beat before she gave one nod. "We should. Okay. Where to?"

They chose a nearby bar called Scully's, and within twenty minutes, they were sitting at a corner table, a glass of pinot noir in front of Monica and a glass of sauvignon blanc in front of Aubrey.

And *now* she was nervous. Of course. All the pep talks in the world couldn't prepare her for actually being in Monica's space, for actually sitting across the table from her. They hadn't seen each other since the wedding, despite Aubrey's attempts. And now, being with her in the same room, close enough to reach across the table and touch her hand, it did things to Aubrey. Did things to her body. Kicked up her heart rate. Made her palms a little sweaty. Switched on her anxiety. But it also made her lower body flutter and tighten, and that was all about desire. She knew that without a doubt. Maybe Monica was giving off pheromones or something, but all Aubrey knew was that when she was close to her, her arousal jacked up into red alert territory.

"You've been avoiding me." Wow, right into the deep end. Head first. Aubrey gave herself a mental shake, both proud and mortified that she'd said the words.

Monica gazed into the moody crimson of her wine and seemed to gather her thoughts. "I have," she said, then lifted her gaze to Aubrey. "I'm sorry about that."

"Can you tell me why?"

"Why I'm sorry?" Monica's gentle grin appeared then.

"Ha ha. You're funny."

"I try."

"Why you've been avoiding me." Aubrey watched Monica's face and heard her sigh softly. She lowered her voice and added, "Is it because of Cody?" That was a surprise, if Monica's raised eyebrows were any indication, and she went on. "I overheard you at the shelter the day of the wedding."

Monica nodded slowly, as if she was absorbing that information but wasn't sure what to do with it. She took a sip of her wine and gazed off into the center of the bar as she spoke. "I mean, he wasn't wrong. I've never really had much of a meaningful relationship."

"So?" Aubrey said, injecting a few drops of indignation into her tone. "Why does Cody get to judge you for that? Let's be honest, he's not an expert. I mean, he broke up with me on our wedding day." She gave Monica a quick wink to show she was joking, then dropped her volume slightly and leaned forward a bit. "I'd bet money Kimmy runs that whole show."

Monica bit down on her lips and Aubrey could tell she was trying to hide a smile. "I bet you're right."

"Listen. I love Cody. I always will. We had something way back, and he's the father of my child. I'll always have love for him. And I know he's been your best friend since elementary school. But he does not get to decide who either of us dates. We are grown-ass adults, and part of being a grown-ass adult is getting to make your own decisions." She stopped, shocked by the vehemence her words had suddenly taken on.

Monica must've felt the same way, because her brows went up again and she tilted her head just a bit. "Wow. I like this version of you."

"What version is that?"

"Adamant. Certain." She paused a moment. "Sexy. I didn't know you had this determined streak."

"There's a lot about me you don't know."

Staring. Lots of holding of gazes right then. The seconds ticked by.

"You've hated me for ten years," Monica said quietly.

"I mean, hate is a strong word," Aubrey said with a sly grin. "I disliked you a lot, though."

Monica laughed softly, a huskier sound than one would expect from her. "Okay. Fine. Disliked. You've *disliked* me for ten years."

Aubrey studied Monica's face, let her eyes follow each dip and curve, slide along her jawline, take in her full pink lips. "I needed someone to blame," she said quietly, bringing her gaze back up to Monica's blue eyes. She felt like she could fall right into them, that they'd catch her and keep her safe. "And I couldn't blame Cody because I was still in love with him at the time."

"I get that."

"For what it's worth, I'm sorry." It felt like too little too late, but Aubrey couldn't *not* apologize.

"Apology accepted." Monica didn't even hesitate before she said it.

"Yeah?"

"Mm-hmm."

"Wow. Well, that was easy." They shared a quick chuckle, but the air still felt heavy, and Aubrey knew there was more to talk about. "And actually, I've found myself feeling the opposite of disliking you lately."

Again with that cute little head tilt. Aubrey would enjoy seeing that more often. "Really."

"Really."

"I mean, we did sleep together. It would be quite the blow to my ego if you still didn't like me."

Aubrey barked a laugh. "That's true." She took another sip of her wine and got serious.

Monica reached across the table and gently grasped Aubrey's hand. Aubrey turned hers so their fingers entwined. She thought about what a cliché it was to think about how well they fit together, but they actually did. Like they'd been molded that way, purposely, so they were meant to link just as they were now. Aubrey looked at their hands, studied them. Monica's hand was a little bit bigger than hers. She wore no polish, but her nails were neatly filed, her skin fading from the bronze of the summer to a lighter shade now that it was midfall. When she glanced back up at Monica's face, she saw a shadow pass over her features.

"What is it?" she asked softly.

"Cody's my best friend." Monica's voice was quiet and firm, but there was an edge of something to it, concern or worry. Maybe both.

Aubrey nodded. "I know."

"I don't want to hurt him."

Aubrey tipped her head slightly. "Monica." She waited. "Look at me."

Monica finally met her gaze, and there was something akin to anguish on her face. It poked Aubrey right in the heart like a long needle piercing her flesh.

"I'm going to say this again, and I need you to listen. Okay?"

A nod. A squeeze of her hand.

"Cody is married. He has Kimmy. And yes, he's Emma's father. But what he doesn't have is any claim on me. Or you." Something struck her then, and she studied Monica's face for a beat before she asked her question. "Have you avoided"—she gestured between the two of them—"this? Because you were worried about him?" Monica's grimace was all the answer she needed. "You know…" She picked up her wine and took a sip, watching Monica's face over the rim. She still held her hand, and now she squeezed it. "I want to be mad at you. I want to be so angry because"—she shook her head and gazed around the bar before bringing her attention back to the woman across from her—"we could've been exploring this." She gave their hands a little shake.

"Let's review, though, and go back to the part where you hated—er, excuse me. Where you *disliked* me for ten years. It wasn't all Cody."

"That's fair," Aubrey admitted. Because it was. Monica was absolutely right. "So, maybe…" She held Monica's gaze for a moment. "Maybe it was meant to be now. Fate and destiny and all that crap."

"You don't believe in all that crap."

"Maybe I'm wrong."

Monica gave her a little half grin. "Maybe you are."

"Don't get used to it. It doesn't happen often."

"I'm sure it doesn't."

They were still holding that delicious eye contact, and Aubrey's mind was playing her previews of kissing those amazing lips again, when her phone buzzed on the table next to her arm. When she glanced at it, she saw a text from her mother.

Call ASAP.

She sighed and let go of Monica's hand. "It's my mom. She has Emma, and she only texts if there's a problem."

Monica waved a shooing motion. "Absolutely. Go ahead."

She dialed and her mother picked up after half a ring. "Hi, sweetie, I'm so sorry. Emma's got a bug of some sort. She started throwing up about an hour ago, and I'd keep her here, but she just wants her mom."

"Okay, I'll be right there." She hung up the phone and blew out a long breath.

"Gotta go?"

She nodded. "I don't want to, if that helps. But Emma's sick."

"Oh no." Monica sat up straighter.

"I'm hoping it's a twenty-four-hour bug, but she's throwing up."

"Then go. I got this. Take care of your daughter." And she meant it, Aubrey could tell. She wasn't just being polite, and for that, Aubrey was immensely grateful. She picked up her purse, gathered her phone. "And please let me know how she is. And if you need anything. Okay?" Monica stood up with her.

"I will." There was a beat right then, a moment where things seemed to stop, just for a second, as their eyes met. Monica smiled, then leaned in and softly kissed her mouth.

"Go," she whispered. "And text me."

She turned and headed toward the door, her lips still sizzling.

❖

Emma's bug turned out to be more of a forty-eight-hour thing, and by Sunday evening, both she and Aubrey were exhausted. The throwing up had finally stopped—thank all the stars above for that—but Emma was weak and sleepy and just wanted her mom.

This was a part of parenting that Aubrey loved—the being needed. It was dwindling as Emma grew. And it was supposed to. She knew that. But nobody really prepared you, as a mother, for that very emotional long game. Every parent wanted their child to grow and become strong and independent. That was the goal. Of course it was. But they didn't tell you how hard it was when, little by little, they no longer needed you. And bouts of the flu or a stomach bug or a broken bone or, hell, even menstrual cramping were all things that made a kid revert back to needing her mom.

They were curled up on the couch where they'd been for pretty much the entire weekend. Disney+ was on the television, and she'd lost track of how many times they'd watched Emma's three favorites: *Frozen*, *Frozen 2*, and *Encanto*. Yes, when Emma was sick, she reverted not only to needing her mom, but also to the movies she'd loved when she was younger. Aubrey knew all three soundtracks backward and forward. Emma was snoring lightly, her head pillowed on Aubrey's chest, and Aubrey herself dozed on and off, having gotten very little sleep the past two nights. Her head was just starting to tip forward when her phone buzzed a text.

She smiled as she read Monica's words. *How's it going over there in Sick Kid Land?*

She typed back. *Hasn't puked in four hours, so I think we're in the clear. Sleeping now.*

The gray dots bounced. *And how is Mom? Have you eaten?*

She scoffed softly, then grinned as she typed. *Not in a long time. Days. Maybe weeks. Not sure. Too faint from hunger to do math. Life is a blur right now.*

Monica's response came immediately. *Good thing I'm in your driveway with a pizza.*

She gasped before she could catch it, and Emma stirred but didn't wake up. "You are not," she whispered, then paused the TV and carefully slid out from under her daughter, relieved when she stayed sleeping. She hurried to the front door, pulled it open, and sure enough, there was Monica's silver SUV.

The car door opened, and Monica slid out, a flat box in her hands. As she got closer, the scent of the pizza hit her, and Aubrey felt her mouth water in anticipation.

"You are a goddess, do you know that?" she asked, pushing up on her toes to give Monica a quick kiss on the mouth.

"Listen, I have other friends with kids, and I've seen them when their kids are sick. They're like camels. They don't eat or drink unless somebody makes sure they do." She held out the pizza. "So here's me, making sure you do."

"Come in."

They were quiet as they went back inside, tiptoed past the sleeping patient, and headed into the kitchen. Aubrey almost couldn't wait to get the box open and a slice of pizza into her mouth, and she did so in about three seconds flat. She looked at Monica with a sheepish grin as she chewed.

"So, you *were* kinda hungry," Monica said, chuckling and opening cupboards until she found plates.

"Just a little bit." She swallowed her second bite and sighed happily. "Thank you so much."

"You're welcome." Monica slid a piece onto her plate, then leaned her back against the counter. "Have you slept?"

Aubrey lifted one shoulder. "On and off."

"That's MomSpeak for no, not really." Monica craned her neck to get a peek at Emma. "She's out?"

Aubrey nodded. "Yeah, I think she's down for the night. Her fever broke about an hour ago. She hasn't thrown up since this afternoon. I think, now, she just needs to sleep. I'd like to try and get her into her own bed, though. We've been on the couch since very early yesterday morning."

"I can do it."

Aubrey looked at her with surprise. "Yeah?"

A nod. "Like I said, friends with kids." She set down her plate. "You eat. I got this."

It occurred to Aubrey then that she didn't know much of anything about Monica's family life, aside from the fact that her dad wasn't always around. But she wanted to know more. Where she'd grown up, were there siblings, what her relationship with her parents was like. There was so much information she found herself wanting that she hadn't cared to know before.

Before.

It was so weird, right?

She watched as Monica went into the living room and, without any visible struggle at all, hefted Emma up into her arms. Her daughter kept sleeping, and Monica carried her to the stairs.

There was a before and an after with them now, she realized right then, in an instant. Before: When she hated Monica. When she was an enemy. When she shouldered all the blame for something that wasn't entirely her fault. After: There was so much to the after, wasn't there? After the hate dissipated. After they'd talked, after they'd kissed, after they'd slept together, after, after, after. Life was different in the after. She liked it. A lot.

She heard Monica coming down the steps, but then the front door opened. Confused, she walked into the living room and glanced out the front windows to see Monica pulling two bags out of her SUV, and then she headed back in, shut the door, and carried the bags into the kitchen.

"What do you have?" she asked, curious now.

"Well, I know that you've been indisposed all weekend with a sick kid, and I figured there were probably some things you'd hoped to do but didn't get to." She reached into one of the bags and pulled out Reese's mini Peanut Butter Cups, fun-size Snickers bars, and mini KitKats, three bags of each. "Halloween is Thursday, you know."

Aubrey gasped softly. "Oh my God, you're right."

"I know your job gets crazy, so I thought I'd take this one chore off your hands."

She didn't know what to say. Really, truly didn't know how to express her gratitude. She was trying to figure out how when Monica reached into the second bag and pulled out a bottle of zinfandel.

"It's chilly out. You've had a hell of a weekend. Allow me to pour you a glass of wine?"

Her eyes filled with tears. She couldn't help it. She couldn't stop it. A small sob escaped, and she covered her mouth with a hand.

Instead of being freaked out by that, Monica just smiled and opened her arms. "Come here, baby."

Her exhaustion, her hunger, and her worry all decided to collide inside her body in that moment. Aubrey walked straight to her and let herself be wrapped up in Monica's embrace while she cried quietly in relief against her shoulder. Monica rubbed her back in soft circles. She pressed a kiss to the top of her head.

"You don't get much help from him, do you?" Monica asked softly.

Aubrey knew exactly who *him* was, and she shook her head, still burrowed into Monica's body, which was fast becoming a spot she never wanted to leave. "Not much, no." She quickly added, "I'm used to it, though."

"That's not something you should have to get used to." Monica's voice was quiet, but there was a steel quality to it.

"I know." What else could she say? It had always been this way. Cody was a once-in-a-while dad. Not because he didn't love his daughter. Because it was all he knew how to do.

"Here's the thing," Monica said. "When Emma is an adult, she'll remember. She'll understand." Aubrey moved back just a touch, so she could look into Monica's eyes. "I am very aware what a crappy father my dad was. When it was important. When I needed a dad. Sure, we're fine now. I love him. He loves me. And maybe he did the best that he could back then. But what I remember is him not being around. For my volleyball games. For my marching band parades. For my college graduation. He wasn't at any of those things, and I noticed." She glanced down at Aubrey. "What are you grinning at?"

"You were in the marching band?" She rolled her lips in and bit down on them. "What did you play?"

"The trumpet. Shut up." But she was grinning, and two little spots of pink blossomed on her cheeks.

"Oh my God. The trumpet, huh?" She squinted at her.

"What?"

"I'm trying to picture you with big cheeks full of air, like that famous trumpet player…What was his name?"

Monica sighed. "Louis Armstrong."

"Yes! Did your cheeks do that?"

"Hey. I brought you Halloween candy. Stop mocking me." She pushed playfully at Aubrey, pretending to be hurt, but she was still grinning.

"You did. You're right. I'll stop." But then she puffed her cheeks up as much as she could, making the face at Monica, who burst out laughing. And then they were both laughing, falling against each other.

And then they were kissing.

They were good at the frantic making out. Aubrey knew that from experience. But this was different. This was gentle. Tender. Monica held her face in both hands and moved her lips against Aubrey's, kissed her softly. Slowly.

It was the slow that was causing the heat to bloom in her center, her blood to speed up its flow. It was the slow that made her stomach tighten and her insides flutter. But mostly? It was the slow that made her feel held and seen and cherished and *safe*.

That last one caught her attention.

Monica made her feel safe.

She pulled back a bit and looked into those blue eyes. Eye contact was intense with Monica, something she'd never known before. It was like she was looking right into Aubrey's brain, into her soul, and could see everything she was thinking, everything she was feeling. She couldn't hide from Monica, and she understood that now. She couldn't. And she didn't want to.

Monica's hand slid down her arm and clasped her hand. "I bet you're exhausted. Let's take our wine and go sit."

It was as if the mere mention of the word *exhausted* manifested all of her actual exhaustion, and she suddenly felt absolutely bone-tired, like it hit her all at once. Her eyes felt scratchy. Her head began a low-key throbbing. Her muscles felt like jelly. They moved to the couch where the TV was still paused on Elsa with gauntlets over her magic hands. Monica arranged herself so she was kind of diagonally lounged in the corner and lifted her arm, indicating the space between her body and the back of the couch. Aubrey wasted no time fitting herself there, snuggling into Monica, and holy absurd relaxation, Batman, had she ever been more comfortable in her life? Like, ever?

No. The answer to that question was a resounding no. She sighed the sigh of somebody who been awake for about forty-three of the last forty-eight hours, and her body felt like it simply melted into Monica's. She tipped her head up so she could place a soft kiss on Monica's chin. Then she burrowed in closer, draped her arm over Monica's midsection, and remembered nothing at all after that.

❖

"Mom!" Emma's voice boomed through the house from upstairs. "Where's my guitar?"

"I haven't touched it," Aubrey called back from the living room where she was straightening up. "It's wherever you left it." She fluffed the throw pillows on the couch and was suddenly hit with a super vivid memory of waking up in the wee hours, cradled in Monica's arms, meeting those blue eyes, asking her how she hadn't fallen asleep at—she'd glanced at the clock on the wall behind Monica's head—three fourteen in the morning.

"I was watching over you," she'd said simply. Quietly. Matter-of-factly. And a line that could have come across super hokey ended up being one of the sweetest things anybody had ever said to her.

"Found it!" Emma shouted.

"Thank God," Aubrey mumbled, shaking her head. They'd pushed themselves up off the couch, to their mutual disappointment—though each of them understood that Emma waking up and finding her aunt Monica asleep on the couch with Aubrey in her arms wasn't something any of them were ready for—and Monica had kissed her softly and headed out into the October chill. At the last minute, Aubrey had whispered to her that she should come trick-or-treating with them that week. The way Monica's face had lit up had been beautiful.

"When's Aunt Monica coming?" Emma's voice startled her, as she was now standing next to her, Aubrey too lost in her daydreaming to have heard her tromping down the stairs.

"Anytime now." She stepped back and took in her daughter, dressed in a big, floofy purple gown and long blond wig. She had her fake guitar slung over her shoulder, and Aubrey had helped her paint her nails in different shades of purple because that's how Taylor Swift did it. "You look fantastic!" she said, beaming at her kid.

"I know!" she said with glee, bouncing on the balls of her feet. The doorbell rang before she could ask again when Monica was coming, and she flew to the door to open it. "Daddy?" she said, equal parts shocked and elated.

Daddy?

Shit.

Of all the days for Cody to step up and surprise his daughter, he picked today? Aubrey hurried to the entryway as Emma was stepping back to let him and Kimmy in.

"Hey, kiddo. Oh, that's an awesome purple dress. Are you a princess who plays the guitar?"

Emma rolled her eyes but didn't seem disappointed that he

didn't know who she was dressed as, and she bounced into the living room and they followed. "You're weird, Dad."

"I try." Cody's dark gaze moved to Aubrey. "Hey."

"Hi," she said. "I didn't know you guys were coming." It came out just a titch on the snippy side, and she winced internally at her tone.

He didn't seem to take offense, just smiled as Kimmy spoke. "We wanted to surprise Emma. Hope that's okay."

Aubrey nodded in approval and chose not to say anything remotely close to *About time* or *Finally* or *Thank you, Kimmy, for making him step up.*

That's when the doorbell rang again.

Please be trick-or-treaters, please be trick-or-treaters, please be trick-or-treaters...

"Is it Aunt Monica?" Emma asked, bouncing back to the door. She pulled it open as Cody shot Aubrey a look. Aubrey pretended not to see it. "It is! Hi, Aunt Monica. What do you think of my costume?"

"Oh my gosh, what's Taylor Swift from her Eras Tour doing here?" Aubrey couldn't see Monica yet, but just hearing her voice brought a tiny smile to her lips. "It's so nice to meet you, Ms. Swift, I love your music. I'm looking for Emma, have you seen her by any chance?"

"You're hilarious, Aunt Mon." Emma snorted her laugh as she turned and came back into the living room. Monica followed her, and shockingly, she didn't miss a beat when she saw Cody and Kimmy standing there.

"Hey, Codes. Kimmy. Good to see you." She shot that disarming smile at them.

Her greeting clearly flustered him, and Kimmy gave him a furrowed brow look. What had he thought would happen? Had he expected Monica to stumble upon seeing him? Stutter in her greeting? "Hey," was all he managed, but Kimmy greeted her with a hug.

Monica kept a safe distance between her body and Aubrey's as she stood next to her. What Aubrey suddenly realized, at that very moment, was just how undeniably sexy that was. To be so close to Monica, but not touch her? To not have Monica touching her in some way? It was like the world's biggest, sexiest tease. How the hell was she going to make it through the evening?

She'd made Emma wear a long-sleeve T-shirt under her purple dress, as the October evening was brisk. No rain or wind, luckily, just a bit of a chill, and they all headed out: Emma and her parents, her father's new wife, and her aunt who wasn't really her aunt and who was also sleeping with her mother. Unconventional families didn't get a whole lot more unconventional than them, that was for sure, and it was so ludicrous that it almost made Aubrey laugh out loud.

"What?" Monica asked softly as they walked.

Aubrey shook her head. "Tell you later."

The streets were busy, filled with little ones dressed as Elsa and Bluey and Dora. As the kids got older, the costumes changed to superheroes, Wonder Woman and Captain America and Iron Man. They only saw one other Taylor Swift, shockingly, and she wore a different outfit, so Emma was happy. They strolled up Aubrey's block, stopping at each house with a light.

"Didn't expect you to tag along," Cody said to Monica. His hands were in his pockets, and he only glanced at her for a second, as if he didn't want to maintain eye contact.

"Just thought it would be fun," Monica replied.

He shrugged, clearly trying to feign nonchalance. "Seems weird, though. You don't often show up for Emma's stuff out of the blue."

"I could say the same about you," Monica said.

Oh, shots fired, Aubrey thought, feeling her own jaw tense as Cody shot Monica a look of surprise. Aubrey glanced at Kimmy, who gave a little eye roll behind Cody's back, and Aubrey felt relief at that.

"I guess I just don't get why you're here. What you're doing." He shrugged again, like he didn't know what other gesture to make, and he still wasn't looking at Monica, but he was clearly trying to make some point.

"Honey," Kimmy said, her hand on his arm. "Maybe that's enough, yeah?"

Emma skipped back to them and called out, "Full-size Snickers!" as she zipped by and moved up the sidewalk to the next house, oblivious to the tension in the air around her adults.

"If you have something to say, just say it." Monica's voice had gone low and quiet and firm. Aubrey could feel the anger, as well as the pain, rolling off her in waves. Cody was her best friend, and he was openly hurting her.

"Fine. I will. I don't like this." He waved a finger between Monica and Aubrey. "I don't like it and I think you're going to hurt her." He pointed at the house where Emma had her bag open for candy. "And maybe her, too. I've seen you leaving women on the side of the road, like passengers you drive just so far. Then you make them get out, and you drive on, and they're left there. You don't let them stay. You never have."

Kimmy murmured Cody's name as the four of them stood there, his words settling around them like snow. Or maybe ash was a better analogy, since he'd just basically burned Monica alive in front of the other two. Her gorgeous blue eyes welled up, and her cheeks and ears had flushed red, and Aubrey put a hand on her arm, but she stepped away, nodding slowly. She kept walking backward, still nodding. When she finally met Aubrey's eyes, she whispered, "Please tell Em I said bye." Then she turned and hurried away, and Aubrey knew she wouldn't be waiting at the house, that she was leaving.

Aubrey had three things she wanted to do, and she couldn't do two of them. She wanted to chase after Monica. She wanted to level Cody. And she wanted to protect Emma from all of it. It was only Emma's bouncing back to the three of them, a big smile on her face, that kept Aubrey from unloading on Cody.

"Hey, where's Aunt Monica?" Emma asked, looking around.

"She had to run, sweetie, but she said to tell you good-bye." Aubrey didn't look at Cody as she spoke.

"Aw, bummer." Like any kid would, she then shook it off when her gaze was caught by something across the street. "Hey! There's Hazel. Can I go say hi?"

Aubrey nodded. "Just watch for cars, please," she called after her daughter, who'd taken off before Aubrey had even finished her nod. She watched until she was safely across the street, then whirled on Cody. "What the hell is wrong with you?"

He looked like he was going to argue with her, but Kimmy stepped between them. "I think we've all said enough for tonight." She met Aubrey's eyes. "I'm going to take him home and maybe you guys should talk tomorrow." She glanced around pointedly. "When we're not surrounded by young ears. Okay?" And before either of them could answer, she was tugging Cody down the street.

Aubrey stood on the sidewalk, now alone, shaking her head slowly. Because what the fuck had just happened? Where did Cody get off, thinking he had a say in her dating life? Why did he think it was okay to humiliate someone—his best friend!—in front of other people? And was this a thing Monica did regularly when things got tough? Run away? Because that was *not* gonna fly. She typed out a quick text to her, asking if she was okay. When it went unread for nearly twenty minutes, she felt her anger go from a simmer to a low boil. Running and avoidance. Terrific.

"Mom, come on," Emma said.

Aubrey tracked her daughter's gaze as she watched her father and stepmother hurrying away, leaving her with just Aubrey. But it was what she was used to, and she shrugged it off faster than Aubrey ever had. "I'm coming," Aubrey said and hurried to catch up with her at the next house.

❖

The next day was Friday, and Aubrey threw herself into her work. When businesses had started to shift employees away from the office to working from home, she was way ahead of the curve, having already worked from home for years. The beauty of a phone-based job, especially one centered around customer service, was that you could do it from almost anywhere. Her small desk fit perfectly in a corner of her dining room, and that's where she sat on Friday just before lunch, deescalating an escalated call.

While most people might worry that their life being stressful would somehow make them less patient with customers on the phone, Aubrey found the opposite to be true. The more chaotic her home life, the calmer she was with the customers, even the ones who were, as her father would put it, losing their shit on her. She hadn't heard from Monica for the rest of Thursday night, and she'd woken up that morning to still no text, and she was just about over these adults in her life who acted like children. She focused on her daughter, and then, once she was off to school, on her job. Aubrey sat down at her desk with her coffee and completely lost track of time.

When her doorbell rang, it startled her so much that she gave a little hop in her chair. The escalated customer was now thanking her profusely for fixing his problem, and she told him he was welcome, nudged him off the phone, then hurried to the door, hoping against all odds it was Monica, coming over to apologize, kiss her, rip her clothes off, anything that wasn't this childish silence that Aubrey was so sick of she wanted to scream.

"Hey," Cody said as she pulled the door open, and her face must've registered her disappointment. "Sorry. It's just me."

"Great," she said and turned away, leaving the door open for him to walk through. She headed into the kitchen to refill her coffee. "What do you want, Cody?" she asked and recognized the tone of her own voice as just tired. Because he had exhausted her just as much as Monica had.

"I came to apologize." He'd followed her into the kitchen and stood there, watching her as she held her mug with both hands and sipped.

"Okay." He grimaced and she said nothing. Maybe she was the one being childish now, but she wasn't about to make this easy on him.

He gestured to the coffeepot. "Can I get some of that?"

She shrugged and moved away. "Help yourself."

He did, taking his time stirring sugar in. She watched him. He sipped.

"Jesus, Cody, I have a job. What do you want?" Yes, it was snarky. Yes, there was anger, but she was justified, wasn't she? For the first time in years, she wondered if she'd be in Cody's life at all today if not for Emma. She'd always thought yes, but maybe she'd been wrong. He was selfish and infuriating and, yes, she still loved him in some way, but my God, he drove her mad.

He had the good sense not to get angry at her sharp tone, and she had to give him points for that. He clearly knew he'd stepped in it. "I need to just tell you how sorry I am for the way I acted last night. I..." He shook his head. "It was all kinds of wrong."

"That's absolutely true. It was a night for our daughter, and you made it about you and your feelings."

He nodded. "I know. That's on me." He gazed off into the distance.

Aubrey set her mug on the counter with a thud. "What is going on with you?" she asked, because there was clearly something. And as she watched his face, she felt a strange sense of surprise work its way up to her brain because right before her eyes, Cody's face flushed a light pink and his eyes filled with tears. Tears! "Cody." Her tone was soft. "What is it?"

He blinked rapidly and ran his palm over his face. "I stayed up with Kimmy last night, just talking about this whole thing, this whole"—he made a gesture around Aubrey—"you and Monica. Because she couldn't understand why it bothers me so much, and neither could I, if I'm being honest."

"*Okay,*" she said, drawing the word out because she was totally uncertain where this was going.

"And I finally—*finally*—realized a couple of things." He moved to the small table, pulled out a chair, and dropped into it as if his legs had given out.

Aubrey followed him, sitting across from him, her eyes scanning his face. It was a face that she'd known so well, once upon a time, and still did. But now, she was having trouble reading it.

"The first thing." He cleared his throat, and Aubrey could see there was some shame around what he was about to say. "I realized that if you and Monica become a thing, which you already seem to kinda be, and you spend time with her and things progress and go wherever they're gonna go, then the likelihood of you no longer blaming her for what happened between us on our wedding day is pretty high. You've always blamed her. I know that." He scratched at an invisible spot on the table with his thumbnail. "And if you no longer blame her, then you'll probably blame me."

She watched as he scratched the tabletop, and when he looked up and met her gaze, there was clear worry there. She almost laughed but realized it probably wasn't a reaction that would help the situation, so she did her best to keep her voice gentle. "How about this—how about it was ten very long years ago when we were *so* young, we both have full lives now, we share a great kid, and maybe this is the way things were supposed to go? How about I don't blame anybody? I kinda like that better, don't you?" The relief on his face was so comical, it was almost cartoonlike, and Aubrey had a hard time not bursting out in laughter. "Was that really so big a concern for you?"

His eyes went wide and he shook his head. "I just didn't want to spend the rest of our kid's life with you hating me."

What she wanted to say was *Wow, you really are self-centered, aren't you?* What she actually said was, "Cody, I never hated you. I was hurt and angry and confused, but I never hated you." And it was the truth. More relief washed over him, she could see it. His shoulders relaxed, and he reached across the table to grasp her hand. She let him, and they stayed that way for a long moment. "What's the other thing," she asked after a while.

"What other thing?"

"You said you realized two things last night."

"I did, didn't I?"

She nodded.

He took in a deep breath and blew it out slowly. Aubrey got the impression he was choosing his words carefully. "I have another stop to make after you. I need to find Monica. Talk to her. Apologize to her."

"I think that's a good idea. She's your best friend and you were a dick to her last night."

His turn to nod. "I know."

"How come?"

"Because I realized something recently. And instead of thinking about it and rolling it around and accepting it, I got pissed off and acted like an asshole." She saw his Adam's apple move as he swallowed. "I realized that Monica has always been in love with you. Like, always. Since college."

She blinked at him. Blinked some more. Cleared her throat. "I, um…" Cleared it again. "I didn't know it at the time, but I've had a few people say she had a thing for me…" She let the thought dangle because Cody's words were specific. He hadn't said Monica had a thing for her. Or that she liked her. Or that she'd wanted to date her. No. He'd said something much more powerful, and she needed to know if he was being hyperbolic.

"No," he said, as if reading her mind. "It was more than a thing. She's been in love with you for years. It's so obvious to me now, I don't know how I never put it together."

"She didn't want you to."

"You're right. She didn't want me to know, and she never did anything about it because…ugh." Again, he wiped his palm over his face. "God, I'm an asshole. How did I not see it?"

And Aubrey understood it all in that very moment. Just like that, it all became clear. "Because you're her best friend."

"Yeah."

"And she thought I hated her."

"Yes."

"To be fair, I did for a while." She gave a sad chuckle when she realized the scope of what Monica had done. She'd saved both her and Cody from making a huge mistake that would have tainted the rest of their lives, yes, but she'd also destroyed her chances of ever being with the woman she'd fallen for, because one thing best friends never did was date each other's exes. "God, she must've been so lonely."

"I know, right?"

She studied his face hard.

"What?" he asked, literally squirming in his chair.

"You guys are very much alike. You both handle crises like children. You get mean, and she runs away." She blew out a breath of frustration. "It's exhausting. You both exhaust me."

Cody grimaced. "Kimmy says the same thing."

She couldn't help but laugh. "Listen to me, Cody—hold on to that girl. She's a keeper."

And then it was his turn to laugh. "I couldn't agree more."

Cody left not long after that, after Aubrey's headset had gone off a few times, reminding her that it was a workday. She wished she could be a fly on the wall during the conversation between him and Monica. She wondered what he'd say about her. More than that, she wondered what Monica would say.

The alarm on her watch went off, reminding her it was time to pick up Emma from school. They headed to her parents' house to order pizza and hang out, which they did often on Friday nights. After a long workweek, it was nice to share some of the load with her parents, and they were always thrilled to have time with their only grandchild.

She'd stopped checking her phone for a text from Monica sometime after the pizza was gone and just before her father brought out a stack of board games.

"Bananagrams first," Emma shouted. "Bananagrams first."

Her father met her gaze. "Well, you're screwed," he said with a twinkle in his eye, knowing just how bad Aubrey was at the word game.

"Doesn't matter. I'll kick all your butts later." She pointed a finger at each of the three of them consecutively, and they all laughed as Emma unzipped the cloth banana and dumped out all the letter tiles. It was fine. It was totally okay that she'd heard nothing from Monica, a pretty clear sign that she didn't really want this after all, no matter what she'd said or how long she'd been in— Nope. Nope. Not going there. Not here. Not now. She had more important things to do with people who wanted to be around her, who wanted to spend time with her, talk to her. People who loved her. She was going to get her ass trounced by her daughter in Bananagrams—and probably by her parents as well because this game truly hated her—and then she was going to return the favor when they played Taboo. They'd stuff themselves full of more pizza and cookies her mother had made, and then she and Emma would head home, and she'd put her daughter to bed and then she'd pour herself a glass of wine, take it up to her room, and read a romance about people who were unrealistic and who actually talked to each other and who would end up living happily ever after at the end. And then she would turn the light off and go to sleep because her book was fiction.

Sleeping alone was her reality.

And she would *not* cry about it, damn it.

Or maybe she would…

❖

November had gone zipping right past chilly and directly into downright cold. Aubrey was very glad she had nowhere to go on Saturday. She'd slept like crap, her dreams—while she couldn't remember vivid details—filled with frustration and confusion. She knew that the second she'd opened her eyes at five thirty-seven, her brain foggy and her heart beating a bit faster than usual for first thing in the morning. She'd lain there for another half hour, trying to drift back off, but it wasn't happening, so she'd hauled herself out of bed and headed downstairs to scrub her kitchen sink. Because why not?

"Mom!" Emma called now from upstairs where she and her friend Jessie were holed up, doing whatever it was that ten-year-old girls did when they had a Saturday afternoon free. "Can we have pizza rolls?"

"On it," Aubrey called back, the box of frozen pizza rolls already in her hand. "Do I know my kid or what?" she murmured to the empty kitchen. Once they were in the oven, timer set, she grabbed the furniture polish and dustcloth from under the sink and went to work dusting the living room. The timer went off just as she heard Emma lumbering down the stairs as if there were four of her.

"Hey, good timing," Emma said as she bounced into the kitchen to the fridge. "Can we have sodas, too?"

Aubrey slid on an oven mitt and pulled out the sheet of pizza rolls. "Sure." Once they were on a plate, she handed it over to Emma, along with two cans of soda and a few napkins she knew wouldn't be used. "Don't make a mess. And bring the plate back down as soon as you're done."

Emma headed toward the stairs with her goodies. "'Kay."

"I mean it, Emma. I don't want to find that plate under your bed with creepy stuff growing on it a week from now."

"'Kay," she said again, louder this time, and Aubrey made a mental note to go up in a little while and grab the plate. She'd learned the hard way that just because her daughter acknowledged what she'd said, that didn't mean she'd actually *heard* it.

With the dusting finished, she pulled the vacuum out of the closet and gave the living room carpet a good once-over. She was rolling it back into the closet when she caught a glimpse of herself in the foyer mirror. She'd piled her dark hair up in a messy bun on her head. No makeup but moisturizer, so her light freckles were visible. She had decent skin, so her face looked fine aside from the slight dark circles under her eyes that told the world she hadn't slept well. She wore black joggers and her favorite long-sleeve white T-shirt that had been washed and worn to the perfect softness.

Just as she closed the closet, the doorbell rang, startling her enough to make her jump. She wasn't expecting anybody, and she figured it might be Jessie's mom, come a little early to pick the girls up for the birthday party sleepover they were headed to tonight. She pulled the door open, and it was not Jessie's mom. Not even close.

"Hi," Monica said, her expression telling Aubrey that it wouldn't surprise her at all to have the door closed in her face. In fact, she looked like she expected it.

"Hey." Aubrey could come up with nothing more to say. No. That was a lie. She could come up with lots to say, but none of it was pleasant, all of it was rude, and rather than be that person, she kept her mouth shut.

"Can I talk to you?" Monica glanced toward the stairs, the loud giggling coming from up there likely clueing her in that Emma was home.

"Sure." Aubrey failed at swallowing her sigh, but she stood aside to let her in, thankful to close the door against the cold fall wind that had picked up.

Monica gave a little full-body shiver. "Cold today," she said, and Aubrey wasn't about to stand there and discuss the weather.

"What's up?" she asked, folding her arms over her chest and leaning on the doorjamb between the entryway and the living room.

Monica shot another glance at the stairs, then moved farther into the living room, forcing Aubrey to follow her. Which was annoying, but Aubrey supposed she agreed that Emma didn't need to overhear any of this conversation. And then Monica moved even farther into the house, to the little dining space between the living room and kitchen.

This time, Aubrey let her sigh loose in an obvious show of annoyance. But she followed Monica anyway.

Once they were both standing in the dining area, Monica wet her lips, took a deep breath, and dived in. "Okay. Listen. First of all, I'm so sorry about Halloween. I should not have gone stomping away like a child."

Aubrey tipped her head one way and then the other. "I mean, Cody was being a dick, so I understood why you wanted to leave."

"You did? Okay. Okay, good. That's good."

"But then you were MIA for the rest of the night. And all day the next day. And all day today, until right now."

Monica hung her head. "I know."

"Like a child, Monica."

A nod. "I know. You're right. I'm so sorry. I shouldn't have done that. I was just so hurt—"

Aubrey held up a hand, stopping her in midsentence. "I know you were hurt. Of course you were hurt. I would've been, too. But you ran. And then you went to radio silence. Just left me dangling out there alone, not knowing if you were okay, not able to talk to you about it. You and Cody both. You acted like children."

Monica's throat moved as she swallowed, but she kept up eye contact, which Aubrey gave her mental points for.

"At least he was here yesterday to apologize. He beat you. Which was disappointing."

"I know. He told me."

"Ah, so you two have talked."

"Yes." Monica clasped her hands together and tapped both index fingers against her chin as if sorting through her words before speaking them. "I called him yesterday, and he told me what he'd said to you. About me." She was blinking a lot, and she swallowed again, and her knuckles were white as she kept her hands clasped, and it occurred to Aubrey in that moment that Monica was very, very nervous. And seeing her like that was slowly chipping away at the icy outer coating Aubrey had built around herself. But she fought it.

"Okay," Aubrey said. She didn't shrug, because that would've just been mean. But she wasn't about to make this easy for Monica.

Monica lifted her arms out from her sides and let them drop. "Apparently, this is what happens when it comes to my feelings for you. I revert to being ten."

Aubrey tipped her head one way, then the other, as she said, "Maybe seven. Emma's ten, and she handles hard stuff better than you have."

A laugh shot out of Monica. "Okay. Ouch. Also, fair point."

"Yeah, that was harsh, but seriously, what's with the running away and silent treatment?"

"It's because it's you!" Monica seemed shocked by her own emotion, and her entire body seemed tense. Tight. Frustrated.

Aubrey blinked at her, and they stood like that for what felt like several minutes. Finally, Aubrey asked quietly, "Can I ask you something?"

"I think you just did."

"You're hilarious."

"I try."

"Your timing could use work."

"Not the first time I've heard that."

"I'm being serious right now."

Monica nodded, inhaled, then let it out slowly, as if bracing herself for Aubrey's inquiry. "Of course you can ask me something."

Aubrey watched her face for a moment before she spoke, took in the worn jeans, the deep blue of her sweater that really brought out her eyes. God, she was beautiful. Aubrey cleared her throat. "There have been a few people we know who've sort of mentioned in passing that they thought you had a thing for me back then. In college."

"They've mentioned that, huh?" Monica chewed on the inside of her cheek and glanced away.

"Yes. And you said your heart has always been with somebody else."

"I did say that."

"And I asked you who, and you avoided answering me."

More nodding from Monica. Aubrey waited. Watched the different emotions play out across Monica's face. Worry. Uncertainty. Resignation. Fear. And they all seemed to chase any anger Aubrey still held not only out of her head, but out of the room, like it had been herded right out the window and into the windy November day, blown away down the street. She felt like her heart had leapt into her throat and got stuck there, keeping her from swallowing and making breathing difficult.

A moment went by. Another. Then Monica finally said, "I didn't hear a question in there."

And Aubrey couldn't wait any longer. She had to know. She *had* to. "Your heart has always been with somebody else." Her voice dropped to barely a whisper as she asked, "Is it me?"

The world seemed to cease spinning. Time stopped. Blue eyes sparkled in the afternoon light coming through the windows. Monica reached out and closed her warm, soft hand over Aubrey's, tugged her closer, right into her space. She hooked a finger under Aubrey's chin and lifted until she looked up at her face, looked her in the eyes, and then she said, very quietly, "It's always been you, Aubrey."

Before Aubrey could stop them, tears filled her eyes, then spilled over, tracking hot moisture down each cheek.

Monica brushed one away. "You're not supposed to cry when somebody says something like that to you."

Aubrey laughed. "They're good tears. They're happy tears." She sniffled and used her fingertips to wipe the tears away. "I'm so relieved."

"How come?"

Aubrey gave her a look of disbelief. "Seriously? How do you think it would've felt if I asked that question and you said something like *Oh no, it's not you. It's this super hot chick at my gym* or something?"

Monica gazed up toward the ceiling as she tapped her forefinger against her chin and said, "I mean, there *is* this super hot chick at my gym—" Aubrey gave her a playful swat before she could finish, and they both laughed, even as Monica kept hold of Aubrey's hand. Their laughter died down, and then it was just the two of them, alone in the dining room, holding hands and reveling in a possible future that neither of them knew had existed only five minutes earlier.

Aubrey spoke first. "This is…" She shook her head, trying to find the exact perfect word.

"Amazing? Terrifying? Hard to believe? Confusing? Concerning? The most incredible thing ever?"

"All. All of the above." Aubrey studied her face for a moment, still grinning, and said with sincerity, "You're actually very funny."

"If you hadn't spent ten years avoiding me, you'd know this already."

"Valid." Their gazes held, and it was suddenly very comfortable, like these were the eyes she was supposed to be looking into all the time. Just as she stepped closer, Monica pulled her in and their lips met. The kiss was soft, tender, and full of promise.

"Here's my plate, Mom." Emma's voice reached her ears as if it had started from far away and then was right next to her and screaming. She jumped back from Monica with a gasp of surprised horror, and she turned as Emma walked past them and into the kitchen with her dish, calling over her shoulder, "Hey, Aunt Mon."

Aubrey knew she was wide-eyed because she could literally feel it, the air on her eyeballs. She gaped at Monica, who had a stricken look on her face that likely matched hers. And seriously, every other time Emma came down the stairs, she sounded like a herd of bison, but this time, she—what—tiptoed? With one last mortified look at Monica, she turned to her daughter. "So, honey, what you just saw—"

"You guys making out? Yeah, I know."

Aubrey squinted at her. "You know what?"

"I know you like each other and might be dating." She shrugged like what she just said was no big deal at all.

"I...what..." She shook her head and gaped at Emma. "How?"

Emma sighed and rolled her eyes because, clearly, adults were so annoying. "The night I was sick. I came down to get a drink of water and you guys were sleeping on the couch."

Aubrey turned to look at Monica, who looked just as stunned as she felt. She remembered when they'd woken up in the middle of the night, Monica's arms wrapped around her, the two of them twined together like vines. Monica brought her hand to her forehead, shook her head, and shrugged in clear apology.

"What?" Emma said, obviously irritated to be kept from her company upstairs. "Aunt Monica's gay. You're bi. You guys like each other. No big." She shrugged again and headed through the living room. "Jessie's mom's coming at four to take us to the slumber party," she called back, and then the running of the bulls was back as she rumbled up the stairs loudly enough to make the pictures on the wall shake.

Silence reigned where they stood. Finally, she turned to Monica, frowning. "What the hell just happened?"

"I think your kid just outed us," Monica said, and then she did something so unexpected that Aubrey stood there watching in horrified fascination.

She laughed.

It started softly, like a little snort-laugh through her nose, but then it grew. Steadily. She clearly tried to stop, but that just made it worse. Aubrey tried to stay stoic and serious because this *was* serious, damn it, but watching Monica laugh made that so difficult, and the next thing she knew, she'd joined in, laughing with her until it grew so much that they were full-on cracking up, complete with gasping for breath and eyes that leaked tears of humor and leaning against walls and furniture to keep from falling down laughing.

Another earthquake hit, and suddenly Emma was at the bottom of the stairs, peeking around the doorjamb at them, clearly wondering what the noise was. They both stopped laughing instantly, which made Emma blink at them exactly twice before she rolled her eyes, shook her head, and informed them, "You guys are so weird," before heading back up to her company.

Both of them laughed again but were able to get themselves under control after a moment. Then Monica stepped closer and took Aubrey's face in her hands. "Where were we?"

Aubrey lifted her chin until their lips were but a hair's breadth apart. "Right about here, I think?" she whispered, and she didn't think she could wait one more second to kiss Monica's mouth again.

"Did I hear Emma say she was going to a slumber party tonight?"

"You did."

"Wanna have one of our own?"

"More than anything."

❖

Aubrey stood with the front door open, waving good-bye to her daughter, who was climbing into Jessie's mother's car.

Thank Jesus, Mary, and Joseph.

"Have fun!" she called as the chilly November wind did its best to coax goose bumps out onto her arms. She watched as the car backed out of the driveway and headed down the street, and only then did she shut the door and turn around.

Monica was right there. Like, right there, waiting for her, and before Aubrey could say a word, her back hit the door, and Monica's mouth was on hers, and oh my God, how had she waited so long to kiss these lips and not died of deprivation? Of starvation? Of loneliness? Of going mad?

She grabbed Monica's face with both hands and deepened the kiss, pressed her tongue into Monica's mouth, and was rewarded with a soft moan that only kicked her arousal to the next level. She wrenched her mouth from Monica's, grabbed her hand, and tugged her toward the stairs. "I can't wait any more," she said, the huskiness of her own voice surprising her.

"Same."

They practically ran up the stairs.

It started out fast. Hurried. Desperate. As if having sex would cure every problem in the world. Clothes flew off. They undressed each other and themselves at the same time until both of them stood naked, face-to-face, and then it all slowed down. Because diving right in would be easy. And Aubrey could do it, absolutely. It wouldn't be hard because Monica had the most gorgeous body she'd ever seen, and who wouldn't want to grab it and have their way with it? But tonight was different. They hadn't talked about it, hadn't mentioned it to each other, but Aubrey felt it in the air, and she was certain Monica did, too. The importance. The reverence. That this was *something*.

She stepped closer, into Monica's space, and tilted her chin up to kiss her. And this slowed down, too. She took her time, explored Monica's lips, took a moment to taste her, really taste her, before easing her tongue in. Monica melted into her. That's what it felt like. Like a melding, as if they were simply becoming one.

They moved to the bed, and Aubrey followed Monica, crawling up her body until she was on all fours above her, looking down into those captivating blue eyes. They were glistening with emotion, and Aubrey could see it so clearly. Aubrey stroked fingertips down Monica's face. "I know," she whispered. "Me too."

It wasn't sex. Not this time. Not with Monica. No, for the first time in more than ten years, Aubrey made love with somebody. They moved slowly, but together, their bodies almost fluid, gliding together, moving as one, but there was *more*. So much more. Aubrey wanted to touch, explore, taste every single part of Monica. She wanted to memorize her. Every dip. Every curve. Every intake of breath, every whimper, every moan. She wanted to categorize them, store them in her mind and in her heart forever, and she wondered—no, she *hoped*—that Monica was feeling the same way. She closed her mouth over a nipple and sucked gently on it until Monica began to writhe under her. Eventually, she switched to the other one. Back and forth, back and forth, until Monica was turning her head from side to side, biting her bottom lip, moving her hips, her breathing ragged. Only then did Aubrey trail her tongue down Monica's torso, stopping to kiss, suck, nibble various spots.

Pushing herself up onto her knees between Monica's legs, she gazed down at her. This beautiful woman was laid out before her, legs open, completely vulnerable to her, and Aubrey felt a sudden wave of emotion, a wave of such honor, joy, and privilege. How lucky was she?

Monica's gaze never wavered, their eyes locked to one another, and she reached up to touch Aubrey's chest, to grasp a nipple between her fingers, to give it a gentle tug, and Aubrey felt that tug between her legs, as if there was a string connecting the two.

Aubrey opened her mouth to say something, but the words lodged in her throat, and the welling of her eyes surprised her. She closed her mouth again, but Monica's gaze never wavered.

"I know," she whispered. "Me too."

"Yeah?" Aubrey asked softly.

Monica nodded, and they stayed that way for a moment before Monica spoke again. "God, you're beautiful," she said. "I really like this view."

"Do you?"

"Oh yeah."

"Well, don't get used to it because I'm busy." With her hands on Monica's inner thighs, she pressed them open farther, then lowered herself to Monica's glistening center. Again, she took her time, kissing and tasting Monica's thighs, behind her knees, that sensitive skin just above her center. Monica's fingers dug into her hair, and Aubrey watched her body as she hovered close. Breaths ragged and hips undulating, Monica glanced up and caught Aubrey's gaze.

"Please?" she whispered, and her fingers tightened in Aubrey's hair. "Please, Aubrey?"

It was all she needed. With no more preamble, she swiped her tongue over Monica's wetness, from top to bottom, and pulled a long moan from her, so deep it was almost a growl. It was so fucking sexy, so Aubrey did the same thing again and got the same sound.

"God, I love listening to you," she said before pressing her entire mouth against Monica's center. That was all it took. Monica came, hard and loud, grasping Aubrey's hair so tightly it was almost painful, her other hand clutching the edge of the comforter. She arched her head back, and Aubrey could see that glorious straining column of neck as Monica's hips rose up off the bed and Aubrey held on in order to keep her mouth in the right place. She rode the orgasm out with Monica, her own center throbbing deliciously, until Monica's hips slowly lowered back down to the mattress.

As she caught her breath, Monica threw an arm over her eyes but also gestured to Aubrey with a rolling of the other hand. "You," she said, not uncovering her eyes. "Here." She pointed at her own chest. Aubrey laughed, gave her one last swipe with her tongue, which made Monica's entire lower body spasm, then crawled up her warmth and settled her own on it.

"*Yes*," Monica said, drawing out the *S*. She wrapped both arms around Aubrey and squeezed her. "I like you on me."

"It's a nice fit. Gotta admit that." She wiggled her hips a little bit.

And then they were quiet. Their quiet breathing was the only sound as Aubrey lay there, enjoying every inch of their bodies that touched. The smoothness. The heat. The safety. She lifted her head off Monica's chest and propped her chin in her hand. "I could do this," she said. It was vague at best, but she could tell by the expression on Monica's face that she got it.

"You think so?"

"I do. And more than that, I *want* to do this." She reached up and brushed some hair off Monica's forehead, and she heard her swallow. This time, it was Monica's eyes that filled.

"So do I."

The rush of happiness Aubrey felt in that moment was something she'd hold on to for years. She knew it right then. "Two things, though."

Monica narrowed her eyes. "Ooh, ominous. Okay, hit me."

"Number one, you can't go running away every time we fight."

Monica scrunched up her nose and slowly nodded. "I know. You're right."

"None of this avoidance shit. If we argue, we stay put and we talk it out. Deal?"

"Deal."

Aubrey made a show of searching her face. Satisfied, she gave one nod. "Good. Number two, we're gonna get crap from people."

"What people? Cody?" Monica scoffed, which made Aubrey laugh.

"Yes, Cody, for one."

"We can handle Cody. Besides, he's already getting used to it."

"You think?"

"He might need a bit more time, but he'll be fine. Who else?"

Aubrey nibbled on her bottom lip as she thought about it. "I mean...Emma?"

"Didn't seem too fazed earlier."

Aubrey grinned. "That's so true. Wow." She glanced upward for a beat before saying, "Okay, yeah, that's it."

They laughed together quietly, and then Monica's expression grew serious. "I think..." She swallowed and cleared her throat, and her eyes started to glisten again. "I think we could have something, Aubrey. Something incredible. All we need to do is take the chance."

It sounded so simple.

Monica reached up to tuck some hair behind Aubrey's ear. "What do you say? Wanna take a chance with me?"

She looked at this woman. Really looked at her, looked beyond the sparklingly gorgeous exterior, looked inside. She felt like she could see everything about her. Her heart. Her soul. Her love. Oh yeah, it was there. She remembered Cody saying Monica was in love with her, and how it had surprised her, but it didn't now. It was right there, plain as could be. There was no way Aubrey could not see it. Monica was most definitely in love with her.

Good thing, because she was in love, too.

"I do," she said, then lowered her mouth to kiss her. "I do," she whispered again.

WEDDINGS DOWN: 5
SUCCESS AT AVOIDING MONICA WALLACE: NOT EVEN TRYING

Epilogue

Aubrey and Monica
December 12, 2026
Small Church Service

Aubrey McFadden *is* getting married.

Today.

Twenty-six months later

"Oh, Mom." Emma stood still, her eyes wide and shimmering, the fingertips of one hand covering her lips.

"Don't cry," Aubrey said over her shoulder with a tender smile. "You'll ruin your makeup."

Emma nodded and seemed to take a moment to collect her twelve-year-old self. Their eyes met in the mirror that Aubrey stood in front of. "You look so beautiful."

Aubrey's smile seemed like it never left her face lately. She gazed at her own reflection, then that of her daughter, and her heart felt like it got a little bit fuller—something she didn't think was even possible in the recent two years and change. "You're one to talk," she said, turning to regard her kid face-to-face. "Look at you, my little bean. You're so…" She searched for a different description than the one that popped into her head, but with no luck, so she resigned herself. "You're so grown up."

Emma reached out and picked at some invisible lint on Aubrey's gown, then toyed with a curl at the end of her hair. "You should wear your hair like this more often. It looks great."

Aubrey didn't have the heart to tell her that it had cost an arm and a leg to get her hair looking like this, and after today, she'd be going back to her regular shampoo and the flat iron she'd purchased from Amazon. But today? Today was all about the best. She wanted to look her best. She wanted the food to be the best. She'd bought her daughter the dress she'd liked the best. All because she was about to marry the best. Not just the best woman she'd ever known, but the best person. The best human. How the hell had she gotten so lucky?

The door to the back room of the church opened again, and this time it was Trina, back from her mission to find—

"Got it!" She pulled an opened bottle of white wine from behind her back.

"Oh, bless you," Aubrey said with a laugh, holding out her hand and wiggling her fingers. "I'm so damn nervous. I just need to take the edge off." Realizing there were no glasses or cups, she bent forward to keep her dress out of the way and sipped directly from the bottle. It wasn't expensive wine, but it was cold and it was alcohol, and it did the trick. She handed the bottle back to Trina, who took a sip herself, then handed it to Emma. At Aubrey's incredulous look, she lifted one shoulder in a half shrug.

Emma sipped, made a face, and handed the bottle back. When she turned away, Trina sidled close enough to Aubrey to whisper, "Lightweight. Just like her mother."

Aubrey bumped her with a shoulder.

"Wait until you see the church," Trina said. "It's so pretty out there with the twinkle lights and mistletoe and silver garland and stuff. It's like a magical Christmas land."

Then they stood there in front of the mirror. Emma joined them, and Aubrey just stared at the three of them. Her, her maid of honor, and her matron of honor. They looked stunning in their matching red gowns. Her own gown was gorgeous. Off the shoulder, tapered waist, lace trim, hugged her hips in the most flattering way. No veil, just some baby's breath and mistletoe woven into her dark hair.

"Monica's gonna faint when she sees you," Trina said softly, and Emma nodded her agreement.

Aubrey met Trina's eyes in the mirror, then Emma's. "You two," she said, and keeping herself from choking up suddenly became the hardest thing in the world. She reached for their hands and held one in each of hers. "I don't know what I'd do without you. Thank you for being here." When she noticed that all three of them were on the verge of tears, she added, "I'd kiss you both, but I can't afford to have your makeup redone." Trina and Emma both laughed, and then Aubrey said, "Can you guys give me a minute?"

"Time for a pep talk," Emma said, but her tone was affectionate. Aubrey brought her daughter's hand up to her lips and kissed it, then let it go and watched in the mirror as she and Trina left, closing the door quietly behind them with a soft click.

She took a deep breath, then let it out slowly. "Okay. This is it. You've been waiting for this day your whole life. Since you were little. Soak it in. It's gonna go by in a blur, but do your best to take it in. Remember it forever."

There was a knock on the door. It opened just slightly and Cody peeked in. "Everybody decent?"

To say Aubrey had a mild flash of panic would have been an understatement, as her heart rate kicked up to jackhammer speed, and she looked at Cody in disbelief, the sense of déjà vu so strong it almost knocked her off balance.

Cody must've realized it because he stepped quickly toward her with a small laugh and grabbed her arm. "Oh no. No, no, don't worry. Everything's fine. You're getting married today."

There was a beat of silence where the two of them just stood and looked at each other before Aubrey released a breath of relief. "Oh my God, what are you trying to do to me?" She pressed a hand to her chest and let out an uncertain laugh.

"I guess I didn't think it through," he said, his eyes crinkling at the corners as he smiled. "Sorry about that."

She looked at him, waiting.

"Listen, I just needed to come in here for a minute because I wanted it to be just us." He glanced down at his hands, then back up. "And getting you alone for the rest of today will be pretty much impossible. So…" He cleared his throat and met her eyes. "I wanted to tell you how happy I am for you. I know I haven't been the most supportive, but seeing you two together over the past two years…" He shook his head. "It makes sense. You just fit."

They did. It was true. She and Monica were like two puzzle pieces that simply clicked together, meant to be side by side.

"Anyway." Cody shrugged. "I'm sorry I was a dick in the

beginning, and Monica's a really lucky woman." His eyes welled up, and he moved in for a hug.

"Thank you, Cody," she whispered against his ear.

Another knock on the door, and then Aubrey's father peeked in. "Hey, sweetie, you ready?"

She and Cody parted. "See you out there," he said, then moved around her father and left the room.

When Aubrey's father walked fully into the room, he stopped in his tracks, his eyes on her. His eyes filled with tears immediately.

"Not you too!" Aubrey said with a laugh, and she went to him and hugged him and heard him whisper in her ear, "You're the prettiest sight I've ever seen."

She wasn't sure how much more emotion she could take.

They parted and sniffled and wiped their faces and eyes, and then an usher was at the door telling them it was time. They walked out of the small room, down a hall, and stood by the double doors, which were pulled open to reveal their small crowd.

"Oh God," Aubrey said quietly as she watched Trina, then Emma walk down the aisle, holding their festive Christmas bouquets in front of them. She glanced up at her father as she tucked her hand into his elbow. "I think I'm going to actually make it down the aisle this time."

Her father chuckled and patted her hand. "Damn right, you are."

The Wedding March began for the second time, and she walked down the aisle, guided by her dad. She knew that Monica's father had walked her down first, and they hadn't wanted to see each other ahead of time, but now, Aubrey was very aware that there were people filling the pews, but she couldn't tear her eyes from Monica, standing there at the altar in a gorgeous sleeveless white gown that dipped low in the front and even lower in the back. Her hair was in a complicated updo that only accentuated the beauty of her face. Her eyes shimmered in the holiday lighting, and when Aubrey finally reached her, when her father had kissed her on the cheek and set her hand in Monica's, all her words flew away. All she could do was stare at the most exquisite woman she'd ever laid eyes on.

"Hi," Monica said, giving her hand a squeeze.

"Hi," she managed to say back. Next to Monica, looking devastatingly handsome in his tux with a red bow tie, stood Cody. His eyes danced and his smile was wide. He hadn't been fibbing—he was happy for them, and it showed.

The ceremony went by in a blur. She must've said everything correctly because Monica slid a ring onto her finger and kissed her lovingly, and then the whole place burst into applause. They made it down the aisle and through the photo shoot as well as the receiving line and finally—*finally*—they sat at the head table to eat.

Monica leaned over to her and asked quietly, "Do you think we'll remember any of what's happened today?"

"Not a damn thing."

Monica pointed at her. "That. That right there is why I married you. You get me."

"But that's why I married *you*," Aubrey said with a grin. "Stop copying me."

They sat there facing each other, smiling at each other, and the entire room seemed to fade away. The sound muted. The background blurred until there was nothing before her except Monica. She leaned a little closer, until her nose almost touched Monica's, and whispered, "I love you so much."

"I love you more," Monica whispered back, and then she captured Aubrey's lips with hers. When they parted, sound came rushing back in the form of guests tapping their glasses with their utensils. Monica gave her a little wink and then stood. Once the small crowd quieted, she spoke.

"First of all, we want to thank all of you for being here. For celebrating us. For lifting us up." She smiled and seemed to take a moment to gather her thoughts.

Aubrey watched, her eyes glued to her wife. And then her smile grew at that phrase. *Her wife.*

"We did not get here quickly or easily," Monica said, and a ripple of laughter went through the crowd. "It's taken over a decade, most of which, Aubrey hate—er—*disliked* me. A lot." More laughter. "What she didn't count on was my patience." And with that, applause broke out, along with a couple of hoots. Monica laughed, then looked down the table at Emma, at Trina, at Cody. Her eyes stopped on Aubrey, and she held her gaze as she said, "All of us at this table, we are nothing if not unconventional, but we are a family. That's the most important part. The best part." She picked up her glass of champagne and held it up. The crowd followed suit. "I'd like to propose a toast. To love and family and not giving up on a dream." She turned her gaze to Aubrey, who didn't think her heart could swell any more. "And to my wife, Aubrey, for making me the luckiest girl in the world."

Cries of *Hear! Hear!* and *yeah!* rippled through the room as glasses were lifted and clinked together, and champagne was sipped. Waiters appeared with plates of food, serving the bridal table first, as Monica sat back down. They ate happily, Aubrey long past the feeling of *I can't eat anything or I won't fit into my dress*. The mashed potatoes were first into her mouth.

People came and went as they ate, stopping by the table to wish them well. It was when a friend of Monica's from work stopped to chat that Aubrey was able to just watch. Monica still looked fresh as a daisy, as her grandmother would say. How did she do that? After all the stress and nerves of the day, her wife still looked like she'd just gotten ready.

Her wife.

There was that phrase again.

Her wife.

"You good?" Monica asked once her friend had moved along.

"I'm better than I ever thought I'd be," Aubrey said, then gestured around the room. "I mean, look at this. Who came up with this scenario? Who'd have thought life would go this way?" She scanned the room, full of her people and Monica's people, and not for the first time, she was humbled by her good fortune. Her life hadn't always been easy. She hadn't had the smoothest path to walk. But she'd done it. She'd waded and slogged and struggled, and it had been so worth it to sit where she was now, surrounded by people who loved her, sitting next to the most amazing human being she'd ever known. When Monica looked up at her, Aubrey knew there were tears glistening in her own eyes.

"What is it?" Monica asked softly.

"I'm just so happy." She failed at holding back the tears. "This is the happiest day of my life."

Monica shook her head with a sly smile. "Well, then, you'd better brace yourself, my love. I plan on doing everything I can to top that. For the rest of our lives. I consider it my mission."

"Then your toast was wrong. *I* am the luckiest girl in the world."

"I love you," Monica said and leaned in for a kiss. Not the first that day, but the first of many. The first of a lifetime.

Aubrey was ready.

WEDDINGS DOWN: 6
SUCCESS AT AVOIDING MONICA WALLACE: COMPLETE FAILURE
MARRIED HER INSTEAD

About the Author

Georgia Beers lives in Upstate New York and has written more than thirty-five novels of sapphic romance. In her off-hours, she can usually be found searching for a scary movie, sipping a good Pinot, or trying to keep up with little big man Archie, her mix of many little dogs. Find out more at georgiabeers.com.

Books Available From Bold Strokes Books

A Case for Discretion by Ashley Moore. Will Gwen, a prominent Atlanta attorney, choose Etta, the law student she's clandestinely dating, or is her political future too important to sacrifice? (978-1-63679-617-8)

Aubrey McFadden Is Never Getting Married by Georgia Beers. Aubrey McFadden is never getting married, but she does have five weddings to attend, and she'll be avoiding Monica Wallace, the woman who ruined her happily ever after, at every single one. (978-1-63679-613-0)

The Broken Lines of Us by Shia Woods. Charlie Dawson returns to the city she left behind and meets an unexpected stranger on her first night back, discovering that coming home might not be as hard as she thought. (978-1-63679-585-0)

Flowers for Dead Girls by Abigail Collins. Isla might be just the right kind of girl to bring Astra out of her shell—and maybe more. The only problem? She's dead. (978-1-63679-584-3)

Good Bones by Aurora Rey. Designer and contractor Logan Barrow can give Kathleen Kenney the house of her dreams, but can she convince the cynical romance writer to take a chance on love? (978-1-63679-589-8)

Leather, Lace, and Locs by Anne Shade. Three friends, each on their own path in life, with one obstacle…finding room in their busy lives for a love that will give them their happily ever afters. (978-1-63679-529-4)

Rainbow Overalls by Maggie Fortuna. Arriving in Vermont for her first year of college, an introverted bookworm forms a friendship with an outgoing artist and finds what comes after the classic coming out story: a being out story. (978-1-63679-606-2)

Revisiting Summer Nights by Ashley Bartlett. PJ Addison and Wylie Parsons have been called back to film the most recent *Dangerous Summer Nights* installment. Only this time they're not in love, and it's going to stay that way. (978-1-63679-551-5)

All This Time by Sage Donnell. Erin and Jodi share a complicated past, but a very different present. Will they ever be able to make a future together work? (978-1-63679-622-2)

Crossing Bridges by Chelsey Lynford. When a one-night stand between a snowboard instructor and a business executive becomes more, one has to overcome her past, while the other must let go of her planned future. (978-1-63679-646-8)

Dancing Toward Stardust by Julia Underwood. Age has nothing to do with becoming the person you were meant to be, taking a chance, and finding love. (978-1-63679-588-1)

Evacuation to Love by CA Popovich. As a hurricane rips through Florida, so too are Joanne and Shanna's lives upended. It'll take a force of nature to show them the love it takes to rebuild. (978-1-63679-493-8)

Lean in to Love by Catherine Lane. Will badly behaving celebrities, erotic sex tapes, and steamy scandals prevent Rory and Ellis from leaning in to love? (978-1-63679-582-9)

The Romance Lovers Book Club by MA Binfield and Toni Logan. After their book club reads a romance about an American tourist falling in love with an English princess, Harper and her best friend, Alice, book an impulsive trip to London hoping they'll both fall for the women of their dreams. (978-1-63679-501-0)

Searching for Someday by Renee Roman. For loner Rayne Thomas, her only goal for working out is to build her confidence, but Maggie Flanders has another idea, and neither is prepared for the outcome. (978-1-63679-568-3)

Truly Home by J.J. Hale. Ruth and Olivia discover home is more than a four-letter word. (978-1-63679-579-9)

View from the Top by Morgan Adams. When it comes to love, sometimes the higher you climb, the harder you fall. (978-1-63679-604-8

BOLDSTROKESBOOKS.COM

Looking for your next great read?

Visit BOLDSTROKESBOOKS.COM
to browse our entire catalog of paperbacks, ebooks,
and audiobooks.

Want the first word on what's new?
Visit our website for event info,
author interviews, and blogs.

Subscribe to our free newsletter for sneak peeks,
new releases, plus first notice of promos
and daily bargains.

SIGN UP AT
BOLDSTROKESBOOKS.COM/signup

Bold Strokes Books
Quality and Diversity in LGBTQ Literature

*Bold Strokes Books is an award-winning publisher
committed to quality and diversity in LGBTQ fiction.*